MW01028120

KILL FEE

KILL FEE

BARBARA PAUL

CHARLES SCRIBNER'S SONS · *NEW YORK*

Library of Congress Cataloging-in-Publication Data
Paul, Barbara.
Kill fee.
I. Title.
PR6065.E9K5   1985   813'.54   85-14633
ISBN 0-684-18426-5

Published simultaneously in Canada
by Collier Macmillan Canada, Inc.—
Copyright under the Berne Convention.

1 3 5 7 9 11 13 15 17 19 F/C 20 18 16 14 12 10 8 6 4 2

Printed in the United States of America.

KILL FEE

CHAPTER

1

Leon Walsh was the first one they found out about. Walsh got rattled easily and consequently did a poor job of covering his tracks—or of covering that other man's tracks, rather, the man everyone was looking for. Walsh was a good editor, even inspired at times; but he was all thumbs at everything else. His intentions were good and he tried hard, and yet the world steadfastly refused to fall neatly into place for him. Two wives had left him. Dogs bit him. Automobiles broke down when he tried to drive them. The normal abrasions of everyday life defeated him utterly; department store clerks made him feel inferior. He certainly had no head for business—which was why he'd needed a partner in the first place.

Leon Walsh got rattled easily and knew it; he deeply resented the intrusion of the mundane. The New York offices of *Summit* magazine made up Walsh's world, and anything that didn't pertain directly to *Summit* belonged off on Uranus or Neptune, to Walsh's way of thinking. As long as he stayed inside his fenced-off domain, he had life under control. He was a careful reader; he respected his writers' copy as much as he could, and he had an instinct for spotting talent that was fast becoming a lost art in the shovel-it-through-and-print-it world of periodical publishing.

Walsh's partner sometimes laughed at him, not exactly good-naturedly, for being a purist. *Purist* was a dirty word in the personal lexicon of Jerry Sussman, the partner, a man who said "between you and I." *Summit* carried both fiction and nonfiction, but Walsh insisted upon literate if not literary style in everything he published. Above his desk hung a sign:

AVOID EMBARRASSMENT:
dangle no modifiers, split no infinitives.

Jerry Sussman laughed.

He was laughing right then, or maybe sneering was closer to what he was doing. "Leon, you don't 'explain' things to advertisers. You either listen to them or kiss the account goodbye. And don't say—"

"Good riddance."

"—'good riddance.' Grow up, for chrissake. You don't just write off an advertiser like Mueller Electronics. Even you know that," he added, insultingly.

Walsh leaned back in his chair and stretched his legs out under the desk, trying to look relaxed. "IBM didn't threaten to withdraw when we ran a computer-menace story."

"Because computer-menace stories are so old hat nobody pays attention to them any more," Sussman growled. "Look, Leon, I know how great it must be, sitting up there above all the petty bullshit like keeping the advertisers happy and seeing the bills are paid. But you

2

ought to try living in the real world like the rest of us once in a while. That story you're so hot to run makes the entire electronics industry look like it's made up of self-seeking incompetents who don't give a damn about the product or even consumer safety."

Look as if, Walsh thought, *not look like. Number one.*

"Why are you so dead set on running it?" Sussman went on. "It's not that great a story."

"Have you read it, Jerry?"

"A summary, that was enough."

Walsh muttered under his breath. Somebody in the office was keeping Jerry Sussman notified as to what was scheduled for publication. Not that there was any reason Sussman shouldn't know; he was the majority stock-holder. But the behind-the-back-ness of the way Sussman kept himself informed irritated Walsh. He wondered who the "spy" in the office was.

Walsh cleared his throat. "You're meddling, Jerry. This is my bailiwick." They'd had that out when the partnership was first formed; Sussman would not inter-fere with the creative side of the magazine and Walsh would leave all money decisions to his partner. It was an agreement that Sussman had violated almost from the outset. Walsh let a little of his anger show. "Damn it, Jerry, I'm getting tired of this. *I* choose what goes into *Summit.*"

"Of course you do, of course you do," Sussman said hastily, falsely soothing, insincere and not giving a damn who knew it. "If it was an exposé sort of thing, a re-searched article, one of those kind, I wouldn't say a word!"

Number two—one of those kinds (plural) or one of that kind (singular).

3

"But it's not," Sussman went on. "It's only fiction. I don't see why you're so stuck on it."

Only fiction. "What have you got against fiction?" Walsh asked mildly, pleased with himself for keeping his temper.

His partner was at the window, looking down on Sixth Avenue. "It's chickenshit writing," he said bluntly. "Like that electronics story. Guy doesn't have any facts, so he calls his story fiction and says whatever he damn well pleases. No responsibility to the truth. I want you to kill the electronics thing, Leon. We can't afford to offend Mueller. They haven't been in this country long enough to roll with the punches. Between you and I, Mueller Electronics is running scared."

Number three. "How do you know that?"

"I know." That was *his* bailiwick. "They're not going to advertise in a mag that undercuts their line of work in the fiction department. I want you to kill that story."

Leon Walsh got rattled easily; and just then he felt his certainty about the story oozing away under the onslaught of that flat voice of authority Sussman could turn on and off at will, a voice that never questioned itself nor permitted questions from others. Walsh knew better than to make any decisions while caught in the throes of berattlement, so he said what he always said when he wanted to get rid of Sussman: "I'll think about it."

Sussman stared at him suspiciously for a moment, but then nodded curtly and left without another word. A big, florid man, Sussman always left a wake behind him when he moved.

Walsh sat motionless for a while, waiting for his resentment to abate. He picked up a pencil and made a notation on his desk calendar: JS = 3. Only three errors today; that would lower Sussman's average for the week.

Walsh had started counting his partner's mistakes in English nearly two years ago, as a way to amuse himself during a long, boring conference that seemed as if it would never end. But when he'd done it once, he found he couldn't help but keep on doing it. He'd actually developed a compulsion to count his partner's grammatical lapses! Adolescent. Every day that the two men talked, Walsh would make a little note on the calendar. He had close to a two-year record. Of value to no one, but unthinkable to discontinue it.

Leon Walsh hated Jerry Sussman. He hated his appearance, his voice, his success, his vulgarity. He hated everything about him. But most of all he hated what Sussman had done to *Summit*. Walsh had often tried to moderate his hatred by telling himself that any profit-oriented partner would have taken the same steps that Sussman had taken—but it didn't help. In his more melodramatic moments, Walsh cursed the day he'd agreed to a partnership.

Not that he'd had much choice. It was either Sussman or bankruptcy court and fold the magazine. Things had been so simple when he'd first started out; twelve years ago he'd founded a literary journal to be published four times a year in Summit, New Jersey—the town just west of Newark that gave the periodical its name. Walsh's goal had also been simple, almost pristine (he liked to think) in its simplicity: he wanted to publish the very best short fiction and nonfiction available to him. That was all. He didn't want to shape people's tastes or expand anybody's consciousness or make the world a better place in which to live. He just wanted to publish quality writing.

Thinking of it that way always gave Walsh a warm glow; it was that self-generated aura of noble aspiration that kept him going. The only advertisements he'd accepted in *Summit* were for books. Since he knew nothing about distribution, he'd contracted out to a jobber who didn't exactly strain himself pushing what to him was just one more egghead rag that didn't have a chance in hell of making it. But *Summit* had attracted an enthusiastic (although minuscule) readership; Walsh's choice of material struck a responsive chord in those who could get hold of copies. He would have done much better if he'd had an efficient subscription department. His subscription department was his first wife, who knew just as much about circulation procedures as her husband did, which is to say nothing at all.

From the day the first issue appeared, Walsh had been in debt. Some bills he forgot to pay, others he couldn't pay. But bill-collectors soon found he was easy to intimidate, so Walsh first sold his wife's car, then took out a second mortgage on the house, then went to work part-time elsewhere just to keep *Summit* going. It killed him to admit it, but he finally faced up to the fact that he couldn't do it alone. He needed help. He needed a partner well versed in the mysteries of accounting and marketing and circulation and keeping the IRS placated.

Enter Jerry Sussman. Sussman had an eye for spotting potential in the publishing business and realizing a nice profit from that very convenient talent. He'd looked at the *Star Trek* subindustry in this country—and had taken a Trekker fanzine and promoted it into a full-scale, big-selling professional periodical. He'd bought up a printing outfit that specialized in seed catalogues and the like, and through the printer's contacts had built a staff that put out a successful rival to *Farmer's Almanac*. And somewhere he'd learned there were quite a few people who would like to read *Summit* if the dumbhead editor could ever figure out a way to make copies available to them.

Sussman had been quite blunt. "I run this show or my money stays in the bank. When it's my own dough I'm putting into a project, I gotta have majority ownership."

Walsh had bristled at hearing *Summit* referred to as a "project" and said well, now, he didn't know about that.

"Not open to negotiation," Sussman had said, shaking his big head. "We can argue about the exact figures later because we'll have to put some shares on the market—but either I end up with a majority or I'm pulling out."

"I can't agree to that!" Walsh had sputtered. "I have to retain creative control—I built *Summit* from nothing and I'm not just going to hand it over to you. Why, you could even fire me if you wanted to!"

"Oh hell, man, I'm not going to fire you." Sussman's thick lips had spread in a big grin. "Leon Walsh and *Summit* magazine are the same thing. I wouldn't *want* the mag without you to run it."

Walsh had liked hearing that, but he didn't know whether to believe Sussman or not. The big man repeatedly gave his word that he would never interfere in editorial matters—in exchange for majority ownership. Walsh muttered under his breath, eyed the stack of unpaid bills on his desk, and agreed.

That had been eight years ago, and every day since then Walsh had kicked himself for being such a fool. There must have been some other way to save the magazine. He just hadn't looked hard enough.

He realized he'd been staring at the same page of manuscript for twenty minutes. He looked at his watch: six-thirty. Might as well call it a day; he was in no condition to give anything his full attention.

The changes Jerry Sussman had made were drastic. The first thing he'd done was move the magazine from Summit, New Jersey, to Manhattan. Dealing with suppliers, printers, advertising agencies, mail services, lawyers, and the like right on the spot had enabled them to cut *Summit*'s lead time from ten months to six, and then later to three. *Summit* had gone from quarterly to bimonthly to monthly as the subscription lists and newsstand sales grew more or less steadily.

Of course, for all that to happen, Walsh had had to give in on a few things. Advertising was the main point of capitulation. Instead of restricting its advertising to books as it once did, *Summit* now aggressively solicited the patronage of the airlines and the big computer firms and the insurance companies and the automobile industry and the tobacco and the whiskey and the oil businesses. Jerry Sussman's procedure was to raise the advertising rates every year, to tap *Summit*'s advertisers for as much as traffic would bear. The advertisers in turn looked at the magazine's circulation figures and asked for breakdowns—what percentage of *Summit*'s readers were high earners, what percentage academics, etc. When most of the advertisers had balked at the latest rate raise, the word Sussman got was that the advertisers wanted their messages to reach a greater number of that amorphous creature known as "the man on the street"—a euphemism for *Use shorter words*.

Use shorter words, avoid subjects that get too esoteric or require the reader to think for more than four minutes, insist on a snappy and easy-to-read style, simplify, simplify, simplify. Sussman had started the ball rolling in that direction by asking Leon Walsh to include occasional articles on sports and pop music. Impressed by Sussman's obvious know-how in the magazine-rescuing business, Walsh had acceded to these early requests. But it very quickly became a habit. A representative of one of the airlines would indicate his company's willingness to take out more advertising space in an issue that featured a story set in a certain romantic, out-of-the-way place. A place that only *his* airline serviced, of course.

Walsh had objected, but to no effect. Several times a year, and against his better judgment, he'd commission a story catering to an advertiser's special interests, feeling slightly whorish every time he did. He knew that kind of mutual payoff was a common practice; what shocked him was the utter lack of awareness of wrongdoing on the part of the participants. *That's business,* Sussman had shrugged. Walsh didn't like it at all; he could never fully accommodate his sense of ethics to that way of doing business. One time the commissioned work for a promotional tie-in was so poor that Walsh had paid the writer his kill fee and refused to print the story.

Sussman had promptly informed him that next month his manuscript budget was being cut one-third.

That was Sussman's way of handling any resistance on Walsh's part. He'd *punish* him—as if Walsh were some recalcitrant schoolboy. He'd punish him by withholding the money Walsh needed to attract the writers he wanted. Back in the early pre-Sussman days, Walsh would publish an occasional story by a name writer who'd accepted far less than the usual fee just because he or she liked *Summit* and wanted to give the struggling quarterly a hand. But *Summit* had gone big time since then; no more handouts from anybody.

"How do you expect me to put out a quality magazine without the money to pay the writers?" Walsh would protest, even though he knew protest was useless.

"You pay those writers too damn much anyway," Sussman would say dismissively. Subject matter was what mattered to Sussman, not good writing. If he'd been editing *Summit,* he'd have installed a staff of competent hacks who could grind out stories and articles on any subject on demand.

So Leon Walsh burned with a fury he could find no safe way of expressing. Slowly, watching Sussman take over by inches, Walsh had witnessed the gradual cheapening of his once-meritorious publication. Very few of his original readers were still with him; now he was publishing for the sort of reader who looked up answers to crossword puzzles and called it doing research. Walsh was no longer proud of *Summit*.

Perhaps I should resign, he thought for the hundredth time. He wasn't happy seeing his name associated with some of the pieces *Summit* carried, but he could never quite bring himself to make the break. Twelve years, two wives, and several hundred thousand dollars later— he couldn't just walk away. *Summit* was a much-loved child who had fallen in with bad company. You don't abandon a child who has been led astray.

If only he didn't feel so damned helpless. He went into the small private restroom next to his office and washed his hands and face. The strain of the past few years hadn't improved the face any. Thin nose, slightly hooked; black, staring eyes; two deep furrows in his cheeks, bracketing the thin lips like parenthesis marks. Noticeably receding hairline.

Jerry Sussman had a head of hair of the sort called leonine. He wore it slightly long because he was all too aware of the effect created by his big veldt-colored mane. Walsh grimaced at his own appearance; his name was Leon, *he* should have been the lionlike one. In America hair was still equated with virility, and Jerry Sussman played the King-of-the-Jungle bit for all he could get out of it. Walsh had once told him the male lion didn't even rule his own pride much less the whole jungle, that he was only a follower kept by the females for stud purposes. Sussman liked that even better.

Leon Walsh made up his mind. He would publish the short story that presented the electronics industry in such an unflattering light. It was good fiction and that was all that mattered. If Mueller Electronics withdrew its advertising—well, that was too bad.

He closed his office door behind him. The tapping of a word processor sounded from down the hall; someone working late. Walsh found himself wondering which of his employees it was that kept Sussman informed of what was scheduled for upcoming issues.

A name immediately popped into his head: Fran Caffrey. Walsh smiled sheepishly; he'd been quick to suspect her simply because he didn't like her. Fran Caffrey was his fiction editor, and she was only twenty-six or -seven, young enough to be his daughter. She had this overly careful way of speaking to him, as if he were growing more senile by the day and she had to take extra pains to make sure he understood everything. But Fran did her job well; Walsh had no real reason to get rid of her. He'd always thought personal animosity a poor reason for firing a good worker, and he liked the feeling of fair-mindedness that attitude gave him.

Just the same, he thought, she's the type to play *I Spy* for Jerry Sussman. Maybe he could get a friend in one of the publishing houses to offer her a job. Who owed him a favor?

In the elevator a man stood on his foot. Walsh had to ask twice before he moved. On the street, two pushy young women crowded in front of him and took his taxi. As usual, he muttered under his breath when he was frustrated.

As usual, it didn't do any good.

CHAPTER

2

As if the Russian army had marched through barefoot.

That's the way his mouth tasted. He'd first heard the phrase twenty years ago but hadn't fully appreciated it until now. The pounding in his head didn't help. He finished his Alka-Seltzer and wished he'd stayed at home.

"Would you like me to repeat it for you?" Fran Caffrey asked.

Don't get mad, Walsh told himself. "No thank you, dear, I managed to get it the first time."

"My name's not 'dear,' Leon."

He muttered to himself. Aloud: "Don't be so damned touchy, Fran."

She made a noise of exasperation. "Will you listen to yourself? Now you're telling me how to *be*."

Just what he needed. "You're making something out of nothing. All I said was 'dear.' "

"I've never heard you call any of the men 'old buddy' or the like. The men in this office you treat with respect—whether they deserve it or not. But you treat the women with a kind of offhand familiarity that's just plain insult-ing. As if we were cute little performing dogs instead of professionals."

Is that what had turned this intense young woman into an enemy? "I'm not a sexist, Fran." His head hurt.

She laughed. "Why, Leon, you're one of the worst kinds! The kind who's convinced he's so open-minded he doesn't need to make any special effort to treat people fairly."

An echo from the past that made him wince: his second wife had once said something of the sort. He certainly didn't intend to be discriminatory in the way he treated his staff. Why hadn't she said anything before? "Fran—are you feeding information from this office to Jerry Sussman?"

She stared at him blankly. "What?"

"Would you like me to repeat it for you?" he asked sar-castically, echoing her own words.

"I heard what you said—I just don't know what you mean. *Feeding* information to him? Illicitly? Are we sup-posed to be keeping secrets from Mr. Sussman?"

It was either a great act or Fran Caffrey honestly didn't know what he was talking about. "No, no—just forget I said anything. Now beat it, will you, Fran? I've got a hangover and I feel lousy."

"All right," she said amiably enough, and left.

Walsh dropped his head into his hands, elbows on the desk. He'd reacted to bad news like any manual laborer: when things get rough, go out and get drunk. He'd really tied one on the night before. Dumb. And how had he allowed himself to get trapped into that childish argu-ment with Fran? He wasn't thinking clearly today.

How could he, after yesterday? He never read the *Wall Street Journal* himself. But, oh my, he had a lot of "friends" who were quick enough to call the day before and tell him about that little item tucked away in the inside pages.

He should have known something was up. He'd gone ahead and published the anti-electronics-industry story and Jerry Sussman hadn't said a word. That should have told him right there. Then Mueller Electronics withdrew its advertising, just as Sussman had predicted . . . and still he hadn't said anything.

And Simple Simon congratulated himself on having won a victory, Walsh thought bitterly.

Sussman had stopped coming around to *Summit*'s editorial offices. At first Walsh had thought nothing of it; his partner had a business office elsewhere and *Summit* was only one of Sussman's "projects"—albeit his most important one. A year or so ago Sussman had acquired a bike-racing magazine, and rumor had it he was buying into one of the supermarket tabloids. Sussman was a busy man, driving himself with the kind of energy Walsh sometimes envied. So a prolonged absence of the majority owner wouldn't attract any particular notice.

But then Walsh realized he hadn't seen Sussman at all since he'd published the electronics story. *Count your blessings,* he told himself nervously. Yet he couldn't help worrying; Sussman was not a man who tolerated opposition quietly. Walsh had called Sussman's office a couple of times. *In conference,* the secretary had said. Then the answer had appeared in yesterday's *Wall Street Journal.*

Suddenly Walsh had to get out of the office. It was too early for lunch, but he just couldn't sit there any longer. "I'll be back," he called to his secretary as he rushed by.

"When?" she asked. "Where are you going?"

He left without answering. Secretaries hated bosses who didn't keep them informed of their whereabouts, but

14

this time they'd all have to plug along without him for a while.

He'd vaguely had it in mind that a hair of the dog was what was needed to cure his hangover. But the elevator's swift descent brought out the wave of nausea he'd managed to keep suppressed so far. *Walk it off,* he told himself.

He turned left and headed uptown. The air was still nippy—it was April—and he had to move along at a fast pace to keep from getting cold. His near-jogging stride jarred his headache, and for some reason all of Sixth Avenue seemed to be permeated with the odor of frying onions that morning. Feeling worse, he hurried across Central Park South and went into the park. He veered off to the right, toward the Pond. Looked for a place to sit. Found it. Sat.

After a while the throbbing in his head began to ease. And he seemed to have found a relatively odor-free corner of the city. He hadn't gone far enough into the park to escape the traffic noise—but the sound was muted, tolerable. He was chilly, sitting still; but the nippy air was starting to brace him up. He decided to live.

To live, but not to go back to the office. No— he changed his mind immediately; that was cowardly. He shouldn't let his staff see how defeated he was. He shouldn't even have let Fran Caffrey see he was hung over. They all knew what was happening—they must know, it was in the paper. Yet no one had said a word to him, although they had to be talking about it among themselves. Other than that, it had been business as usual. Waiting for him to make the first move? Well, he'd made it. He'd run away.

Leila. He wanted to talk to Leila. Needed to, *had* to talk to her. He got up and left the park, looking for a phone.

Leila had been his second wife, the one he kept in touch with. She'd remarried after their divorce—a little too soon to please Walsh. He'd once tried to rekindle the flame. It had been a time he was in special need of comforting—another instance when Sussman had made his life miserable, come to think of it. So he'd gone to Leila.

She'd turned him down flat. "You'd just love that, wouldn't you?" she'd said. "You'd like me to cheat on Jack with *you*—that'd make you the big man after all. Sorry, love. I'm not interested in making you feel big."

They hadn't spoken for three months after that.

But something had gone sour in the marriage to Jack; Leila was once again an unmarried woman and swearing to stay that way. For once she and Walsh were agreed: two marriages were enough. Leila and Leon didn't see each other often—lunch every month or so. It suited them.

Walsh had to walk all the way to Columbus Circle before he found a phone that worked. He dialed the television production company where Leila worked.

"Leon? How are you? Haven't heard from you for ages."

He couldn't wait for the amenities. "Leila, Sussman is selling *Summit*."

There was a small pause on the other end, and then she said cautiously, "Couldn't that be a good thing? You've been wanting to break with that man for years."

"He's selling to UltraMedia."

"Oh. Oh, my god. Oh, Leon—I'm so sorry!"

As well she should be. UltraMedia Corporation was an ultrabuck conglomerate that had grown (astonishingly, to Walsh) out of a single acid-rock bimonthly that had been considered hot stuff back in the sixties. Now Ultra-Media had fingers in just about every aspect of pop entertainment—gossip magazines, music videos, record albums and tapes, TV production, a dozen other things Walsh couldn't even guess at. UltraMedia had pioneered the one-issue magazine. A personality would capture the public interest, and UltraMedia would put out a one-shot magazine devoted solely to that personality. They'd started off in the sixties with Jackie and Elvis and Liz and moved through the seventies with Farrah and Burt and Liz and into the eighties with Bo and Prince Charles and Liz. And that was the outfit that was buying *Summit.*

"Maybe they've decided to go straight," Leila said wryly. "Do you know what their plans for *Summit* are? What does Sussman say?"

"I haven't seen him for over a month. And he won't come to the phone. It's still in the negotiation stage, but the *Wall Street Journal* says they're close to an agreement. That's how I found out about it, Leila. From the goddam *news*paper."

"Sussman didn't tell you he was selling?" The astonishment in her voice was real, indignant.

"No, he didn't tell me he was selling," Walsh said bitterly. "I'm only the minority owner—but I *am* his partner, damn it." Walsh knew why Sussman hadn't told him, but he didn't want to say so to Leila. Sussman was punishing him again. For being a naughty boy. "He should have let me know."

Leila agreed. "Have you talked to anybody at Ultra-Media?"

"No." He hadn't even thought of it.

"Seems to me that's your next step. Jerry Sussman may be ashamed to face you, but the people at UltraMedia can hardly refuse to talk. Maybe you can find out what their plans are."

"That's a possibility."

Another pause. Then: "Leon—maybe UltraMedia won't interfere with *Summit*. You might end up just going on doing what you're already doing."

"Hah."

"No, listen—*Summit*'s a major periodical, a paying proposition. Why would they want to meddle with a winning formula?"

Walsh thought of Mueller Electronics. And a few others. "We've had a little advertiser attrition lately."

"Oh. Well, I'm sorry to hear it. But they still might not want to change the magazine. Talk to them, Leon," she urged. "Find out what their plans are."

Yes, that was what he should do. Find out from the enemy what his own partner wouldn't tell him.

Rain pounded New York's streets and buildings for three days, the three days it took Walsh to set up an appointment with UltraMedia. Finally someone by the name of Hartley Dunlop agreed to meet him. What kind of name was that, *Hartley Dunlop*? Walsh didn't even know Dunlop's position in the firm. He supervised publications, the secretary had said. That could mean anything, Walsh muttered under his breath. What rank? Manager, vice president, department head? *A supervisor*, said the breathy, girlish voice on the phone.

Through the secretary Walsh had invited Dunlop to come to the *Summit* offices; no dice. Then he'd tried for a meeting on neutral ground, a restaurant for lunch. That didn't work either. So Walsh was going to have to go into Dunlop's turf, hat in hand, begging for a crumb of information.

He shouldn't be treated this way, Walsh told himself uncomfortably. *Summit* was *his* magazine, he'd created it out of nothing. And yet people he didn't even know were deciding the magazine's future. No one had consulted him, no one had asked his opinion. He'd never heard of doing business this way; simple courtesy dictated that at least a telephone call be made.

UltraMedia's corporate headquarters were in Los Angeles (naturally), but there was a New York office, on Lexington. The rain was still pouring from a livid sky when the time for Walsh's appointment approached; he got water down the back of his neck as he bent to climb into the cab. Visibility was poor and the driver swore all the way during the short trip from *Summit* to Ultra-Media.

UltraMedia's reception area looked like a set for a science fiction movie—colorful, futuristic, and boastfully plastic. Music from Jupiter filtered through invisible speakers. Walsh was directed through a tunnel of rotating lights (an ordinary hallway when the plug was pulled, he was sure) and emerged at the other end with a slight feeling of nausea. And waiting for him there—well, she was either a fashion model or a movie star or the Queen of Venus, at least. But no, it was only Hartley Dunlop's secretary—she of the breathy voice.

She was an absolutely stunning young woman, and Walsh stared in open admiration. She noticed (in fact, she was waiting for it), and she gave him an open, sweet, professionally shy smile in return. "Mr. Walsh?" she whispered. "This way, please."

She was an expensive-looking young woman: clothing, haircut, make-up—all reeked of money. Walsh followed her down another hallway and wondered how long it took her to get ready in the morning. But it was her personal style that was most disconcerting. Her manner was soft, friendly—but with just a touch of hesitation in it.

19

As if she were saying: *Here I am, a great beauty, but I'm still vulnerable. You won't hurt me, will you?* Walsh didn't buy it, but it was obviously the pose UltraMedia liked in its female employees. He had half a notion to send Fran Caffrey over here on an errand so she'd see how well off she was at *Summit*.

Having found a reason to feel superior, Walsh was able to enter Hartley Dunlop's office in a fairly self-confident mood. But that good feeling began to evaporate the second he caught sight of his new surroundings. From a science fiction set he had stepped into one of those display rooms of fine period furnishings at the Metropolitan Museum of Art. His own office was a paper chase: desk and work tables piled high with manuscripts, galleys, layout pages, paste-up boards, all the accouterments of putting together a magazine. It was a *working* office. This, on the other hand, was the office of a man who sat in luxury and thought big thoughts, made big plans—which others would implement at the flick of a finger.

Walsh sat down gingerly on a Louis Somethingth chair and stared at an ornate tapestry on the opposite wall. Miss Vulnerable Beauty whispered something in his direction and disappeared through a door. This wasn't even the inner office. This was an audience hall where the King entertained petitions from the peasantry.

Hartley Dunlop came in; Walsh found himself standing up to meet . . . *a little boy.*

Well, he looked like a little boy. He had to be in his twenties, but he appeared even younger than that. Clean, all-American features; dark hair in an ostentatiously youthful cut—he would have looked at home in a Boy Scout uniform. But Dunlop's "uniform" came from Savile Row; the expensive clothing and his half-closed eyes gave him an effete air, a poise far beyond his years.

"I'm Hartley Dunlop, Mr. Walsh. Let's sit over here, shall we? So much more comfortable than those." He dismissed the Louis Somethingth chairs with a graceful wave of his hand.

Walsh lowered himself on to the indicated settee and found himself staring at Dunlop's suit, wondering if UltraMedia gave its people a clothing allowance. He sat admiring Dunlop's tailoring until Dunlop asked what he could do for him.

Walsh roused himself and said, "You can tell me what the hell is going on. Why do I have to read in the newspaper that you're buying *my* magazine?"

Dunlop tilted his head back and looked at Walsh through his eyelashes—easier, Walsh supposed, than opening his eyes all the way. "I would have thought your partner had kept you informed," Dunlop said.

"Do you know Jerry Sussman?"

"We've met, yes."

"Then that's your answer—you know the kind of man he is. He's been negotiating with UltraMedia behind my back—and you know it."

"Do I?" Dark eyebrows raised a fraction. "What goes on between you and Mr. Sussman is not our concern."

He wasn't getting anywhere. "Look," Walsh said, "I've been in the magazine business longer than you've been alive. There's no way you can understand what creating your own magazine means. I did donkey work in periodicals you never heard of, and then twelve years ago I started *Summit*—from nothing I started it. Sussman came along with the money when I needed it, but *I* built the magazine. And yet you don't even bother to consult me when you negotiate a purchase?"

"Mr. Sussman is the majority shareholder. He's the one we'd have to deal with in any event."

21

"Damn it, Dunlop, that's not what I'm talking about! I'm talking about just plain good manners. How can you think of buying a magazine and *not* talk to the editor? You should have consulted me. UltraMedia is way out of line."

"Well." Dunlop crossed one impeccably tailored knee over the other. "I'm sorry you feel that way." Not exactly an apology.

"How the hell should I feel? My life is being manipulated by strangers and nobody bothers to tell me—that's supposed to make me feel good?"

Dunlop spread his hands, made no comment; the effect was to make Walsh feel he was behaving in a tacky and self-pitying way. *Get a grip on yourself,* he thought. It was the age of his adversary that was throwing him off stride. Walsh should be calling him "son" and teaching him the rudiments of the business. Instead . . .

Instead, this twerp had one-upped him from the moment he walked into the room. And how had he done it? Just by being there, in that office, in that corporation. By sitting quietly while Walsh ranted and complained about being left out. By being *in.*

Walsh made the effort to assume a posture of dignity and speak in a level voice. "*Summit* is totally different from your other publications—I can't see how it fits into UltraMedia's corporate image. I need to know what your plans for the magazine are. My staff has a right to be kept informed."

"Ah." Dunlop played here's-the-church-and-here's-the-steeple with his hands. "It would be inappropriate for me to detail our plans before the sale is final—but I do understand your position." He smiled to show how understanding he was. "I can give you an idea of the general thrust we have in mind. We'd like to see *Summit* concern itself with issues and writers that people are interested in right now."

Walsh stared. "I thought that's what we *were* doing."

Dunlop managed a pained smile, as if afraid of hurting Walsh's feelings. "When I say right now, I mean this very minute. *Now.* So far *Summit* has done an admirable job of publishing for, well, shall we say for posterity?"

Don't patronize me, sonny.

"But we'd like *Summit* to go more current, more contemporary. For instance, a few months ago you published an article on Ernest Hemingway—"

Walsh barked a laugh. "You mean to say people aren't interested in Hemingway any more? Come on, Dunlop— you know better than that."

Again that pained smile. "There are always some who still read him, I'm sure. If you'd titled it 'Macho Man Revisited' and gone at it from that angle—well, then maybe it would have said something to the modern reader. But it was the same sort of old-fashioned critique I was forced to read in school."

"When was that?" Walsh snapped. "Yesterday?"

Dunlop smiled the smile of the man who cannot be offended. "I make no pretense to literary expertise, Mr. Walsh. Frankly, it doesn't even interest me very much. We are not in the elitist business here—we deal with *popular* culture. Today's reader doesn't give a damn about the emasculation imagery in Ernest Hemingway. What he wants is input from *today's* writers—people like Derek Stanton and Shana Burleson and Kristy Lee."

Walsh had heard of none of them. Admit it? Hell, no. "Flash-in-the-pan stuff. A year from now nobody'll even remember their names."

"Quite possibly that's true," Dunlop conceded. "But we don't want *Summit* to be for the reader a year from now. We want to publish for right now, for this very minute."

Walsh smirked. "Kind of hard when you have a three-month lead time, isn't it?"

"That's something else—we think three months is too far ahead to schedule. Not really cost-effective, you know. We're going to try for one month."

Walsh's mouth dropped open. "That's impossible," he said flatly.

Dunlop smiled and shook his head.

"I tell you it's impossible," Walsh repeated. "You need time to make alternate arrangements when things get screwed up. You can't always get the grade of paper you want, writers don't always meet deadlines, printers go on strike at the drop of a hat—"

"Mr. Walsh, we know what we're doing. The primary reason UltraMedia has an office here is that New York is the center of the country's publishing industry. Everything we need is here. Have you forgotten we put out *weekly* magazines? *Personalities, Homemaker's Weekly, American News Magazine.* We have the techniques, the equipment, the right people. We can put *Summit* out with only a month's lead time."

"But the *quality* . . . only a month . . . !" Walsh was appalled. "It'll be a junk magazine!"

"So you see with only a month's lead time, it's quite possible to deal with matters of contemporary interest," Dunlop went on as if Walsh had not spoken. "It's what advertisers want now—immediate feedback. Even Mueller Electronics."

Pow. So he'd saved Mueller for the stinger. Walsh said nothing. He looked at Dunlop sitting opposite him. So young, so sure of himself. The young were always positive they had all the answers—but they didn't sit in offices like this one telling editors of literary periodicals what was wrong with their magazines. What was Dunlop doing here in so responsible a position, where had he come from? Even as he asked himself the question, Walsh knew the answer. Dunlop was here because it had become a young man's world. Walsh was fifty-four and feeling every minute of it; it was only the members of his generation that started at the bottom and worked their way to the top. Today's kids came *in* at the top, the young *did* sit in expensive offices and tell experienced men how to do their jobs.

"I'm sorry, Dunlop," Walsh heard himself saying. "I can't ask my staff to do a complete turnabout. It's unthinkable."

Dunlop opened his eyes wide for the first time. "We don't expect you to ask them, Mr. Walsh."

Walsh was confused. Did Dunlop mean that Ultra-Media would give the orders? Or the staff would be replaced by UltraMedia people? Or . . . oh. Oh god. Oh god, no. Finally, it sank in on him. It must have been lurking in the back of his mind all the while—he just hadn't wanted to acknowledge it.

"You're replacing me as editor," he said numbly.

Dunlop spread his hands. "It's simply that we think you'd be happier at a magazine with a more literary orientation."

"*Summit* has a literary orientation." Woodenly. "Had."

Dunlop actually looked sympathetic. "I know how you're feeling—"

"How could you possibly know? You haven't the first idea of what *Summit* is all about. How dare you tell me you know how I feel?"

Walsh didn't wait for Dunlop's response. He was on

his feet, brushing past the younger man, out of the fancy room. Miss Vulnerable Beauty materialized and steered him toward the tunnel of lights. The revolving colors disoriented him and the feeling of nausea returned. Then he was out of the tunnel, out of the building, on the street.

Head whirling with humiliation, he paid no attention to where he was going. *That's the first thing normal people think about when ownership changes hands—Is my job safe? But good old Head-in-the-Sand Walsh, I manage to make it the last.*

The rain had stopped, but Walsh didn't notice. He let himself be carried along by the flow of sidewalk traffic until he came to a saloon. Inside, at the quiet end of the bar, one scotch later, he began to come out of his daze.

Fired. By a Boy Scout.

He ordered another drink. Why were they doing this? It seemed to him as if the hydra-headed UltraMedia Corporation had come into being for the sole purpose of destroying Leon Walsh and *Summit* magazine. His lovely magazine—what were they going to do to it? If they wanted a magazine of the sort that Dunlop described, why not start a new one? Why change *Summit* into something it was never meant to be?

For the advertisers, dummy. Summit already had the big-money advertisers; but if Sussman was right, they were all whispering the same word: *Change.* Former advertisers like Mueller Electronics could be brought back into the fold by using that same magic word, *change,* as bait. Why should UltraMedia start from scratch when there was a nice little setup like *Summit* just waiting to be taken over?

And Leon Walsh could do nothing but sit there helplessly and watch his life's work go down the drain. *Sum-*

mit was the one thing in his life he was proud of, his one real accomplishment. *Had* been proud of. Sure, it had gotten a little tainted lately—but nothing that couldn't be cleaned up, made right. The magazine was his life. Take *Summit* away—and what did he have left? He paid for a third scotch without noticing the bartender had short-changed him.

What was he going to do now? What the hell was he going to do now? He couldn't live without a magazine to edit. Start over? Build another *Summit*, start from nothing again. No, he wouldn't have to start from quite nothing, he could get financing now, he wouldn't have to depend on the Jerry Sussmans of the world this time. He could do it. He could start over.

A little voice inside his head laughed unpleasantly. *At age fifty-four?*

A lot of people start over in middle age, Walsh answered himself.

But you're not a lot of people, are you? the little voice asked.

He was too tired, too defeated. Well, then what? He could go to *Saturday Review,* wherever it was now, with his tongue hanging out, begging for a job. But *SR* didn't publish fiction. *Harper's,* then? Or the *Atlantic,* in Boston? He wouldn't have anything like the authority he'd had at *Summit,* but he could probably get some sort of job.

Couldn't he?

Third possibility. Pack it in. Take one grand leap from one of the World Trade Center towers. To hell with everything—who cared anyway? Nobody gave a damn if UltraMedia flushed *Summit* down the toilet. And would anyone even notice if Leon Walsh simply disappeared from the face of the earth? Why keep fighting?

27

"He's been on that phone twenty minutes, I tole him it was a emergency, but he don't pay no attention," came a voice from the next barstool.

"What?" Walsh said, startled.

"That fella over there," said the man next to him, gesturing with his head toward a wall phone. "I tole him I gotta call the hospital, but he won't get off." The speaker was a man well into his seventies and stick-thin. "He won't get off," he repeated.

"Yeah, some people are like that."

"I gotta call the hospital to see if they got a room for me. I got cancer and they're gonna cut my stomach out and I don't know if I got a room to stay in. I gotta call the hospital."

A pause. "Ah, I thought the doctor arranged for the hospital room," Walsh murmured, not knowing what to say.

"I thought so too, but he tole me to call. My kids won't do it, they don't take care of me. I wrote 'em all and tole them I was dying and not one of 'em would come. They all had excuses. The doctor tole me not to get my hopes up, he'd just do what he could but he didn't think he could get it all out. Not one of 'em would come."

"I'm sorry," Walsh said, shaken.

"Thanks, mister. Huh—about time." He headed for the wall phone the talkative man had just relinquished.

Walsh slipped an ice cube from his glass and held it on his tongue. Here he'd been thinking of suicide, while that old man—who probably had nothing at all in the world—was fighting for his life right down to the wire. Fighting and needing to talk about it. Well. Wasn't that inspiring. *What am I supposed to do?* Walsh thought. *Feel renewed?* Maybe the old man ought to give up too.

I despised myself and the voices of my accursed human

education, D. H. Lawrence had written. Walsh had read somewhere that the more educated the individual, the more likely he was to turn his anger inward, on himself. Educated people were more apt to commit suicide; the uneducated tended to turn to murder to resolve their problems. It was the uneducated man who found it easy to direct his anger outward, toward another person.

It was certainly another person who deserved his anger. Jerry Sussman had gotten him into this fix. Sussman knew how much *Summit* meant to Walsh, he knew it was his life. But did that stop him? Walsh wondered if Sussman had so much as hesitated before selling him out to Ultra-Media. He doubted it. Sussman had ridden roughshod over Walsh and *Summit* from the very day he had first bailed them out. Money is power. *And Sussman is shit.* Walsh sat thinking of the man who had destroyed him; he thought about him in a detached, almost impersonal way.

The cancer victim finished his call and left. Walsh went to the phone, dropped in a dime, and dialed Leila's number.

CHAPTER

3

Fifteen minutes. In fifteen minutes James Timothy Murtaugh went off duty, and he was leaving whether the goddam paperwork was finished or not. He pecked away at the typewriter, filling in the form on some stupid kid who'd tried to lift his billfold. Normally he'd have given the kid a kick in the ass and sent him on his way. But Ansbacher had announced before a squad room full of people that Murtaugh hadn't made a personal collar in two months; and when Captain Ansbacher spoke, the world rolled over with its paws in the air.

So there he sat, making out a report on some thick-witted teenager who hadn't even known it was a cop's billfold he was boosting. Murtaugh was a lieutenant, for chrissake, not some patrolman in a prowl car; he was supposed to oversee busts, not make them. "I like my ranking officers to keep in touch with the street," Ansbacher had said, overarticulating as usual. The man was an artist at dealing out small indignities. So Lieutenant James Timothy Murtaugh put the collar on an adolescent pickpocket and typed up the report in quadruplicate. *Keep in touch with the street.* Hah. The wonderful Captain Ansbacher himself never put in an appearance at the scene of a crime until after the shooting was over, when the arrests had been made and the hooraw had died down and it was safe once again for God-fearing people to walk the streets.

Ten minutes. Murtaugh hadn't watched the clock like that since he was a rookie. The phone rang.

Speak of the. "Murtaugh?" Ansbacher said. "We've got a street shooting, near Fifty-third and Park. I want you to cover it yourself."

Murtaugh groaned; only ten more minutes. "Right, Captain." He hung up. *Bastard knows it's the end of my shift.*

Fifty-third and Park. Not your usual setting for a street shooting. Murtaugh stuck his head out of his office door to see who was available. "Eberhart! You're coming with me."

Sergeant Eberhart nodded and got up from his desk with no particular show of resentment; he'd just come *on* duty.

The scene of the shooting was oddly quiet in spite of the number of people there. The rotating light on top of the medical examiner's van served notice to passersby (some of whom stopped to gawk) that something was wrong. Officers in uniform, two patrol cars. Sergeant Eberhart pulled up to a fire hydrant and parked.

A man's body lay dramatically spread-eagled on the sidewalk in front of an office building; an Oriental named Wu from the medical examiner's office was inspecting the dead man's hands. Three uniformed officers were standing guard. Murtaugh knew one of them. "Fill me in, Sodini."

"Hello, Lieutenant. Victim's name is Jerry Sussman, and he has an office upstairs here." Officer Sodini jerked his head toward the office building behind him. "Shot at approximately ten-fifteen P.M. That's forty-five minutes ago, Lieutenant."

Murtaugh closed his eyes. "I know what time it is, Sodini. Who called the police?"

"Sussman's secretary. She witnessed the shooting, sir. My partner took her back inside."

Murtaugh nodded to Sergeant Eberhart, who went into the building to talk to the secretary. "You have his billfold?"

"I didn't touch the body, Lieutenant."

Very proper. "Anybody else see the shooting?"

"The secretary says not. None of these people saw anything." He meant the gawkers.

"I want you—and you and you," including the other two officers, "to do a door-to-door—say one block each side of the street. Anybody who saw anything, heard anything. Look for nightwatchmen, like that. Get going."

The three officers moved off on what they all knew was most likely a time-wasting expedition. Murtaugh hunkered down beside the Oriental examining the body and said, "Doctor Wu," by way of greeting.

"Evening, Lieutenant. Looks like a straightforward one this time."

"What can you tell me?"

"Only that he was shot within the past hour at fairly close range. Could be a forty-five—look at the size of that wound. We'll have to find the bullet to be sure."

"I'm going to need his billfold."

Wu gestured with one hand. "Help yourself."

Murtaugh fished out the billfold and a ring of keys. The billfold said Gerald M. Sussman, home address Central Park West, business cards, credit cards, membership cards to private clubs. A fat cat. "When do I get the autopsy report?"

The doctor shrugged. "When it's done. You got a rush on this one?"

"Not particularly. Mostly I want a confirmation on the caliber of the bullet. We don't see forty-fives so much any more. Everybody's moving to nine-millimeter."

Wu grunted. "I'll call you as soon as I have it. Anything you want here or can we take him?"

"You might as well take him." Murtaugh stood up and watched as Wu's assistants zipped the body into the plastic carrier with some effort. The victim had been a big man; the body was heavy and bulky. They were driving away when Murtaugh went into the lobby of the office building to see what Sergeant Eberhart had found out.

"Lieutenant, this is Mrs. Janice Kluvo, kay ell you vee oh. Lieutenant Murtaugh. Mrs. Kluvo saw the shooting but she didn't get a look at the killer's face. Guy was in a car."

Janice Kluvo was in her fifties, tired, and obviously under a strain even though the initial shock had worn off. She was sitting on a folding chair the young police officer standing nearby had scrounged up for her somewhere. She focused on Murtaugh with effort and said his name.

"I'm sorry, Mrs. Kluvo—I know you want to go home, I'll try not to keep you. You say the killer was in a car?"

"That's right, Lieutenant, he shot from the car."

"How? Bang-bang Chicago style?"

"No, it wasn't like that. He was just driving along like everybody else. Then he pulled out of the line of traffic—"

33

"Dark two-door sedan, no make," Sergeant Eberhart interrupted.

"He drove right up to the curb. We'd just come out of the building—we were working late tonight. Then the man in the car said, 'Jerry Sussman?' Like asking a question. Mr. Sussman went over to the car and the man shot him—just like that!"

Murtaugh and Eberhart exchanged a quick glance. A professional checking to make sure he had the right target? "Did you go over to the car with Mr. Sussman?"

"No, that's why I didn't get a look at the driver."

"Only the one man in the car?"

"I think so. I'm sorry to be so unhelpful, but it was dark and it happened fast and it was Mr. Sussman I was concerned about. I didn't even think to look for a license number." Her face was strained.

"Don't worry about it, Mrs. Kluvo, it was probably a rental anyway. Did you and Sussman work late often?"

"No, almost never. It's just that this month has been especially hectic and the work piled up. Mr. Sussman was selling one project and buying another, and between the two transactions we got a little behind."

"What projects? What line of work was he in?"

"Mr. Sussman is a publisher." She paused, and the men watching could see her think: *was*. "He was selling *Summit* magazine and buying into *Q.T.*"

"*Summit* I know—what's *Q.T.*?"

"A supermarket tabloid." She pressed the tips of the fingers of both hands against her eyes; Murtaugh could see her hands were trembling.

Suddenly the young police officer who'd been hovering discreetly in the background stepped up to her. "You all right, ma'am?"

Mrs. Kluvo nodded and mustered up a smile for him.

34

Murtaugh felt that quick wave of sympathy he always felt for eyewitnesses. Especially if the witness knew the person he or she had watched die. Mrs. Kluvo probably wanted to scream and scream and scream; but she was still making the effort to be civil.

He handed her Sussman's key ring and asked which was the office key. She picked out the right one and told him the office number. "Is this going to take much longer, Lieutenant? I'd like to call my husband. I know he's worrying."

Murtaugh pressed his lips together and thought. "I don't see any reason why you can't go on home now. We can finish this tomorrow." He arranged with her to come in and make a statement the following morning and turned to Sergeant Eberhart. "You have her home address?"

Eberhart looked pained. "Yes, Lieutenant, I've got her home address."

Murtaugh suppressed a smile; he didn't like being asked obvious questions either. "Thank you for your help, Mrs. Kluvo. The officer here will drive you home." He didn't know the young man's name.

In the elevator on the way up to Sussman's office, Eberhart said, "Couldn't have taken more than ten seconds, the way Mrs. Kluvo tells it."

"Yeah. He pulls up to the curb, pops Sussman, and drives away. Nice and neat."

"Sure looks like a hired job."

Murtaugh agreed.

Sussman's office was rather characterless, although someone—Mrs. Kluvo, no doubt—had tried to pep the place up with an array of houseplants. Murtaugh guessed that Sussman didn't spend a whole lot of time in the office; his desk had that look to it. A man on the go, then.

Murtaugh sent Eberhart into the file room while he himself went through Sussman's appointment calendar and unanswered correspondence. Twenty minutes later he still didn't have a picture of the kind of man Jerry Sussman had been. He was big physically, Murtaugh had seen that for himself. He was pretty big financially as well—that meant he'd made some enemies along the way. What little Murtaugh could glean from the correspondence made Sussman sound like a hard case, a touch ruthless in his business dealings. So far, no surprises.

There was much about Sussman he still needed to know. Who stood to profit from his death? What about his business associates—who were they and did they have the kind of connections that could put them in touch with a professional killer? What happened to Sussman's various holdings now? Who was his lawyer? Did he have any family? What happened to the two deals he'd been making when he was shot down—did they fall through or were the papers already signed?

Sergeant Eberhart came in from the file room with a slightly dazed look on his face. "Lieutenant, we got a hell of a lot of work ahead of us."

"Um. I'd just come to that conclusion myself. I think we'll start with the two things he was working on. The sale of *Summit* magazine and the purchase of *Q-Tips* or whatever the hell it is."

"*Q.T.* Like, what we're telling you is on the q.t." The Sergeant grinned. "They pronounce it 'Cutie.' "

"Eberhart, you amaze me. All right, pull the files on those two. We might as well get started."

Two days later the phone call Murtaugh had been waiting for came.

"He's here, in his office," Sergeant Eberhart's voice

said over the phone. "Says he's been out of town and didn't know about Sussman. Came back as soon as he heard."

"Sit on him." Murtaugh slammed down the receiver and hurried out of his office.

In the past two days Murtaugh had learned quite a lot about Jerry Sussman. The man used his money to bully people. Nothing new about that; an uncomfortably large segment of the population thought that was what money was *for*. But Sussman had had a way of making the intimidation a personal matter, as if he fed on other people's discomfort. One-upmanship was the air he breathed.

None of his business associates had really liked Sussman; they did business with him because he was a good money risk or because they had no alternative. His secretary, Mrs. Kluvo, liked him; he'd paid her a good salary and delegated a lot of authority to her. She admitted he wasn't in very often and she could run the office pretty much as she pleased.

Sussman had been married and divorced; his ex-wife and their fifteen-year-old daughter were now living in Scottsdale, Arizona. Sussman had provided for his ex-wife in his will—rather generously, Murtaugh thought. *Just generously enough,* Sussman's lawyer had remarked dryly, *to prevent the former Mrs. Sussman from making trouble.*

The bulk of Sussman's money was tied up in his various projects. In all of his partnership contracts, there was a clause to the effect that in case of the death of one partner, the surviving partner or partners had first option to buy up the deceased partner's shares. Whether they exercised the option or not, the proceeds from any sale were to go to Sussman's daughter.

So a teenager in Arizona who hadn't seen her father

since she was six years old was on the road to becoming a very wealthy young lady. Mrs. and Miss Sussman's presence in Scottsdale at the time of Sussman's death had been satisfactorily attested to. In addition, Mrs. Sussman had cut all her ties to New York; she didn't even exchange Christmas cards with former friends who still lived there. It seemed highly unlikely that she could have engineered Sussman's death.

Murtaugh mentally scratched her off the list and concentrated on the two transactions Sussman had been working on right before he was killed. Both deals were now off; papers had been signed in neither case.

In the case of *Q.T.*, the present publisher and the editorial staff were desolated by Sussman's murder. *Q.T.* had been dying on the stands and in the supermarkets; too much competition. The market was saturated with gossipy tabloids, and only the strongest (that is, the juiciest) were going to make it. The people at *Q.T.* needed fresh money, a financial shot in the arm if they were going to compete on the level needed to survive. *They* had approached *Sussman*, not the other way around. Now, unless they could find another money man fast, *Q.T.* would fold.

Summit magazine, however, was quite a different matter. Sussman had been negotiating its sale to UltraMedia Corporation without the consent or even the knowledge of the editor. The editor, Leon Walsh, had built *Summit* up from nothing and was a part-owner. But he couldn't override the majority owner's decisions and had learned only a few days ago that his magazine was being sold out from under him.

"This Walsh is looking good for it," Captain Ansbacher had said in his meant-to-be-heard politician's voice when he'd called Murtaugh into his office the day before. "You picked him up?"

"Not yet. Mr. Walsh seems to have made himself inaccessible."

"You're telling me you don't have him in custody?" Ansbacher said in a tone intended to carry through the open door toward whoever felt like listening. "What about a warrant? You did get a warrant, didn't you?"

"If we do bring him in, it'll just be for questioning," Murtaugh said quietly, hoping Ansbacher would moderate his own tones.

He just became louder. "Questioning?" He snorted. "Come on, Murtaugh, why the tippy-toe-ing around? A warrant can be a weapon if you know how to use it right."

"It's a matter of evidence, Captain." Murtaugh was sick to death of this cat-and-mouse game. Ansbacher knew perfectly well they didn't have enough evidence to arrest Walsh—hell, they didn't have *any* evidence. Just a motive . . . and a suspicion. "Why don't we talk to him first? Then we can decide how we want to play it."

Captain Ansbacher put his lips together and smiled without opening his mouth. Then, when the silence had grown uncomfortable enough to suit him, he said: "How are you going to talk to him when you can't even find him?"

Murtaugh had left the interview with the taste of bile in his mouth. It occurred to him that Jerry Sussman and Captain Ansbacher were two of a kind: they both enjoyed watching other people squirm. Murtaugh felt a quick stab of sympathy for the missing Leon Walsh.

Murtaugh's wife Ellie had subscribed to *Summit* up to a few years ago but then had dropped it. On impulse he called her at her office and asked why.

"It was getting to be just like every other magazine," she said. "It used to be something special—but now it's trying to be all things to all readers. Why do you want to know?"

"Tell you tonight," he promised.

The change in the magazine—could that have been Jerry Sussman's doing? If so, Leon Walsh would have even more of a motive than ever. Murtaugh sent Sergeant Eberhart over to the *Summit* offices to talk to the staff. Eberhart called to say Walsh was back.

"I'll put it as delicately as I can. I hated the bastard's guts." Leon Walsh smiled wryly. "I might as well tell you. If I don't, somebody out there will." He made a flapping gesture with his hand that Murtaugh took to be a reference to the *Summit* staff.

The Lieutenant sat in a comfortable chair facing Walsh's desk, in the messiest office he had ever seen. "How did you feel when you heard he'd been killed?"

"Shocked, numb—virtually paralyzed." Walsh's face was pained. "And at the same time, underneath the shock —I was pleased, Lieutenant. And the more I thought about it, the less shocked I was and the more pleased I became. To be free of that bastard once and for all—even if I'd lost *Summit*, I'd still be rid of Sussman and *that* was something to cheer about." Walsh didn't try to hide the fact that he was worried. "Then, of course, I came to my senses. I like to think of myself as a relatively civilized man, Lieutenant. I'm not proud of the way I reacted."

Murtaugh nodded, taking it all with a grain of salt. He'd seen too many men admit to something discreditable in that same open, disarming way—admitting it because they were hoping to conceal something even more discreditable. But Walsh's reaction had been identical to that of quite a few of the people who'd known Jerry Sussman: first shock, then pleasure, then shame at feeling the pleasure. Walsh could be telling the truth.

Murtaugh was having trouble getting a fix on the man. As the editor of a magazine like *Summit,* Walsh must be a man of considerable authority. Yet he didn't generate that impression when you talked to him. Walsh had more of an average-guy air about him; he was probably easy to work with and never pulled rank on his staff. His manner certainly showed no signs of the kind of barely restrained violence that could lead a man to murder. Even his admission that he'd hated his partner had carried no residue of smoldering hostility. *I like to think of myself as a relatively civilized man,* he'd said. Was that self-denigrating strain a true part of Walsh's character or was it just an act?

Walsh had been out of town at the time Sussman was killed, in Connecticut, with his ex-wife. He and Leila Hudson had registered in a country inn—a story that could be checked a dozen different ways. But Walsh's physical whereabouts at the time of the shooting probably wasn't important; by now Murtaugh was fairly well convinced the shooting had been a professional job. The question now was whether Walsh had hired a killer to save his magazine for him or not. That was the kind of connection that was so hard to prove.

Murtaugh told Walsh he'd be talking to him again and left the editor's office. The Lieutenant felt a little out of place in the *Summit* offices, a feeling he hadn't had for years.

Sergeant Eberhart, on the other hand, looked right at home. He came up to Murtaugh and said, "Lieutenant, there's a woman down the hall you might want to talk to. Name's Fran Caffrey and she's the fiction editor."

"What's she got to say?"

"As little as possible, unfortunately. She was a sort of unofficial spy for Sussman here. Seems everybody in the office knew about it except Walsh. She wouldn't talk to me, but maybe you can get her to open up."

Murtaugh nodded and went down the hall to the office Eberhart indicated. So Sussman had thought he needed a spy in what was technically his own organization. Interesting.

Fran Caffrey was waiting for him, standing by her desk and leaning slightly forward as if ready to pounce. Had Eberhart scared her or was she always that tense?

Murtaugh barely had time to mention his name before she interrupted. "That sergeant of yours has been asking questions about me! Am I a suspect or something?"

"Good gracious, no." Murtaugh tried to look properly shocked at the idea. "It's just that we can't understand why Sussman would need his own private ear in a magazine he owned."

"I don't know what you mean," she said stiffly.

"Yes, you do. You weren't breaking any law by reporting to the primary owner what was going on in his own magazine. But it does imply Mr. Sussman didn't trust Mr. Walsh."

"Mr. Sussman didn't trust anyone. Not even me." She sounded bitter.

Something worth pursuing there? "He disappointed you in some way?" When she didn't answer, Murtaugh prompted: "Perhaps he promised you something."

She threw him a hard glance. "Shrewd guess, Lieutenant. Or maybe I'm making it obvious, I don't know." She sighed. "Yes, he promised me something. It was a promise I know now he had no intention of keeping."

A promotion, Murtaugh thought. Perhaps even Walsh's job. "Would this broken promise have anything to do with UltraMedia Corporation's plans for *Summit* after the takeover?"

Fran Caffrey smiled a slow, sad smile. "Yes, indeed it would, Lieutenant. That's exactly what it has to do with. Do you know what UltraMedia was planning? They're not going to admit it, but I have a friend who works there and I *know*. They weren't just going to get rid of Leon Walsh—everybody'd seen that coming for months, he and Mr. Sussman were barely speaking. But the Ultra-Media powers-that-be were going to let the entire staff go and bring in their own people. Every single one of us would have been fired, right down to the last file clerk."

"So you could say Jerry Sussman's murder was quite timely," Murtaugh mused. "A whole lot of jobs were saved. Now I wonder who's job meant the most to him?"

Fran laughed in a jittery sort of way. "No, you don't. You don't wonder, I mean. And you can forget it—Leon Walsh never killed anybody. Leon's as nonviolent as they come."

"Ah, but many a man who shrinks from violence up close often finds a solution in hiring someone else to do the job for him. Someone who doesn't faint at the sight of blood."

She was shaking her head. "You're on the wrong track. Leon—hiring a, a *hit man*? That's absurd. He wouldn't know how. Forget about Leon. He's not behind it."

"You don't think much of him, do you?"

She shrugged. "Leon's all right as long as he stays in that office. *Summit* is his whole world—it's all he cares about, it's all he knows. He's a little short-sighted, but he *functions* when he's editing. But negotiating with a hired

43

killer? Unh-uh. He could no more arrange for a murder to be committed than I could fly to Saturn. Forget Leon Walsh, Lieutenant. He's not your man."

Murtaugh examined her closely, trying to read her face, her body language. A lot of tightly controlled anger there. Her position at *Summit* had been saved by whoever put a bullet into Jerry Sussman (a .45 caliber, shattering the spine: Dr. Wu had been right). But *Summit's* fiction editor had thought she was in line for something bigger, not for dismissal. Sussman had promised her something she'd wanted, perhaps the editorship, perhaps something else—and then had betrayed her just as casually as he'd betrayed Leon Walsh. That might be motive enough in Walsh's case; but Fran Caffrey was a young woman—she still had years to go and heights to scale. Her career would not end with the loss of this one job. She didn't have the investment in *Summit* that Leon Walsh had.

"When did you learn Sussman had sold you out?" Murtaugh asked her.

"Just this morning."

"Your friend at UltraMedia called you?"

"No, I called him. He wasn't going to tell me." Her voice was curiously flat.

So Fran Caffrey would have no motive since she didn't know of Sussman's doublecross until after his death. *If* she was telling the truth about when she found out. But she had made no effort at all to shift suspicion on to Leon Walsh, the person with the most to lose. In fact she had stated flatly, several times, that Walsh couldn't have done it.

Murtaugh was inclined to agree with her. Besides, she sounded so *certain*.

· · ·

Leon Walsh watched the two police investigators leave the *Summit* offices with a distinct lifting of the spirits. That hadn't been too bad. It wasn't over yet, he knew— but it hadn't been too bad.

Of course they're going to suspect you—it's only natural, Leila had said. *You've got to prepare yourself for that.*

How do you prepare yourself for being suspected of murder?

Tell the truth, Leila had advised. *Don't try to pretend that you and Jerry Sussman were friends or even that you had an amicable working arrangement. They'll find out how it was from other people. Just tell the truth.*

So he'd told the truth, even to the point of confessing his shameful pleasure upon hearing of Sussman's death— which was probably going farther than Leila meant. But it had felt *so good* to tell that police Lieutenant what he really thought of Sussman. Confession must still be good for the soul.

Leila had been a rock, an absolute rock. (If only she'd been that caring while they were still married!) When he'd thought he was losing *Summit,* she'd talked him out of his near-suicidal depression and arranged for both of them to get out of the city for a few days. They hadn't turned on the TV or looked at a newspaper the whole time they were in Connecticut, and it was only through an accidental encounter at the inn with someone Walsh knew that he learned his traitorous partner had been deliberately killed by person or persons unknown.

Their rush back to New York had been colored by both anxiety and cautious hope; Leila had had to drive, he'd been in too much of a daze. When he found out the deal with UltraMedia had not been "finalized"—one of Sussman's favorite junk words—Walsh had almost fainted from the relief. *Summit* was still his! In fact, it was more his now than it had been ever since the day he'd struck his Faustian bargain with Sussman.

The contract Walsh had signed had one little clause in it that now put him in complete control of his magazine. That clause said that when one partner died, the other had first option on the deceased's shares. Walsh wouldn't even have to buy all of Sussman's shares—just enough to give himself majority ownership. He could raise that much money easily. Then *Summit* would be his, answerable to no one except Leon Walsh.

No more toadying to advertisers, no more slop articles catering to a constantly changing readership that wanted everything made easy. And best of all, Hartley Dunlop and the trendy freakishness of UltraMedia could never touch him now. Walsh picked up a manuscript from his desk, one that had been commissioned on the basis of a Sussman "suggestion"—and dropped it into the out-basket. All those times he'd given in to pressure from Sussman—they didn't matter now. Now he had a chance to redeem himself. How many people ever got a true second chance? Now *Summit* could go back to being what it was always meant to be: a *literary* magazine, by God.

He put in a long and full day, happily doing what he did best. Walsh couldn't remember the last time he'd felt this good. One act of violence and all his problems were solved—and he hadn't even had to commit the act himself. And since he didn't know who *did* commit it, he didn't even have to worry about his conscience bothering him.

When he got home that night, his body hurt with the kind of tiredness that felt good after a good day's work. And the apartment looked good to him; it was the same apartment where he and Leila had lived when they were married. Even *that* was looking good again.

Seven pieces of mail were waiting in the box. One was clearly a bill, in a window envelope, but it was such an odd slate-blue that it caught Walsh's eye. Something else odd: no return address. He opened the envelope.

FEE FOR SERVICES RENDERED

One murder, arranged to coincide
with establishment of Connecticut
alibi

Amt. due $100,000.00

CHAPTER

4

Ellie Murtaugh was worried about her husband. Both of them had long since given up trying not to bring their work home with them; one's work was one's life, not some separate category to be filed away for sixteen hours out of every twenty-four. But now Ellie was beginning to feel a third presence in their marriage. Captain Ansbacher had never set foot in their home—but he was there just the same.

"I don't mind living with one cop," she said one night when her husband couldn't stop talking about Ansbacher, "but two are beginning to get me down."

James Timothy Murtaugh didn't answer right away. They were in bed, but turning out the light hadn't stopped what had become a nightly tirade. Then, stiffly: "I'm sorry. I didn't realize I was imposing."

Ellie laughed. "Relax. Just put the man out of your mind for a while, Jim."

"Easier said than done."

"Then find a course of action. Confront him. *Do* something. Don't let it go on festering."

"Easier said than done."

"You already said that."

He sighed. "I know."

Murtaugh was trying hard not to feel depressed; he could no longer avoid facing an unpalatable truth about his life. More than unpalatable—a nauseating, debilitating truth. And that was: he was as far as he would ever go. All these years as lieutenant, and he knew now he'd never make captain. No matter what he did, he was stuck. Advancement was out of the question, and for one simple reason.

Ansbacher.

Captain Ansbacher had blocked Murtaugh's two attempts at getting himself promoted. In Murtaugh's first try, Ansbacher had shot him down during the board interview. Murtaugh didn't know what his superior had done to sabotage the second attempt. But a sympathetic word had filtered down from above: *Make friends with your Captain.*

It was impossible even to maintain a friendly atmosphere when Ansbacher was around. Murtaugh tried, but everything about the man rubbed him the wrong way—the way he dismissed your theories about a case without even thinking about them, the way he treated his detectives as if they were dirt. Even the way he talked bothered Murtaugh; every syllable was pronounced *so* carefully, *so* distinctly—as if he were making a special effort to spell things out clearly for the moron he was talking to. Impossible to get along with a man who went out of his way to let you know how deficient he considered you to be. And Ansbacher never reevaluated his opinion of anything.

Once the man had his mind set, there was no budging him. There would always be people who thought changing one's mind was a sign of weakness, and Ansbacher was one of them. He'd put Murtaugh into a certain category years ago, and there Murtaugh was going to stay. That category wasn't at the *top* of Ansbacher's shit list; the Captain wasn't out to destroy him, only to prevent his rising any higher in the police hierarchy. Murtaugh was luckier than some.

The man was *weird*. He looked upon himself as a bastion of moral strength in a corrupt and uncaring world. Only Captain Ansbacher knew the real difference between right and wrong. An avid churchgoer all his life, he never quoted scripture at you; consequently newcomers who were unlucky enough to joke about organized religion suddenly found themselves in hot water. The Captain stood foursquare for all the conventional virtues. Murtaugh had gotten on Ansbacher's wrong side because he and Ellie had lived together for two years before they married.

"Decided to make an honest woman of her, did you?" had been Ansbacher's remark at the time of the wedding.

A tacky joke, in terrible taste, but Murtaugh had been going to laugh anyway—when he suddenly realized Ansbacher wasn't joking. He meant it. *Make an honest woman of her*—good lord. The man actually thought that way, in this day and in this place. And the Captain's treatment of those who did not conform to his own personal rules of conduct was downright criminal, in Murtaugh's view. Ansbacher had taken one look at a young officer and decided from the way he walked that he was a pansy. The officer's career in law enforcement came to an abrupt end shortly after that.

How could he do things like that, how could he get away with it? It was something that Murtaugh hadn't been able to puzzle out. Whatever Ansbacher did had the backing of the Commissioner's office, even his meddling in his officers' private lives. There was something warped about Ansbacher, some sexual hang-up that made him rabidly intolerant of any way of life different from his own. There was no he-ing and she-ing among the men and women under Ansbacher's command, no casual talk of affairs. Ansbacher's wife of thirty years was one of the women who "choose to stay at home"; his children were grown and successful and respectable. Murtaugh had no children and his wife worked at a career of her own; ergo, he was suspect.

He was suspect, and he would stay suspect until the day either he or Ansbacher keeled over for good. The Captain would never change his opinion of his lieutenant; he was like a bulldog who'd got a firm grip and wouldn't let go no matter what. Ansbacher even looked a little bit like a bulldog—heavy jowls, pug nose, small eyes.

Albert Payson Terhune—unbidden, the name floated into Murtaugh's mind. My god, he thought, all those dog stories. He'd read them as a boy, all of them, and hadn't thought about them for years. It must have been seeing Ansbacher as a bulldog that called Terhune to mind. Terhune had been a collie man; and while he acknowledged the strength of a bulldog's jaw in never letting go once the animal had a good grip, he had maintained the collie was the superior fighter. Because the collie was constantly on the move, biting here, nipping there, always looking for a better point of attack. He'd mentioned it several times, in different books. For some reason it had been important to Terhune to prove the collie was a better fighter than the bulldog.

So, is there a moral in all this? Murtaugh wondered. Am I supposed to turn collie and keep nipping away at Ansbacher?

"Ellie," he asked, "did you ever read Albert Payson Terhune when you were a kid?"

But she was asleep.

Ansbacher the Bulldog had gotten something else between his jaws and wouldn't let go: he was convinced Leon Walsh had hired someone to kill his partner. Or at least so he said; he could be pressuring Murtaugh into making an arrest that wouldn't stand up. Something for the file, booking a suspect on insufficient evidence, ammo to use against Murtaugh in his next bid for a captaincy. How did you defend yourself against something like that?

Murtaugh was as sure as he could be that Leon Walsh had not arranged the murder of Jerry Sussman, but he could see the day he might have to arrest the editor just to protect himself against Ansbacher. Would I do it? Murtaugh wondered. Arrest a man I knew was innocent just to get out from under the heat? It wasn't as if Walsh would go to prison—he wouldn't even go to trial. He'd be out as soon as the D.A.'s office decided they didn't have a case.

And Captain Ansbacher could make life hell for any subordinate who didn't toe the line. He'd done it before, and to Murtaugh—especially when Murtaugh had disagreed with him about a case. Ansbacher had forced him to close a few investigations before he was satisfied; he'd always wondered about those. But Ansbacher could do it. In time he could probably force him to arrest a totally innocent Leon Walsh.

No.

Damn it, enough was enough. What had he come to, lying there in the dark actually thinking about bringing charges of murder against a man he felt sure was innocent? Just because one narrow-minded, non-thinking, power-happy police captain had got it into his head that the editor of *Summit* magazine had hired a killer to do his dirty work for him.

What have I come to? Ellie was right; he needed to confront Ansbacher, or find some course of action to take instead of letting it fester and fester and fester. He needed to *do* something.

He sighed. Easier said than done.

While Murtaugh lay sleepless in his need to decide what to do, a different man in a mid-Manhattan high-rise was also trying to reach a decision.

"It's just that I don't really trust opera singers, you see," he told the wall in a reasonable manner.

The man liked to call himself Pluto—the whimsy of mixing the devil and Mickey Mouse's pet dog appealed to him. He was in his study; one wall was lined with cork-board. Affixed to the corkboard with push-pins were photographs, newspaper clippings, magazine articles, a map. Dead center was an enlarged glossy of a man wearing the costume of the Duke of Mantua in *Rigoletto*.

"Italian tenors are the worst," the man who called himself Pluto said. "So temperamental."

The Duke of Mantua seemed to wink at him. The singer in the photo was youngish, good-looking, not too much overweight. He had a distinctive voice, one that could never be confused with any other singer's pearly tones. Next year's superstar, if he lived that long.

It wasn't *that* tenor's temperament that worried Pluto.
Oh no—it was the other one who made him uneasy, the
primo tenore: Signor Luigi Bàccolo, supertenor, king of
the operatic hill for lo these many years. Bàccolo the
Great—and he *was* great, at one time, and still was more
often than not. Irregular greatness, must be a pain to
live with. Never knowing whether tonight was going
to be one of the outstanding performances or merely an
acceptable one. Eh, Luig'—whassamadda, you slippin'?

The Duke of Mantua in the glossy photograph was
John Herman, a blue-eyed, blond Canadian who hid his
Nordickness under dark make-up and a wig every time
he stepped out on a stage. Some of the world's greatest
Italian tenors hadn't been Italian at all—the Swedish
Bjoerling, the Jewish-American Tucker, the Spanish
Domingo. And now Canadian John Herman, whose con-
cert fees had risen to equal those of Luigi Bàccolo and
who was singing more and more of the great Bàccolo's
roles.

It was too soon; Bàccolo had years of singing left in
him. But the new boy from up north was beginning to
catch on with the ever-fickle opera-going public. There
were other tenors around, but none to carry the serious
threat that the Canadian posed. John Herman smiled out
of his photograph, a wickedly sensual Duke of Mantua,
a role that once had been Luigi Bàccolo's private property
at the Metropolitan Opera.

Bàccolo would pay, the man called Pluto thought, no
doubt of that. The tenor would gladly pay for the removal
of his rival. But the question was, would he keep his
mouth shut afterward? Would he be able to, overemo-
tional and excitable as he was? It would be a risk.

That was the trouble with free-lance murder. So many
risks.

You just never knew how people were going to react. Pluto knew it was a foolish hope, but he'd still like to see a little gratitude once in a while. When you tell people that their recent good fortune is the direct result of something *you* have done—was it too much to expect at least a thank you? Of course, Pluto always collected his fee—he *always* collected—but still, an occasional expression of appreciation would surely not be amiss.

His clients just didn't realize all that was involved. He couldn't simply push the offending party down a steep flight of stairs and then walk away. That might look like an accident; it was important that the death *not* look like an accident. It had to be quite clearly a case of homicide, the police had to be involved, it had to be in the newspapers and on television. The client had to understand beyond doubt that he personally was benefiting from somebody else's act of murder. Otherwise he might think Pluto was just some nobody trying to cash in on a semi-unfortunate accidental death. The client must be made to understand that he was in debt to *a practiced killer.* That always made collection of the fee a fairly smooth operation.

No one appreciated all the preparation that was involved. He had expenses. Pluto had to research his subjects, even to the point of occasionally employing the services of credit bureaus and detective agencies. When seeking out a prospective source of income, he always looked for a combination of conflict and good money; but he had to know a great deal about the combatants before he took sides. Then too he had to time the killing perfectly; his future client must have an airtight alibi or the whole thing was just so much wasted effort. A client arrested for murder was no client at all. Pluto had actually passed over several rather promising conflicts because one or more of the participants had some remote link with organized crime. In such cases the police would immediately think *contract killing* and haul in Pluto's client without a second thought. A hundred thousand dollars down the drain.

And on top of all that, he also had to convince his clients that his bill did not mark the beginning of a lifetime of blackmail payments. *Fee for services rendered*, that's what his mailed statements said and that's what he intended to collect. One payment, period. He was no blackmailer. This, too, was a risk; Pluto feared there were people in the world who just might take their own lives rather than face a lifetime of being bled dry by a stranger. It hadn't happened yet, but it was a possibility that haunted him.

This last time, for instance—he'd thought the possibility had come true. He'd made a serious mistake: he'd overestimated the *Summit* editor's strength. He may have overestimated his bankroll as well—but that was Walsh's problem. The fee was fixed, one hundred thousand. But Walsh had gone to pieces over the phone, the first time they'd talked. The editor was feeling guilty over profiting from Sussman's death, he was feeling guilty over not calling the police when he'd received Pluto's bill, he was afraid for his own life, he was afraid he wouldn't be able to raise the money, he was afraid he would be hit for payment again and again. A messy mixture of self-blame and self-interest.

Pluto didn't quite know what to make of it. Over the phone he'd said, "You may call me Pluto. I recently sent you a bill—"

And Walsh had burst into tears.

Now what do you do with a man like that? At age fifty-four, a person is just about as grown up as he's ever going to be—yet Walsh had blubbered like a baby. Pluto was exasperated. It was a simple *business* arrangement; all this emotionalism was out of place.

When Walsh finally recovered to the point where he could talk intelligibly, he'd actually asked for some sort of E-Z Payment Plan, Reasonable Rates. One payment, Pluto had said firmly; he wanted as little contact with his clients as possible. How Walsh raised the money was his business; and Pluto kept drumming away that after that payment, Walsh would never hear from him again. *One* payment.

He always allowed his clients a reasonable amount of time to raise the money; in Walsh's case, he suspected, it would take a little longer than usual. But Pluto could be patient when it served his interests to be so. Leon Walsh was adequately terrified; there was no need to push him. He'd get the money.

But what if he couldn't get it all? Pluto mused idly over what he himself would do in such a case; it had never happened before. Would he just take what he could get and forget the rest? Or would he break his long-standing rule and agree to accept payments over a period of time? The answer to that one was *No*. He could kill Walsh—as punishment. But there was no profit in that; it wouldn't even serve as an object lesson, since no one else knew about their arrangement. Pluto found himself halfway hoping Walsh would not be able to raise the whole amount—just so he could find out what he *would* do when the time came.

But all that was for later. In the meantime, it was business as usual. Pluto didn't intend to sit on his hands waiting for Walsh to pay his bill. He was going to need money himself soon, a lot of money. Besides, the War of the Tenors was reaching epic proportions; even people who never listened to opera knew of the enmity between Luigi Bàccolo and John Herman. The time was ripe to cash in on the rivalry.

There remained the difficulty of dealing with Bàccolo afterward. Bàccolo's temperament was legendary, deliberately exaggerated (originally for publicity purposes, no doubt) until it had become an integral part of the man's personality. The singer was theatrical, flamboyant, a regular cliché of an Italian tenor. All of life was to him one *grande passione* after another. Would he be able to keep quiet about what had happened?

It'd probably be safer to remove Bàccolo and collect from Herman. But that presented problems too: Herman didn't have as much money as Bàccolo, and the younger man might balk at paying anyway. The older Bàccolo wasn't that great a threat to the upcoming Herman; all the Canadian had to do was wait, and age and an eventually overworked voice would take care of his rival for him. He didn't need a man with a gun.

Bàccolo, on the other hand, could very well profit from Pluto's services. The very things that were helping John Herman were working against the *primo tenore*—time, primarily. Herman could outwait Bàccolo, but Bàccolo was already losing ground. Pluto never met his clients face to face, so there was no danger the garrulous tenor would identify him. And as to any story Bàccolo told about some unknown gunman who murdered on spec— might that not be taken as simply one more example of the theatrical self-aggrandizement now more or less expected of the tenor? The danger seemed less the more Pluto thought about it, until he at last did make his decision: he would go with Bàccolo.

Ycs, that was best. Bàccolo would be the client, Herman the target. Pluto opened a cabinet drawer and studied its contents. He'd used the .45 on Jerry Sussman; let's see . . . the .357 Magnum this time, he thought. Pluto never used a gun once and dropped it at the scene, as so many other practitioners of his profession did. For one thing, that would look like a contract killing; and Pluto didn't care to encourage the police's thinking along those lines. For another, there was no way for him to acquire a new weapon without personal contact of some kind. So he kept his small arsenal in tip-top condition, replenishing it only when absolutely necessary.

Bàccolo versus Herman—Pluto was satisfied with his decision. If you wanted to be a success in this business, you had to know how to choose the right side in a quarrel. He would help Bàccolo.

Besides, John Herman's top notes did get a bit reedy at times.

At first Leila Hudson had wondered why her former husband had brought her to Luchow's; Leon knew she hated noisy restaurants. But then it occurred to her he was acting like those chickenprick husbands who take their wives to public places to ask for a divorce. To avoid scenes, noisy recriminations, embarrassing outcries of pain. Leon was *protecting himself* against her even while he was trying to get something out of her.

"Let me make sure I've got this straight," she said. "You want me to lend you twenty-five thousand dollars— but I'm not to ask you what it's for? Did I get that right?"

He looked miserable. "That's about it. It's damned unreasonable, Leila, I know that. But I just can't help it. I have to have the money and I can't tell you why."

Now what kind of mess have you gotten yourself into?

she thought. "Can't you raise money on your *Summit* shares?"

"I've already done that," Walsh said tightly. "I need twenty-five thousand more."

More. "That must be one hell of a spot you're in," she said. "Leon, are you being blackmailed?"

"No, not really, I—"

"Not really?! What kind of answer is that—*not really?* Are you being blackmailed or not?"

"Not. It's . . . it's money I owe, that's all I can tell you. For God's sake, Leila, don't make it any harder than it is."

She recognized the pitch for sympathy and ignored it. "Twenty-five thousand isn't all that much. You should be able to get it on your signature alone. Take out a dozen small bank loans, two thousand apiece or whatever."

"I've already gone that route as far as I can go. I had to raise money to buy Sussman's *Summit* shares, enough to give me a majority. And then this other thing came along on top of it, this thing I can't tell you about. I'm tapped out. If I can't get a personal loan, I. . . ." He trailed off, his eyes seeing something inside his head, something hidden to Leila.

"Finish it, Leon," she said, curious. "What happens if you don't get a personal loan?"

"Then I die."

Leila stared at him in disbelief. She was outraged; what kind of fool did he take her for? She was prevented from saying anything by the appearance of the waiter, who gathered up dishes and asked if everything was all right and refused to leave until he got an answer.

When at last he'd gone, Leila said to Walsh, "So you're going to kick it if I don't come up with twenty-five thousand dollars for you, is that it? That makes me responsible for whether you live or die—cute, Leon, real cute." She paused. "You've always been quick to dump guilt on other people, but I swear to God this one takes the cake!"

"Leila, I'm not making it up, it's true! My life depends on my getting the money before next Wednesday. That's as long as I've got."

"Somebody has threatened your life. Is that what you're saying?"

"Well, yes, that's what it comes down to."

"And of course you've gone to the police."

"No! The police mustn't know anything about this! I've already told you more than I should—promise me you'll say nothing to the police."

"I'll promise you no such thing," Leila said hotly. "How do I know what you're involving me in? Leon, what have you *done*?"

"I, have, done, nothing." He gave her his best sincere look. "I have broken no laws, and I'm not being black-mailed. It's just that I'm in this . . . situation. I've got to pay off, ah, *pay* some money I owe, and I've got it all except the twenty-five thousand. This man I owe money to—I'm afraid of him, Leila. I'm afraid of what he'll do. He's dangerous."

She made a noise of nervous exasperation. "All the more reason to go to the police."

Hating himself for what he was about to do, Walsh took a deep breath and said, "That wouldn't solve anything. Leila, this man is dangerous in a way you can't even imagine. He might kill me—or he might kill someone close to me. You know who that would be, don't you?" He looked away from her horrified face, forced himself to go on. "You're the only one I'm close to. You."

Her mouth worked for a moment before she said, "You're telling me *my* life is in danger."

"*Might* be. He could go after either one of us."

She laughed disbelievingly. "Leon, that's preposterous."

He shook his head, praying she would swallow the lie. "I don't know how to reach this man, I don't even know his real name. The police wouldn't be able to stop him— they wouldn't even be able to find him. You're contaminated, Leila, just by your association with me."

Leila looked far away. "You mean," she said in a small voice, "there's a man out there somewhere who goes around threatening to kill people if they don't pay him—"

"No, no—it's not like that. I *owe* him the money, Leila. It's a one-shot deal—I pay him what I owe and I never hear from him again." He hoped. "I wish I could tell you the details, but I truly can't. I *can* buy our safety —I wanted to do it by myself, so you'd never know you were even momentarily in danger because of me. But I just can't swing it. I came up twenty-five thousand short."

Leila was silent for a long time. Then: "I can't get it until tomorrow."

Walsh nodded. "I have until Wednesday," he said.

CHAPTER

5

Sergeant Eberhart shifted his weight uncomfortably. Captain Ansbacher never invited you to sit down. The Captain himself leaned back in his desk chair.

"You did question the *Summit* staff? All of them?" Ansbacher asked in his overly precise speech that always made Eberhart feel like some dumb kid who'd been called into the principal's office.

"Yessir, I did. I talked to every one of them."

"I didn't see any reports."

"I reported to Lieutenant Murtaugh."

"In writing?"

"No, sir—verbally."

Ansbacher narrowed his already small eyes. "What is the matter with you people? How many times do you have to be told? *I want written reports on all homicide interrogations.* Do you understand that? Are you capable of understanding that?"

"Well, they weren't exactly interrogations, Captain."

"Oh? Then what were they . . . exactly?" Ansbacher said sarcastically.

Eberhart cleared his throat. "Interviews, I'd call 'em. We didn't bring anybody in for intensive questioning. The *Summit* staff people aren't suspects, Captain—just sources of information."

Ansbacher looked at him a long time without saying anything, long enough for an already uncomfortable Sergeant Eberhart to start fidgeting. Eberhart tried to meet the Captain's eyes but couldn't; he found himself staring at Ansbacher's pink and white cheeks. Jowls that would do a bulldog proud—and the complexion of a baby.

Then Ansbacher said, softly, "They aren't suspects, you say. You don't consider Leon Walsh a suspect?"

"Lieutenant Murtaugh doesn't," Eberhart answered—and immediately felt like a fink. Buck-passer.

"I know what Murtaugh thinks. I'm asking you what you think."

Eberhart thought furiously before replying. Was Ansbacher offering him a way out? It sounded as if he was building some sort of case against the Lieutenant—and wanted to use Eberhart in some way. "I don't really know whether Walsh should be considered a suspect or not," he temporized, wondering if he could get away with straddling the fence.

"Why not?" Ansbacher persisted. "You've been on the case since the start. You must have formed your own opinion, independent of what other people think."

There it was. He was supposed to side with Ansbacher against Murtaugh, with the captain against the lieutenant. Common sense said go with the higher rank. But Murtaugh was a good cop; Eberhart wasn't sure what Ansbacher was. But one thing he did know: he wanted to go on working with Lieutenant Murtaugh.

"Well, sir," Eberhart started out cautiously, "Walsh

isn't the only one to profit from Jerry Sussman's death. Sussman had other partners in other projects—"

"But Walsh was the only one in danger of losing his magazine," Ansbacher interrupted.

"That's what makes him *look* like a suspect. But his alibi checks out—he was in Connecticut at the time of the shooting. We got witnesses. His former wife was with him all the time. Also, there's the desk clerk at the inn where they stayed, a waitress in the coffee shop, one of the maids. They all say Walsh was there, right up to a couple of days after the killing. They stopped for gas on the way up—we got the dated credit card receipt with Walsh's signature on it. No question, Captain. Walsh was in Connecticut when Sussman was killed."

Ansbacher scowled. "So what? A pencil-pusher like Walsh wouldn't do the job himself. He hired somebody."

"We don't think so, Captain. He doesn't have that kind of connections. He doesn't even know somebody who knows somebody who has that kind of connections. He just doesn't move in that world."

"Bank accounts?"

"Two, checking and savings. No large checks or withdrawals in the past year—just enough for bills and walking-around money." Ansbacher knew all that; Lieutenant Murtaugh had kept him informed.

"Did you search his apartment?" Ansbacher asked.

"On what grounds? We got no probable cause for a warrant."

"Bankbooks for accounts you don't know about. Key to a safety deposit box."

"Excuse me, Captain, but we can't get a warrant because we think Walsh *might* have something incriminating in his apartment. You know we—"

Ansbacher barked a laugh. "You're telling me Murtaugh doesn't have a tame judge in his back pocket? Didn't you even try?"

Sergeant Eberhart was sweating; he was in over his head. "Maybe you ought to talk to the Lieutenant, sir. I personally don't see any probable cause, but maybe if you talked it over with—"

"Are you telling me how to do my job, Sergeant?"

"Nossir, I—"

"I've talked with Lieutenant Murtaugh, and now I'm talking to you. I don't think you've been pushing hard enough. What about Sussman's other business partners? Any prospects there?"

"We're still checking them out."

"Meaning you don't have anything. Well, Sergeant, I hope for your sake this one doesn't go down on the books as unsolved. That's not going to help your record any. But you and Murtaugh are on your own now. I can't help you any more—I'm overloaded. I already have six killings on my desk when some opera singer from Toronto gets shot down at Lincoln Center and now I've got the Canadian consul on my back. You'd better know what you're doing, Eberhart."

God, that sounded ominous. "Doing my best," he said noncommittally. Ansbacher's warning had a double meaning: you'd better know what you're doing when you side with Murtaugh instead of me. "That all, Captain?"

Ansbacher looked him up and down as if inspecting him for leaks and then nodded. The sergeant had almost made it out the door when Ansbacher spoke again. "Eberhart—how old are you?"

How . . . ?? "Thirty-two," he said wonderingly.

"Thirty-two. Isn't it time you were getting married?"

In spite of himself, Sergeant Eberhart let his mouth drop open. He took a deep breath to control his annoyance; and when he could, he said, "Maybe it is." *Not that it's any business of yours.*

"I like to see my men settled," Ansbacher said.

"Yessir." Eberhart made his escape.

Lieutenant Murtaugh found him leaning against the wall in the hallway, looking as if he couldn't decide whether to laugh or cry. "What's the matter?"

"Captain Ansbacher," Eberhart said. "He just told me it was time I was getting married."

Murtaugh grinned sympathetically. "You're in for it, then. He'll keep after you until you at least tell him you're engaged."

"What the hell business is it of his whether—"

"None, but that won't stop him. It's his business if he makes it his business. And he seems to have noticed he has a swinging bachelor among his troops."

"I don't swing," Eberhart said grumpily. "I just sort of two-step a little once in a while. My sister used to complain because the family kept at her all the time to get married. Now I know how she felt."

Murtaugh doubted that, but didn't say so. "Well."

"Damnedest thing," Eberhart went on, "what if I *had* been thinking of getting married? How could . . ." He trailed off.

"Getting married would make it look as if you'd given in to Captain Ansbacher?"

"Yeah, that's it."

"Sergeant, if you don't get married because of the Captain, then he's controlling your actions just as much as if you did get married on command. You can't decide on that basis."

"Yeah, I know. It's just that—*shit*. You know."

Murtaugh knew. He knew something else too: Eberhart was stalling, avoiding talking about something.

And Eberhart knew he knew. The Sergeant made up his mind. He'd already chosen sides, while he was still in Ansbacher's office. He'd done so at some risk to himself; therefore he'd better make sure Murtaugh understood he'd gone out on a small limb for him.

Eberhart jerked one shoulder toward Ansbacher's office. "He called me in there for a reason. He tried to get me to say you'd handled the Sussman case wrong. Specifically, that you should have booked Leon Walsh."

Murtaugh just looked at him, wordless.

"I said I thought you were right about Walsh."

"Thank you, Sergeant," Murtaugh said quietly. "I'll remember."

Leon Walsh was unaware of the police's reluctantly continuing interest in him; that part of his life, he thought, was over and done with. He was not a suspect; he was in the clear. They didn't think he'd killed Jerry Sussman; Lieutenant Murtaugh had made no move to arrest him, had (in fact) treated him with courtesy and respect. Walsh was no longer worried about being charged with murder.

Now he had brand new things to worry about. New, and worse, in a way.

He had guilty knowledge of the murder; consequently he was an accomplice after the fact, he was sure that was the way the law must read. He didn't know the murderer's real name, or where he lived, or even what he looked like. He knew a voice over the phone, that was all. A voice saying: *You may call me Pluto.* When Walsh had finally gotten the last twenty-five thousand, from Leila, he'd gone into the men's room at the Mark Hellinger Theater at exactly two-thirty on Wednesday afternoon. The matinee performance was well into the first act when Walsh removed the paper hand towels from the wall dispenser and placed the money inside. Evidently the pickup had been successful, for he hadn't heard from Pluto since.

Just like that, he'd paid off a murderer. He, Leon Walsh, respectable and contributing member of society— had paid off a murderer! After the fact, of course. But there wasn't much real difference between that and going out and hiring someone to kill Jerry Sussman. Clumsy irony: now that the police no longer suspected him, he looked upon himself as guilty.

How easily he'd yielded to Pluto! The voice on the phone had known all about the enmity between editor and publisher, it had known of UltraMedia's involvement, of Walsh's impending loss of *Summit*. Pluto had known financial details not published in the *Wall Street Journal* story, he'd even known details of Walsh's own personal finances. When Pluto had said he had "disposed of" Sussman, Walsh believed him.

Walsh had put himself into a financial hole, a deep one. Buying up Sussman's *Summit* shares hadn't wiped him out, but it had come close. And then this Pluto had hinted that if he didn't get his money, Walsh himself would never live to enjoy it. Again Walsh believed him. He hadn't slept at all the night after that first phone call; he'd shivered in bed on a warm night and he couldn't sleep.

He felt sick to his stomach every time he thought of the rotten trick he'd played on Leila. What kind of man would do a thing like that to a woman? A terrified one, that's what kind. Walsh tried to console himself by thinking that Leila hadn't been too eager to give him the money when she believed only *his* life was at stake. But oh boy did she come across when she thought she was in danger too. Served her right. If she'd said yes when he first asked her, he wouldn't have had to stoop to such underhanded strategy; it was her own fault.

No use. It was still a rotten trick.

Walsh sighed, and knew he'd do it again if he had to. For a man who'd been thinking about suicide only a few weeks ago, he certainly was doing all he could to stay alive now. His money problems bore down on him; he didn't know how he was going to pay back all he'd borrowed. But the idea of giving up now was inconceivable; because now he had *Summit*. That's what made the difference. All to himself he had the magazine, to do with as he pleased.

Guilt over rewarding Sussman's killer, guilt over Leila. There wasn't much he could do about that now; maybe in time it would take care of itself. Concentrate on the money problems.

It was time to trot out J. J. Kellerman again.

J. J. had been lying in a file drawer for a long time now—in Walsh's personal file, at home. It wouldn't do for carbons of a J. J. Kellerman *parvum opus* to go floating around the *Summit* offices—wouldn't do at all. J. J. Kellerman was the best-kept secret in Leon Walsh's life; even Leila hadn't known about him. If someone like Fran Caffrey should ever find out that Walsh was writing fiction under a different name—well, he didn't even want to imagine that scenario.

Was writing, hah. *Had written* was more like it. Walsh hadn't composed any fiction of his own for over four years now. The *Summit* readers' response to the last J. J. Kellerman story he'd published had been so negative that he had dropped out of the short-story rat race altogether. He'd actually felt his genitals shrivel when he read the letters some of the magazine's readers had taken it on themselves to write. *Amateur* was the word that appeared most often; there were other disparaging terms, but *amateur* was the one that hurt the most.

Walsh had come up with a fair rationalization of the antipathy his fiction had aroused. He told himself those letters must have been written by readers who liked the kind of story Jerry Sussman had manipulated him into printing. Nonliterary readers. There had been no letters of endorsement from readers with what Walsh imagined were more esthetic tastes, but that wasn't surprising. People tended to write letters about things they disliked; when they liked something, they didn't bother. So Walsh had been able to tell himself he just might have a readership out there someplace after all. But he'd written no more stories; the hurt had been too deep.

J. J. Kellerman had been born out of a combination of modesty, professional ethics, and an unwillingness to take risks. In the pre-Sussman days when *Summit* was just another struggling quarterly, Walsh had been inundated with manuscripts from beginning writers. They all subscribed to *Writer's Digest* and they all felt that if they were ever paid thirty-five dollars for something they'd written, they were a success. But Walsh had never meant *Summit* to be a testing ground for learners; he'd wanted the best, right from the start. But to find the good ones he'd had to wade through floods of quasi-realism, pseudosymbolism, countersurrealism, neo–New Wave, god knows what else. There was even a short-lived university-nurtured movement that called itself "holistic fiction"—Walsh got a lot of good laughs out of that one.

Most of what he read was so bad that Walsh felt that old itch to write coming back once again. It was the same trap so many readers fell into: *I can do better than that.* Walsh had tried writing when he was younger but had given it up when he decided he didn't really have anything to say. He was an editor—an *improver*, to his way of thinking. But still, there was that itch.

So he had turned to his typewriter and had laboriously produced an earnest little story called "Talking of Michelangelo"—he was still in his T. S. Eliot period then. But what to do with it? Editors of fiction anthologies included one of their own stories as a matter of course, but it was considered shabby for periodical editors to print their own work—except for editorials, of course. Obviously the thing to do was send "Talking of Michelangelo" to another editor; but Walsh hesitated, worried about what a bad story might do to his growing reputation as an editor. He couldn't judge his own work as objectively as that of others.

He thought of trying to work out a back-scratching arrangement with the editor of some other literary quarterly; there must be dozens of editors with writing aspirations who'd be willing to swap stories with him. But Walsh could never bring himself to propose such an exchange. *Modesty*, he thought—hoping it wasn't really cowardice that kept him from acting.

So because he didn't have the nerve to publish under his own name, Walsh invented a pseudonym for himself—J. J. Kellerman. "Kellerman" because at the time he'd recently seen the movie *Who Is Harry Kellerman and Why Is He Saying Those Terrible Things about Me? Keller* was German for cellar, basement; Keller-man was the man in the cellar, the leading character's subconscious that was acting against his own best interests. Walsh wanted to draw on his own subconscious; and one way of bringing the man out of the cellar was through the creation of art, wasn't it? Walsh liked the neat way that worked out. So he'd paid himself a token fee of ten dollars and published "Talking of Michelangelo" (by J. J. Kellerman) in the next issue of *Summit*.

The story didn't draw one single word of comment.

Nobody objected to it, nobody said *I like it*, nobody so much as mentioned it. Even Walsh's first wife, who was not at all shy about expressing her opinion, didn't have anything to say about it. Walsh was nonplussed, but not discouraged. He published three more of his own stories; and when two letters arrived from readers faintly praising J. J. Kellerman's "potential," Walsh duly published them in the *Correspondence* column.

But when Jerry Sussman moved in and *Summit* turned big time, Walsh found that the readers of a national magazine were not nearly so flexible or willing to experiment as the readers of literary journals. His stories were not, to put it politely, well received. The last one—it was called "Mithridates, He Died Old"—had been written because Walsh wanted to vacation in Norway that year but was running a little low on funds. So he'd paid himself a generous five thousand dollars and had had a marvelous time in Norway, but "Mithridates" marked the end of Walsh's attempts to build a writing career for himself. The story had drawn, without qualification, the most hostile mail ever received in *Summit*'s twelve-year history. Walsh couldn't buck that kind of resistance; he simply gave up.

But now—now it was time to bring the man out of the cellar again. This time, however, there'd be no artsy delusions about creating great literature. This time J. J. Kellerman was writing for money, and Leon Walsh would pay it to him. He'd write the story and simply tell Fran Caffrey to publish it. *Summit*'s fiction editor wouldn't like that—but *Summit* was now his to do with as he pleased.

Walsh went into his study and pulled the cover off the old Remington that had served him for more years than he could remember. All of *Summit*'s editorials had been written on that machine, every one of them. The *Summit* offices were equipped with word processors, but Walsh liked the noisy banging and clacking of the old type-writers; his model wasn't even electric. He liked the physical act of punching out words on a bulky black machine. He rolled in a yellow second-sheet and got to it.

> Leon Walsh W Leo n Walsh***H*Y*M*A*N***
> K*A*P*L*A*N***SUMMIT's at the summit let us
> sit upon the ground and tell sad stories of
> the death of kings Leon Walsh

He hated that initial period when it was so hard to get going. He always used the old trick for breaking up writer's block, the one that said start typing, just type, the alphabet, the weather report, your name, anything—the physical movement involved in hitting the keys was sometimes enough to get you writing. Type *anything*.

> Leila Hudson   Leila Hudson Walsh
> Leila Hudson   Leila Hudson Baxter
> Leila Hudson   Leila Leila Leon
> Walsh the voices of my accursed education the voice
> on the phone said, "You may call me Pluto."

Walsh stopped. A chill ran up his back at the same time little drops of sweat broke out on his forehead. He put his hands back on the keyboard.

> It was a Noel Coward voice, an Oscar Wilde voice.
> It was young Sebastian Flyte in BRIDESHEAD RE-
> VISITED. Young? Ageless, rather. Precise, artic-
> ulate, and immensely pleased with itself.

Walsh went into the kitchen and took a bottle of scotch out of one of the cabinets. He poured himself a drink, took it back with him to the study.

"It's a *business* arrangement," the voice said with a touch of petulance. "I kill, you pay. What could be simpler?"

He stood up and walked around the room a few times. Did he really want to do this?

Suddenly he knew he *had* to write about Pluto. He had to let the world know what was going on even if it was only in disguised form as fiction *(only* fiction, Jerry Sussman had said). Yes, that was it: he'd turn *Summit* magazine into a . . . a newspaper. No, that was too close. A movie studio, a ballet company, something. A radio station, maybe—a classical music radio station easing over into pop in order to pay the bills.

Those were details that could be worked out. Walsh felt suddenly excited, more excited than he'd felt in years. He had a story to tell and he knew how to tell it. He *had* to tell it; he had to get it out of his system. Writing should be more than just therapy for the writer, he firmly believed; but for some reason it felt *right* to put his shame and guilt down on paper.

Especially if it was a way he could pay himself a big writer's fee, he thought gleefully. He could start paying on what he owed, some to Leila, some to the banks. Already Walsh was wondering what the reader feedback would be *(feedback,* ha, the UltraMedia influence). My god, wouldn't that be something?—if Pluto's murderous intervention in his life turned out to be the spur needed to prod him into becoming the writer he'd always wanted to be?

He wanted very much to make contact with The Reader, whoever and wherever he might be. He wanted *someone* to understand what he had gone through when that first telephone call from Pluto came. At that time he'd been sitting on top of the world; *Summit* was his and his alone, Jerry Sussman would never bother him again, UltraMedia's takeover bid had been foiled, he himself had been reprieved. Walsh had been uttering nightly prayers of thanksgiving to Fate, Chance, Providence, Fortune, Destiny, and just plain old good luck. Everything had broken right for him, for the first time in his life.

Then Cloud Nine had collapsed right out from under him. His dream of perfection had been interrupted by that blue envelope in the mail, by that mannered voice on the phone demanding payment, that effete bill-collector . . .

. . . and Walsh suddenly had his title. "The Man from Porlock"—yes: it was perfect. He would tell his story, he would tell of his collaboration with a conscienceless killer who thought of himself as some sort of worldly trouble-shooter, a cleaner-up of messes. A self-styled superior man who wouldn't for one minute allow himself to get boxed into the kind of situation that had had Leon Walsh thinking of suicide. That was important, to get that ego into the story, to sketch out that glamorous picture Pluto so obviously had of himself.

Walsh hunched over the typewriter and started working on "The Man from Porlock" in earnest.

CHAPTER

6

She allowed the mayor's gofer to go for her second martini. She smiled pleasantly at the owner of a plumbing and heating supplies firm, a heavy-breathing man who'd grown fat on city contracts. The man was talking too fast, trying too hard to make an impression. She nodded vaguely and let her gaze wander; a man and a woman quickly looked away—talking about her? How nice to be *persona grata* again.

"She's a real beauty," the plumbing and heating man was saying. "A forty-foot ketch. Real mahogany hull—no fiberglass anywhere! Ever sailed on a two-masted vessel? Whole different feel to it . . . you ought to try it. We're taking her out next weekend—want to come along?"

"Perhaps," she said, luxuriating in being able to temporize without having to worry about repercussions later. "I have something I have to see to."

"Well, if you get finished—look, if you'll tell me where you can be reached, I'll check back with you."

"I'm not sure where I'll be. Why don't you leave your number with my secretary? I'll call you."

He didn't like that, but he had to settle for it. Just then the mayor's gofer returned with her martini. "Here you are, Ms Randolph."

She thanked him with her eyes and took a sip. What game-playing! She must try not to look too smug; these people were trying to be agreeable, trying to make up for the wrong done her. The cocktail party had been somebody's idea of the way to mark a festive finale to what had been a rather nasty piece of business.

It was the first time Carolyn Randolph had been in Gracie Mansion, but she didn't intend it to be her last. Now that she had her foot in the door, she meant to keep it there. She knew a few more city contracts would be coming her way, a backwash from *l'affaire Parminter*. Enough to establish her, perhaps.

Her garrulous companion had switched his line of patter from ketches to private drinking clubs; when Carolyn realized he was one of those people who love to talk about how much alcohol they consume, she murmured an excuse and slipped away. Immediately someone from the mayor's office materialized at her side—the unofficial guest of honor mustn't be left alone. But this someone was more important than the martini-toting gofer, and more attractive as well.

She knew him slightly. "Hello, Jeffrey." Nobody called him Jeff. "Haven't seen you since you were trying to get me to sit down and shut up."

He laughed easily, not offended. "Unfair. I think I was the only one on that committee who did *not* tell you to shut up. Give me credit."

That was true. The whole thing had been a fiasco—an investigating committee that investigated but found nothing. "Some committee. We both know I wouldn't be here right now if Parminter hadn't gotten himself murdered."

"I know." Jeffrey's mouth was grim. "Hell of a way to find out the truth. But it's all over now, Carolyn, and I'm glad you're here."

"I am too."

William Parminter had been a thief. He had stolen Carolyn Randolph's designs for a new park and recreation facility the city was planning for the White Hall area. The city had announced an open competition, and Randolph Landscape Architects (consisting of Carolyn, two draftsmen, and a secretary) filed its intention to compete. Exactly four nights before the deadline, Carolyn's office was broken into and every drawing, every diagram, every doodle—every scrap of paper in the place was stolen. Four days didn't give her enough time to start over; Carolyn was out of the running.

The rules of the competition stipulated that the winning design be made available for public examination. When Carolyn recognized her own designs (carefully copied by Parminter's draftsmen), she raised holy hell. She accused Parminter of theft, in letters addressed to everyone even remotely connected with the project and in a long one to the *New York Times* as well. Parminter sued Carolyn for libel. Carolyn hired a lawyer.

The mayor appointed a committee to look into this most distressing affair, as he put it. Carolyn's two draftsmen swore the winning designs were indeed the property of Randolph Landscape Architects. But Parminter had *eleven* employees who swore the designs were the work of *their* boss. The committee could not agree upon a statement, but some of the members made it clear to the news media that they considered Carolyn Randolph a troublemaker, a sore loser, an also-ran trying to cash in on the success of her betters. Carolyn hired another lawyer.

And there matters stood until someone put a .38-caliber bullet into William Parminter's head. Carolyn had been in Montego Bay in Jamaica at the time, consoling herself with her new lawyer. When the police investigated the murder, they found some of Carolyn's original designs in Parminter's safe. Down in the corner of each sheet the words *Randolph Landscape Architects* were clearly legible. Confronted with this evidence, one of Parminter's lesser assistants had broken down and admitted the theft. They'd kept the incriminating designs because Parminter had held back some of Carolyn's detail work from the plans he'd submitted to the city; the idea was to insert it later, with an eye to raising construction costs to the point where new and generously remunerative contracts would have to be negotiated. Parminter had an "understanding" with certain construction and landscaping firms in the city.

The city of New York apologized to Carolyn Randolph.

The White Hall recreational park project contract was re-awarded (to the accompaniment of drumbeats, fanfare, and general hoop-de-doo)—this time to Randolph Landscape Architects. Carolyn was completely exonerated. The thought occurred to quite a few people who mattered that Carolyn Randolph must have a lot going for her if a prestigious firm like Parminter's would steal from her. So Carolyn was getting more and more calls for consultations, at least some of which were bound to lead to contracts. She doubled her staff, and thought about tripling it. The icing on the cake was her new lawyer's explanation that, because of Parminter's fraud-

ulent libel suit against her, her countersuit should give
her a claim on the murdered man's estate.

"They still don't know who did it, do they?" Carolyn
said to Jeffrey.

"From what I hear, they don't even have a suspect."

"I don't understand that at all. A man like Parminter?
He was bound to have enemies."

"Yes, that's just the problem—he had too many enemies. He was not a well-loved man," Jeffrey said dryly.
"When almost everybody he dealt with could have had
reason for hating him, then no one person stands out as
a suspect, you see. There are quite a few people who are
better off because Parminter's dead."

"Including me," Carolyn sighed. "You know, when the
police questioned me, I got the distinct impression that *I*
would have been a suspect if I hadn't been in Montego
Bay at the time it happened. Can you imagine?" That
Lieutenant Murtaugh had openly intimated he suspected
her of involvement. Dreadful man.

"Now, now—mustn't dwell on morbid details," said a
voice from behind them; it was the fast-talking plumbing
and heating man. "Clean slate, start over. And it wouldn't
hurt you to get away from work for a while. Come along
on my sailing party—it'll be good for you."

"I'll see," Carolyn said, and decided that sounded too
abrupt. "I really do have something to take care of first,"
she added. "I don't know when I'll be free."

"How about you, Jeffrey? Want to come along?"

"Sorry," he smiled. "I get seasick crossing the George
Washington Bridge."

"You don't get seasick, do you?" the man said to
Carolyn, and then plunged on without waiting for an
answer. "Two masts, eight sails—well, that's something
special, let me tell you. That kind of sailing makes you

feel alive. Try to come, dear, you'll enjoy it. We'll take good care of you—give you lots of TLC." When she didn't say anything, he added: "You know what TLC is, don't you?"

"Certainly," she deadpanned. "Thin layer chromatography."

The fool was actually going to explain what TLC stood for when Jeffrey stepped in smoothly with a murmured explanation of an appointment elsewhere and steered Carolyn out of Gracie Mansion and into a taxi.

"Thanks," she said sincerely. "It was getting harder and harder not to be rude to that man."

"He does have that effect on people," Jeffrey grinned. "Hungry?"

She allowed him to buy her dinner on his expense account. When he tried to invite himself into her apartment, she pleaded fatigue but made a date for later in the week. When he'd left, she started the process of shifting mental gears, preparing herself to wait.

She'd been waiting every evening for ten nights now. And it wasn't the sort of waiting one got used to—wondering whether tonight would be *the* night. Tucked into a small leather notebook by the telephone was the bill typed on that odd blue paper. *Fee for services rendered.* She doubted that he would call her at her office—not much privacy there. But he would call; that she was sure of. Carolyn had never spoken to a murderer; she wondered what one sounded like. All she could think of was Richard Widmark's maniacal giggle as he pushed the old woman in the wheelchair down the stairs.

He was a careful man, whoever he was. He'd probably watched to see if she'd contacted the police when she received his bill—she didn't much care for the thought of *that*. But he must have been watching her before, both her and Parminter. He'd planned it all so carefully. Parminter had been shot in an elevator. The doors had slid open to reveal the body slumped on the floor; nobody else was in the car. He had been careful about protecting her, too. *One murder, arranged to coincide with establishment of Montego Bay alibi.*

The call came at eleven o'clock.

"Hallo, is that Carolyn Randolph there?" Pseudo-English accent, an American trying to sound British. "You may call me Pluto. I recently sent you a bill."

"Yes, I have it right here."

"Do you understand the terms?"

"You made yourself quite clear, Pluto."

"Good. I hate misunderstandings. Have you raised any of the money yet?"

"I have all of it. One hundred thousand."

There was a pause. "Well, that was fast work, I must say. Does this mean I don't have to threaten you with dire and calamitous events to get you to pay?"

"That's what it means. I honor my debts—I don't like owing people."

"Excellent! I'm glad we understand each other. Do you have the money where you can get your hands on it tomorrow morning?"

"It's in a safety deposit box."

"What time does your bank open? Nine?"

"Yes, nine."

"You may have to change the money. I want nothing larger than hundred-dollar bills."

"They're all hundreds."

"Then there's no problem. You do know not to try anything clever, don't you? I refer to marking the bills or using sequential serial numbers or whatever technique for tracing money the police favor this year."

"There won't be anything like that—I'm not stupid. Where do you want me to meet you?"

"Alas, Ms Randolph, we don't meet. As sure as I am that the acquaintanceship would prove mutually enjoyable, I find it more prudent to remain merely a voice on the telephone. You understand?"

"Perfectly."

"Very well. Do you know Carlyle and Piper's excellent establishment?"

"Carlyle and Piper's? Never heard of it. What is it?"

"It's a bookstore dealing rare editions. On Fourth Avenue, between Ninth and Tenth—are you getting this?"

"Yes—go on."

"Across the back wall of the store are shelves with closed storage boxes on them. The boxes hold old and very rare magazines. Look for the one marked *The American Gentleman, 1909–1910*. It's an extremely large box that either Mr. Carlyle or Mr. Piper bought in a moment of unwarranted optimism. The box contains exactly one thin magazine—plenty of room in there for a hundred-thousand-dollar-sized package. A regular grocery bag should do nicely. I want you to be there when the store opens at ten—not many customers around that early. Now I think it would be best if you said all this back to me. We don't want any slip-ups, do we?"

Carolyn repeated what he'd told her. "It seems awfully public. What if I'm seen?"

"Wait until you see Carlyle and Piper's. One could hide in there for *years* without being discovered. Now, do you have any questions?"

"Only one. Am I correct in assuming this one hundred thousand is payment in full?"

"Oh absolutely, dear lady. You do your part tomorrow and you'll never hear from me again. One service, one payment. I like to keep things clean, don't you?"

"I do indeed. And Pluto?"

"Yes?"

"Thank you."

There was a long pause. Then: "Why, you are most welcome! Most welcome indeed!" He was almost burbling. "I must say, Ms Randolph, it has been a real pleasure doing business with you. You don't know how refreshing it is to find someone who doesn't muddy a simple business transaction with all sorts of emotional complications. What a pity we shall never meet! Ah well—it can't be helped. Good-bye!" He hung up.

Carolyn smiled as she replaced the receiver. What a strange man. All business right up to the end, and then he'd practically gushed at her. You'd think no one had ever thanked him before.

Captain Edward Ansbacher climbed out of the patrol car, told the officer who'd driven him he'd take a cab back.

He took a moment to examine the restaurant's façade before he went in. Not bad; expensive-looking. Inside, the maître d'—whom Ansbacher had never seen before in his life—knew who he was. In fact, the whole staff seemed primed; there was a satisfying amount of bowing and scraping. Ansbacher followed the maître d' past tables covered with rich white linen and heavy-looking silverware to a semisecluded alcove on a level three steps above that of the main seating area.

A man was waiting for him—white-haired, expensively tailored, nails manicured. Ansbacher noticed all that as he reached across the table to shake hands.

"Captain Ansbacher, this is a pleasure. I'm Joseph Sutton. Please—sit here."

A waiter had placed a whiskey sour in front of Ansbacher almost before he'd got settled. So, they'd "researched" him, knew his tastes.

"So how is the car?" Sutton asked. "Running nicely?" He pronounced it *cah*.

"Very nice indeed. Just what Mrs. Ansbacher wanted—the exact model." *But then you researched that too,* he thought. (Captain Ansbacher never referred to his wife by her own name, or even as "my wife"—she was always and only Mrs. Ansbacher. A conversational mannerism that led some of his less charitable acquaintances to suspect the Captain liked hearing the sound of his own name.)

Ansbacher waited. If Sutton was disappointed because his guest had failed to thank him for the gift of a *cah,* he hid it well. Ansbacher always avoided saying thank you; it tended to make the other fella think he had a claim on you. But *this* other fella was chatting amiably about this and that, very smooth. The waiter brought the soup. Ansbacher could wait; he had plenty of time.

The pitch came halfway through the meat course. "Howard Dudek tells me you might be able to help me with a little problem we're having," Sutton said. Dudek was the contact man, the one who'd arranged for the delivery of the car.

The Captain looked across the table at the distinguished-looking man who wanted a favor of him. If he was only a regular businessman who was having a little trouble and just wanted a helping hand—well, that was one thing.

But if he was mob-connected, fronting for that sleazy
bunch . . .

"What kind of problem?" he asked Sutton.

"It's my brother's boy," Sutton said. "The kid just
started his own business a couple of years ago, and I'm
afraid he hasn't been as discreet as he ought to have
been."

Ansbacher waited.

"Not that he did wrong, mind you," Sutton went on.
"But you know kids. Too eager for their own good, always in a hurry. My nephew has a nice little landscaping
business, my brother and I throw him some work, you
know how it goes."

Ansbacher nodded. He'd done some research of his
own; the Sutton brothers owned a construction firm that
wasn't exactly scrambling to survive. They made a lot of
money and they spent a lot of money. It was the other
brother who knew the construction business; this oily-
tongued Sutton was the greaser of wheels, the smoother of
rough spots. "So what did the kid do?"

"He had some correspondence with a man named William Parminter."

Ah. That was the connection. "And?"

"Let me tell you, it was a blow to all of us when Parminter got killed. My brother and I'd been doing business with the man for years. So of course when he landed
the White Hall project we bid on the contract, and we
wanted to throw a little business to the kid. So my nephew
gets all excited and starts telling Parminter what he's
going to do—on paper, no less. We had no idea those designs were stolen."

So far, no problem; Ansbacher couldn't see what they
were worried about. "So your nephew jumped the gun a
little, so what? Happens all the time."

"Well, you see, the letters mentioned several earlier jobs we'd done for Parminter. The boy was just showing off, trying to prove to Parminter he was part of the team. But he used several ambiguous phrases about our earlier arrangements that might, ah, might be misconstrued. You understand? In themselves, the letters prove nothing— how could they? But they could lead a curious investigator to start prying into Sutton Construction Company's business affairs. Affairs that have nothing at all to do with Parminter's death, I might point out."

Murtaugh, Ansbacher thought darkly.

"One of your investigators has been using his authority to stick his nose into our business," Sutton said. "His name is Lieutenant James T. Murtaugh. We were wondering if he's pursuing this line of inquiry under your direction?"

"He is not," Ansbacher growled.

Sutton allowed a small smile to appear. "Well, then. It is possible that Lieutenant Murtaugh's time could be better spent elsewhere?"

Ansbacher scowled, didn't answer.

"Is there a problem?"

"There could be. Let me think."

Of all his ranking officers, Murtaugh was the only one who ever gave Ansbacher any flak when he pulled him off a case. It had happened a few times before—besides which, Murtaugh was well aware Ansbacher had twice blocked his promotion. Ansbacher was frankly worried that Murtaugh might be reaching his flash point.

The waiter brought dessert and coffee. Say Murtaugh refused to take his dismissal from the Parminter investigation quietly; what could he do? He had no evidence of anything—he couldn't bring any charges against Ansbacher. Murtaugh could transfer out; Ansbacher hoped he would. Or he could start a bad-mouthing campaign against his superior officer. Ansbacher didn't much like the thought of that. He wanted to help Sutton out. The man obviously had no connection with the mob; he was just a businessman caught in a bind. Good family man. But still . . .

"I can pull him off the case," he finally said to Sutton, "but not without a lot of backlash. More backlash, frankly, than I care to have to deal with—it could get out of hand. I'm not sure I can do anything for you, Sutton."

The other man didn't bat an eye. "I understand. You have your problems. But we would all be grateful if you could see your way clear to do this one favor for us. We wouldn't forget. My nephew especially would be grateful. Did I mention he drove past your home last week? He came in just bursting with ideas for landscaping the grounds."

Ansbacher took his time and thought about it. Might not be a bad idea. Mrs. Ansbacher was always complaining about the gardener. She'd probably welcome a little outside help.

"I'll see what I can do," he said.

CHAPTER

7

Lieutenant Murtaugh sat in his car in a no-parking zone in front of Murray Hill Academy, a high-priced private school where Ellie reigned as director. On her down days, Ellie tended to grumble that she was willing to settle for promising the parents only that there'd be no muggers or pushers inside the school, and that their offspring would be able to read and write a little when they graduated. Murtaugh thought even that was aiming rather high.

Ten o'clock. He'd been waiting fifteen minutes when she came through the double doors of Murray Hill Academy in the company of a few of the teaching staff. Ellie was walking heavy: tired. Nobody liked night meetings, but sometimes they were unavoidable. The school's director was the only one who ever had a lieutenant of police waiting to escort her home; he hoped Ellie wouldn't ask him to give lifts to any of the others.

She didn't. She settled herself primly on the passenger side, opened her mouth, and screamed.

"Rough day?" he asked sympathetically.

Ellie hadn't had time to eat, so they stopped at a deli for something to take out. Only when they were home and Ellie had kicked her shoes off and worked her way through half a sandwich did she ask, "Well? Decide what you're going to do?"

He nodded. "I've decided to find out *why*. Not only this time, but the other times as well. There's got to be something. I'm going to try to keep it under wraps, but if I can't . . . well. But there has to be a reason Ansbacher pulls me off when I'm getting close. I'm going to find out what it is."

"What are your chances?"

"Pretty good, I'd say." Murtaugh had already started the long procedure of calling in every favor owed him, from everyone from the detective who'd replaced him on the Parminter case down to a few beat patrolmen whose minor mistakes Murtaugh had overlooked at one time or another.

"Then what?"

"Depends on what I find. If he's been bought off, I'll bring charges of malfeasance. I have to have damned good evidence before I can do anything like that. But a man can't be on the take for years without leaving some sort of trail."

Ellie wiped mustard from her mouth and shook her head. "Hard to think of Ansbacher as taking bribes. He doesn't seem the type."

Murtaugh laughed wryly. "He's exactly the type. Remember the saying, 'Never do business in the amen corner'? These self-righteous bastards are the most double-dealing of the lot. Ansbacher probably has the whole thing rationalized away to fit in with his personal brand of ethics. What a hypocrite."

"You sound already convinced he *is* on the take."

"What else could it be? There was something fishy
going on between Parminter and the Sutton brothers—
they've probably taken the city for a bundle over the
years. I'm just beginning to put the pieces together when
out of the blue Ansbacher tells me I'm off the case. How
would you interpret that? I tried to tell him what was
going on, but the man just *would not listen*. The only
thing I can figure is that he already knew what was going
on and had been paid to stop me. What else could it be?"

"I don't know. Did he give you a reason?"

"He said he wanted me to concentrate on solving the
Sussman murder. Gave me Sergeant Eberhart to help
with the leg work—he's down on Eberhart too right now.
But he reassigned all the cases that had come to my desk,
not just the Parminter investigation. You see what he's
doing? He's putting Eberhart and me on a dead-end case
where we can't do *anything*, where we can't interfere with
whatever else he might have going. We've been benched,
grounded, whatever."

"He's clipped your wings."

"Yeah. I'm supposed to be overseeing the investigation
of half a dozen criminal cases, yet he assigns me to investigate personally the one case that everybody knows is
going nowhere. Now he wouldn't do that, Ellie, unless
he was afraid I'd find something. Well, he's outsmarted
himself in a way. Limiting me to the Sussman investigation is going to give me a lot of spare time. I'm going to
use it to nail Ansbacher."

Ellie got up from the kitchen table. "This whole thing
makes me uneasy. You could be the one that gets nailed,
Jim."

"I know," he said. "But I don't see that I have much
choice. Ansbacher's as much as warned me my days are
numbered." He forced a smile. "Besides, aren't you the

one who's always telling me I ought to decide on a course of action?"

She kissed him lightly. "I'm going to take a shower."

Murtaugh sat at the table for a while longer, feeling tireder than he had any right to feel. Eventually he decided a shower was what he needed too. When he stood up, he inadvertently kicked over Ellie's book bag that she'd propped against the table leg and then forgotten. He bent over to pick up the scattered papers and notebooks, and found himself holding a copy of *Summit* magazine.

He took the magazine to the bedroom with him and leafed through it. He read Leon Walsh's editorial, about the way contemporary America takes its language from advertising instead of from books. It was a familiar argument; Murtaugh had been expecting something more original from Walsh. An off-month, perhaps—the time of Jerry Sussman's murder? He didn't know how long ago the editorial had been written.

When he heard the water stop, he went into the bathroom. "I thought you didn't read *Summit* any more."

"What?" Ellie was drying herself. "Oh—well, I got interested again, since you were investigating those people. I was curious, too."

"About anything in particular?"

"No, I just wanted to see if the magazine was going to go back to what it used to be. You know, quality material aimed at a limited readership. I think it might be—it's a little early to tell."

"I suppose they're committed to print things months in advance."

"Mmm. Funny thing, Jim, it actually has a murder story in there. Utterly unrealistic premise, but the story's kind of interesting just the same."

"What's it called?"

" 'The Man from Porlock'—I forget who wrote it."

Murtaugh turned to the contents page. "J. J. Kellerman."

"That sounds right. I'm finished here—do you want to take a shower?"

Murtaugh showered quickly and climbed into bed clutching the copy of *Summit*. Ellie was lying on her stomach, grimly making her way through an article in an educational journal.

"There's no written language anywhere in the world as awful as *Educationese*," she groaned. "It always makes me move my lips."

Murtaugh patted her bottom absently and turned to "The Man from Porlock." He read casually at first, and then with increasing concentration. By the time he'd finished, he was holding his breath.

Was that it, could that have been how it happened? The story was about the near loss of a radio station instead of a magazine, but other than that it was an almost literal retelling of the Leon Walsh/Jerry Sussman conflict—with a bizarre explanation of the murder tacked on. Crazy. He went back and read again the part about the free-lance killer's first phone call to his "client"—and Murtaugh found himself believing it. But he'd heard Ellie say fiction was supposed to be a transformation of fact, not a literal reporting of it.

"Who's J. J. Kellerman?" he asked.

"Mm?"

"Kellerman—the author of this story. Do you know anything about him?"

"No, I don't think I ever heard of him."

"I don't get the title. 'The Man from Porlock'—Porlock isn't even mentioned in the story. What is it?"

"A little town in England. The title's an allusion to how Samuel Taylor Coleridge came to write 'Kubla Khan' and why the poem was never finished."

Murtaugh raised one eyebrow. "Coleridge isn't mentioned in the story either."

Ellie smiled tiredly. "You're supposed to know the story. Coleridge was staying out in the country somewhere near Porlock. He woke up from an opium dream with his head so full of images that he sat down and started writing the poem. You remember it, Jim—'In Xanadu did Kubla Khan a stately pleasure dome decree. . . .' "

Murtaugh shook his head. He must have read it in high school, but it was too many years ago.

"Anyway," Ellie went on, "while he was writing, he was interrupted by a knock at the door. It was a bill-collector from the town of Porlock. Coleridge finally got rid of him—but when he sat back down to write, his mind was blank. The vision was gone. And so the poem was never finished."

"So 'The Man from Porlock' refers to . . . ?"

"An interrupter, a destroyer of dreams."

"Or a bill-collector?"

"Yes, that too."

A bill-collector.

"The idea is preposterous," Ellie was saying. "Whoever heard of anyone going around killing people and then later collecting from other people who had nothing to do with it! Have you ever run across anything like that?"

"No."

"The story's not badly told, though. A few intrusive writerish tricks. But on the whole not too bad."

Murtaugh didn't say anything; he was thinking. The idea *was* preposterous, Ellie was right. But he'd run into even more preposterous things during his seventeen years on the force. People were capable of performing any absurd act the mind could conceive. Could J. J. Kellerman be Leon Walsh? Murtaugh tried to compare the styles of the short story and the editorial Walsh had written, but he didn't really know what to look for; he'd ask Ellie to do it tomorrow. Had Walsh written fiction before? Ellie said the story had a few writerish tricks in it but on the whole wasn't bad. Murtaugh didn't know anything about literary values.

But he thought he recognized a plea for sympathy when he ran into one.

The voice on the answering machine said, "For crying out loud, Leila, why don't you return my calls? What do I need—a note from my mother?"

Leila Hudson turned off the machine. Leon always understood only what it was convenient for him to understand.

He'd paid her back twenty-five hundred of the twenty-five thousand he owed her. "Ten percent for a start," he'd smiled, trying to be charming. It was wasted effort. He'd already killed any chance for a reconciliation when he pulled that stomach-turning stunt on her—just to talk her into a loan.

Leila had sat at that table at Luchow's and listened to Leon lying to her about how her own life would be in danger if she didn't come up with twenty-five thousand dollars immediately. She'd sat there thinking *I don't believe this* while he went on embellishing the story. Leon was so transparent a liar that a child could see through him. This was something he was never able to understand, even though he'd been told so several times. Leila had told him once herself.

In the end she'd decided to let him have the money because obviously he had to be desperate to resort to such underhandedness. Leila didn't know what kind of trouble he was in, but it had to be serious. And the money did seem to do the trick; Leon was able to buy his way out.

But at what cost! Whatever respect and sympathy and concern for his well-being that had been left over from their marriage—now it was all as dead as Jacob Marley and his doornail. *My supply of charitable understanding is exhausted,* Leila thought. Used up. Gone. How could Leon have done such a thing to her? He'd always used her to a certain extent; that's what had caused the divorce in the first place, his tendency to assume her primary function was to make him feel good. There'd been no malice in it; only thoughtlessness and a seeming inability to learn.

But telling her that grotesque and melodramatic story, trying to make her *feel afraid*—oh, that was unforgivable. Before he did that, they'd actually reached a point where Leon had begun hinting that maybe this time they could make a go of it. But now she didn't even want to talk to him on the telephone.

Leila was sick at heart. Once again she'd allowed Leon Walsh to let her down.

Pluto was displeased. He was displeased with the weather, he was displeased with having to use the .45 again so soon, he was displeased with having to do so many jobs close together. But most of all he was displeased with a smartass young millionaire named Roscoe Malucci.

It had finally happened. Pluto had often wondered

what he'd do if it ever did happen, but without really believing that it *would*. But now it had. Roscoe Malucci had refused to pay his bill.

Prudence said, *Let it go, forget it, write it off.* Pride said to Prudence, *Get stuffed.* Still, if he failed to collect this one time, nobody would know about it. "Not true," Pluto said aloud in the back seat of the taxi. "*I* would know about it."

"You say something, Mac?"

"No, no—just drive."

Pluto's normal workload was three jobs per year. He'd found he could live quite comfortably on three hundred thousand tax-free dollars a year. (It used to be only two jobs a year, but what with inflation, etc., etc.) Pluto wasn't avaricious; his needs were moderate. He prided himself on not being like rock stars or advertising executives or ballplayers. Or like pretty-boy anchormen who were paid $650,000 a year for reading the news on local television—*local*, not even network. Pluto tut-tutted at that; no sense of proportion. He, on the other hand, charged a reasonable fee for doing a dangerous job that others didn't want to do.

That was the way it used to be. This year, however, he'd already done eight jobs—and he was behind schedule. Because now he needed money. He'd thought about raising his rates but decided against it. People with money were willing to pay a hundred thousand to have their problems solved for them, but over that amount they tended to get panicky. Pluto didn't want to push his clients over the edge; they were no good to him that way. A hundred thousand was just about right.

He wanted to buy a chalet in Switzerland. He had come upon it quite by accident last year while on vacation, and he'd immediately fallen in love with it. The chalet was tucked away among the vineyards between Geneva and Lausanne, on an estate that itself produced a modest four thousand bottles a year. Pluto had tried the wine and found it a typical Swiss white with no great pretensions; a pleasant wine. The idea of inviting the neighbors over for a glass of wine from the back yard appealed to Pluto. The chalet itself was a work of art, designed to house other works of art. Suddenly Pluto's middle-class, three-hundred-thousand-dollars-a-year way of living no longer satisfied him. He aspired to better things.

As a result he was having to work harder than he'd ever worked since the day he first discovered where his natural talents lay. There was danger in such increased activity; Pluto was convinced the one reason the police had never made any connection among his various jobs was that he'd never gotten greedy. The killings were spaced far enough apart not to attract undue attention, and he followed a strict rotation system governing which weapon he used. But now the chances of the police tumbling to what was going on grew with each new job. The risks were increasing geometrically.

He got out of the taxi at Ninety-first Street and Second Avenue; he was carrying a briefcase. He walked away from the corner, making a moue at the sky. It wasn't raining yet, just threatening. Pluto needed a rainless day. Otherwise the small restaurant he'd selected would not put its café tables out on the sidewalk. Aha! The tables were out. Pluto told a waiter, "I say, I am glad to see these tables! Good show!"—and seated himself with his briefcase between his feet where he had a clear view of Roscoe Malucci's townhouse. The waiter asked him how he liked New York and whether he was planning to stay in America long.

99

That started him wondering, once again, whether he should work outside New York for a while. Until things cooled down a bit. He sipped his wine and thought about it. Pluto wasn't too happy at the idea; he knew New York and New York was where he operated best. Even after he had his chalet he planned to divide his time between the two places. New York was where he *worked*. He didn't know how to go about checking credit in Boston or finding a private investigator in Chicago he could rely on. He could learn, but it was all such a bother. Besides, he didn't like Boston or Chicago.

Besides again, he had this deadbeat Roscoe Malucci to take care of before he could do anything else. If only there were more people like Carolyn Randolph! That woman had understood immediately what he'd done for her and she knew *exactly* what it was worth. She'd not quibbled over the price; she knew a bargain when she saw one. She'd even thanked him. And she'd not lingered in the neighborhood of Carlyle and Piper's bookstore in an attempt to get a glimpse of him when he went in to pick up the money. Her behavior had been impeccable from start to finish. Unfortunately, there weren't many Carolyn Randolphs in the world.

At one time Pluto had toyed with the idea of notifying his clients ahead of the fact, of telling them what he was going to do before he did it. That way there'd be no doubt or tears or panic afterward. But that way there was also the danger that some misguided soul might notify the police. And too, if his clients knew ahead of time what was going to happen—well, that piled a complicating burden of guilt on them. Pluto had learned early that all guilt feelings were to be avoided as assiduously as possible.

Pluto was convinced that everyone in the world yearned for some strong person to come in and solve their problems for them, make the nasties go away, even kill for them if necessary. That way they'd get what they wanted without having to dirty their own hands. *Let George do it.* Pluto's solution: allow the clients to wear their little blinders until the dastardly deed is done, then slap 'em with a bill. That way they can feel shocked, horrified, outraged—and secretly pleased as punch. But not guilty. Oh no, never *guilty*.

Leon Walsh had felt guilty. But Pluto thought Walsh must be the kind of man who wallowed in negative feelings no matter what happened. He was the exception, not the rule. Funny those two extremes should come so close together—Leon Walsh and Carolyn Randolph.

But the *extreme* extreme was the do-nothing young nitwit who lived in the expensive townhouse across the street. It wasn't even his townhouse—well, it was now, thanks to Pluto's intervention. But until recently Roscoe Malucci had been living in a roach parlor in the Village; the townhouse had belonged to Roscoe's grandmother, who'd been on the verge of disinheriting her only son's only son in favor of a remote second cousin's brother's grandnephew umpteen times removed or whatever, some vague male relative she hadn't seen in twenty years.

Pluto wondered whether Roscoe really understood how close he'd come to losing Grandma Malucci's millions. Grandma had been fed up with Roscoe; she was convinced he'd never make anything of himself. (She was undoubtedly right.) All Roscoe wanted to do in life was play his guitar. The only thing he talked about was "my music"—and he talked about it soulfully, with stars in his eyes (a look he must have practiced in front of a mirror). Roscoe was a twenty-four-year-old child who'd learned five or six chords on the guitar and called himself a musician. Roscoe was lazy, and not too bright, and not at all concerned about the difficulties of living in the real world. His family had always had money. Somebody would take care of him.

The thing that really irritated Pluto was that this job had been his most difficult in years. Grandma Malucci wasn't exactly a recluse, but catching her alone out of the house hadn't been easy. And catching her at a time Roscoe had an alibi—for a time it had looked impossible. Roscoe's behavior was totally unpredictable; there was no pattern to his life at all. Roscoe just followed the trail of whoever happened to cross his path that day. If only he'd had a girlfriend! Or even a boyfriend. Leon Walsh had been snuggling up with his former wife in Connecticut; Luigi Bàccolo had taken a soprano from the chorus for an illicit weekend in a borrowed house on Fire Island; Carolyn Randolph had been enjoying her lawyer's special services in Montego Bay. Thank god for sex; it provided so *many* alibis! But not for Roscoe Malucci. As far as Pluto could determine, Roscoe had no sex life at all. Damn the boy.

But Pluto had finally gotten to Grandma on a weekend when Roscoe had piled into a car with five other "musicians" and headed for a rock festival at Cape Cod. They didn't make it all the way; the car broke down outside New Bedford. But Roscoe's alibi was established. Pluto had typed up his bill on his usual blue paper; but when he'd made his follow-up phone call, he'd been greeted with, "Whaddaya doin', man—puttin' me on?"

All in all he'd made four phone calls, not one of which got through to the two-watt brain of Roscoe Malucci. Pluto had been in turn threatening and sinister, stern and paternal, whimsical and cajoling. Nothing worked.

Pluto's rapidly evaporating sense of dignity had left him sputtering into the phone, "I am not a man who takes no for an answer! I *always* collect my fee!"

The only sound coming back over the receiver was that of a guitar being strummed.

Pluto gave up. Roscoe Malucci was unreachable. That bird-brained thud-plunker had defeated him.

Let it go, his common sense told him. But he couldn't. He just couldn't let that little worm get away with it.

Pluto dropped some money on the table and picked up his briefcase. Roscoe was coming out of the townhouse.

There were many things that Roscoe Malucci could not do, and one of them was drive a car. Eventually it would dawn on him that now he could afford to have a chauffeured limousine waiting for him, but for the time being he still depended on the passing taxicab. Cabs didn't cruise Ninety-first Street, so Roscoe would have to wait until one arrived to deliver a fare. Or else walk back to Second Avenue (but Roscoe was lazy).

Pluto trotted up the steps of a residential building almost directly opposite from where Roscoe was standing. Pluto had checked several buildings on the street before he made his choice. The one he now entered was an elegant brownstone that had been divided into two luxury apartments. That meant elaborate security systems for the individual apartments but only an ordinary lock on the common street door; the second pick he'd tried had opened it. Now he slipped inside and kept the door open.

The foyer was empty. The building had a back door that opened on to one of a series of connecting gardens: his escape route. He'd have to work fast; one of the building's legitimate inhabitants might walk in on him. Pluto opened his briefcase and took out the .45. The street was narrow; easy shot.

Just then Roscoe spotted a taxi coming down the street. He stepped off the curb to signal. He raised his arm into the air; Pluto carefully squeezed the trigger; and Roscoe's left hand exploded.

"I *always* collect," Pluto murmured.

CHAPTER

8

"I want you to run a credit check on Leon Walsh's finances," Murtaugh said. "Big withdrawals, loans he's taken out, like that."

Sergeant Eberhart looked puzzled. "We already did that."

"We checked for the time around the Sussman killing and right before. I want to know what's been happening lately."

"You got something?"

"Maybe." Murtaugh told him about the story in *Summit* magazine and laughed at the you-gotta-be-kidding look on the Sergeant's face. "No-down-payment murder— outlandish notion, isn't it? But it's not as far-fetched as it sounds. You have to read the story." He rummaged through the drawers of his desk, found the copy of the magazine he'd brought from home. "Here—read it when you get a chance. It's 'The Man from Porlock' by J. J. Kellerman."

"Kellerman? Who's that?"

"I think it's Leon Walsh. I got Ellie to compare the story to an editorial Walsh had written. She said it was possible both had been written by the same person, but there was nothing distinctive enough in either style to make it a certainty. So before we go charging in and accuse him of paying off a killer, I want to know if he's needed money recently, a lot of money. The story says a hundred thou—but that could be literary license."

"You know he had to come up with a fistful to buy Sussman's shares of *Summit*."

"I'm allowing for that—I got a contact on Wall Street tracking down the exact figure. I want you to check the loan departments of banks, credit bureaus, and so on. And you read that story."

"I'll do that," Eberhart said with interest. "My god, if you're right—huh, maybe we should have booked Walsh just the way Captain Ansbacher said!"

"Don't remind me," Murtaugh groaned. "We'll cross that bridge when we come to it. Now git."

He wished Eberhart hadn't mentioned Ansbacher.

Murtaugh had had to put that little matter on the back burner. He was now one hundred percent convinced that Ansbacher had been on the take for years—but after several weeks of inquiry he still didn't have any evidence. At first Murtaugh had been content to find that a personal enemy was turning out to be so thoroughgoing a bad guy. Justification! But the elation quickly faded as the proof he needed persistently failed to materialize. Instead of hard evidence he had indications, maybes, might-bes, could-have-beens. For instance, Ansbacher had had lunch with one of the Sutton brothers; a waiter at the restaurant had been willing to talk in exchange for a generous gratuity. What Sutton and Ansbacher had talked about the waiter couldn't or wouldn't tell him, but the day after the lunch Ansbacher had pulled Murtaugh off the Parminter investigation. The *inference* was clear, but there was no *proof* of a connection between the two events.

Murtaugh had found out about the lunch meeting from the police officer who'd driven Ansbacher to the restaurant. He'd come to Murtaugh with the information on his own—and that was something else Murtaugh had discovered. He was surprised at the extent of cooperation he was receiving; a lot of it he didn't even have to ask for. His not-completely-legitimate investigation of his superior was supposed to be a secret, but he couldn't ask questions without raising questions. Word had slowly leaked among Murtaugh's fellow detectives and lower-ranking officers, and to a man they wanted to help. Until he'd started his investigation, Murtaugh had had no idea of how widely hated Captain Ansbacher was.

Take the young officer who'd reported driving Ansbacher to the restaurant. He admitted frankly that he wanted to "get" Ansbacher. Why? Because certain slum landlords had been paying him off for years. The officer himself was a product of one of those slums. Years ago when he was a boy, his older brother had organized a strike against the landlords. The strike had been broken up by club-swinging cops directed by Ansbacher, still a lieutenant at the time. One of those swinging clubs had caught the officer's brother right in the kneecap; he'd walked with a limp ever since.

No, the officer had no evidence of a payoff, not the kind that would be recognized by a departmental hearing. Just a series of things observed throughout his youth; it was common knowledge in the neighborhood that the cops were paid off by the landlords. Complaints about rats and broken plumbing and falling-down staircases would get lost in the files. Buildings the Health Department was investigating would mysteriously catch fire in the night: people died, the landlords collected insurance, investigations headed by Ansbacher uncovered no definitive evidence of arson.

That story had particularly disturbed Murtaugh. If the officer's allegations were correct, Ansbacher was guilty of complicity in a felony (arson) that resulted in death— making the Captain an accessory to murder. And if Ansbacher had been able to rig things in the landlords' favor over a period of years, that meant he was not only corrupt himself but he would also have had to corrupt other policemen in order to make the scheme work. Ansbacher was even worse than he'd thought, far worse. Murtaugh tended to believe the young officer's story, and not just because he wanted to believe him. He'd checked the officer's record. The younger man may have joined the force as a way of getting at Ansbacher, but the record showed he was a good cop, doing a good job; he already had a couple of commendations even though he'd been on the force less than two years. He just wanted to help get the goods on Ansbacher.

So did a lot of other people. The stories came trickling in, sometimes duplicating each other, never offering evidence of any sort. The stories ranged from the horrible, such as the slum fires, to the absurd: a policewoman told Murtaugh that Ansbacher had once instigated an investigation of her personal life because he'd seen her in an off-duty dress he thought was too revealing. The charge became absurd only when it was dropped; before then, it had caused the policewoman a great deal of distress. Which was probably Ansbacher's sole intention in the first place.

Murtaugh was feeling more frustrated than ever. There was no longer any doubt in his mind but that Ansbacher was as dirty a criminal as any that had ever been hauled in on the wrong end of a pair of handcuffs. Nor was there any doubt that Murtaugh's unauthorized investigation had the tacit backing of his fellow police. What was very much in doubt was the probability that he'd ever be able to prove anything against Ansbacher. There had to be something, some way of getting the man. When he'd just started out, Murtaugh would have been content simply to get Ansbacher off the force. Now he wanted to see him in prison.

The phone rang. "Murtaugh."

"Lieutenant? This is Carlos Montoya in Ballistics. I've got something for you."

"Jesus, I sure could use something. What is it?"

"You know the shooting on East Ninety-first yesterday? The one where the kid millionaire got his hand blown off?"

"Yeah, what's his name, starts with an M—"

"Malucci, Roscoe Malucci. We recovered the bullet—"

"That's not my case, Montoya. I think Billings has that one."

"I already told Billings. Now I'm telling you. The bullet was a forty-five. We did a computer run for unsolved crimes involving forty-five-caliber weapons within the past year, matter of routine—"

"And you found a match?"

"We sure as hell did. The gun that was fired at Roscoe Malucci yesterday is the same gun that killed Jerry Sussman."

Murtaugh skipped a breath. "Montoya, you old sonuvagun, you will be remembered in my will. Where's the Malucci kid now?"

Montoya had to ask someone, got an answer. "Doctors Hospital."

East End Avenue. "Thanks." He hung up and rushed out into the squad room. "Eberhart! We're going."

Sergeant Eberhart hurriedly ended the phone call he was making and ran to catch up with Murtaugh. "What's up, Lieutenant?"

Murtaugh told him about the .45-caliber bullet on the way down to the car. "You drive."

"Now wait a minute," Eberhart said as he slid behind the wheel. "If the guy with the forty-five popped Sussman and then collected from Walsh for it—do we assume the same thing is going on here? Is somebody going to profit from this Malucci guy's death? Who?"

Murtaugh scowled, trying to remember details. "Maybe the killer isn't trying to collect on Roscoe Malucci. Maybe he's trying to collect *from* him."

"Meaning what?"

"Well, the kid himself just profited from somebody's death—his grandmother's. And the old lady was murdered. Shot. But not with a forty-five or Ballistics would have turned that up. I don't remember what caliber was used on her."

"So this guy's got two guns?"

"At least. The fact that he holds on to his weapons instead of dropping them at the scene should tell us something."

"That he can't lay his hands on a new gun any time he feels like it?" Eberhart said. "Which means he's not all mobbed up. A free-lance. A free-lance who doesn't want to fill out registration forms when he makes a buy."

"Sounds like it. Okay, say what we've got here is the real-life version of Walsh's fictional killer. He kills first,

110

then sends a bill, and then calls with instructions for making the payoff—along with a few choice threats if needed. Logically, Roscoe Malucci should be one of the people who pay off, not one of the targets."

"So why'd he try to kill him? Malucci refuse to pay up, shortchange him?"

"Maybe the man with the forty-five didn't try to kill him. Maybe he *meant* to shoot his hand off."

"Jeez." Eberhart was silent a moment. "But Leon Walsh is safe because he paid up like a good boy? Huh. Just when we were thinking the Sussman case was a dead end, things start breaking all over the place."

"What about Walsh's finances—did you have time to get anything?"

"Yep, and it's lookin' good. He sure needed money in a hurry. He borrowed twenty-five thousand from Sterling National Bank and Trust—that's where he has his checking account. He got another thirty thousand from Chase Manhattan, where he keeps a savings account. Neither bank would let him have any more than that because he'd already had to borrow from them to buy Sussman's *Summit* shares. Walsh has cleaned out his savings as well, except for a hundred bucks to keep the account open. I was just starting to call around the other banks."

Both men fell silent, trying to fit the various events into a logical order. Near Doctors Hospital Sergeant Eberhart found another fireplug to park by. Inside the hospital a physician named Riley expressed his annoyance at seeing more police wanting to talk to Roscoe Malucci. "I told Detective Billings that Malucci was so heavily sedated he couldn't talk sensibly. But he insisted on seeing him anyway."

"Dr. Riley, I appreciate the problem, but right now

all we need is a minute." The look on the doctor's face made Murtaugh add, "Well, maybe two minutes. But no more than that."

"Can't it wait, Lieutenant? In a few days he'll be able to talk. Right now he might not even understand what you're saying."

"No sir, it can't wait. We won't disturb your patient, I promise."

Dr. Riley went with them, not believing Murtaugh's promise and resenting having his time wasted this way. Roscoe Malucci was hooked up to monitoring machines, his eyelids fluttering. His left arm ended in a bandage.

"Roscoe?" Murtaugh said. "Roscoe, can you hear me?"

Only a slight head movement answered him.

"I told you," Dr. Riley was quick to say.

"Roscoe, listen to me. I'm Lieutenant Murtaugh and I've come to help you. Do you hear?"

Roscoe opened his eyes and looked straight at Murtaugh. After a moment he smiled the sweet smile of a child who's just been told daddy is here and everything's going to be all right.

"Hello, Roscoe," Murtaugh smiled back. "We're going to find the man who shot you. Do you understand?"

"Hngh." Was that a nod?

"All right, I want you to tell me if you've heard from someone claiming he killed your grandmother—somebody who wanted you to pay him for killing her."

But that was too long a sentence; Roscoe drifted away. A wide-eyed Dr. Riley was staring at Murtaugh, horrified.

"Roscoe," Eberhart said, "come back. Roscoe?"

Dr. Riley interrupted. "I can't have you disturbing him with a thing like that! You—"

"All we need is a yes or no, Doctor, and then we'll be

gone," Murtaugh said quickly. "Roscoe? Can you hear me?"

The eyes fluttered open again.

"Roscoe, did someone call you about your grand-mother's death?"

Roscoe was mumbling something. "Shah me."

"Shot me?" Eberhart said. "Who shot you?"

Mumbling.

Murtaugh said, "Roscoe, do you know who shot you?"

"Pluto shah me."

"What's that?" Eberhart asked.

Roscoe's eyes closed. "That's enough," Dr. Riley insisted. "You'll have to leave now."

Murtaugh and Eberhart left Roscoe Malucci's room and walked slowly down the hospital corridor. "Well, he didn't exactly tell us what we came to hear," Murtaugh said. "But at least we have a name to put on the file folder now. Pluto."

"Pluto?" Eberhart said in surprise. "I thought he said Bluto."

"Bluto? What kind of name is Bluto?"

"Oh, you know who Bluto is. He's the heavy in the Popeye cartoons."

"I thought his name was Bruto."

"Naw. Bluto."

"Well, Roscoe said Pluto, I'm sure. I remember wondering why anyone would be named after a planet."

"Hey—that story in *Summit*? What was the killer's name in that?"

Murtaugh frowned. "Damn. I should remember, but I don't."

Back at the station the first thing they did was head toward Eberhart's desk. Murtaugh flipped through the magazine until he found what he wanted. "Here it is. Osiris."

The two men stared at each other blankly. "I'll get a dictionary," Eberhart said.

A memory teased at Murtaugh and then became clear just as Eberhart came back. "Egyptian!"

Eberhart found the entry in the dictionary and grinned. "Right you are. Egyptian god of the dead, sometimes identified with the Greek Hades and . . . huh. And the Roman Pluto." He closed the book. "God of the dead."

"So that's how he sees himself, is it?" Murtaugh mused. "A divinity ruling over life and death. I wonder—when he shot off Roscoe's hand, was that meant as a warning? I think we'd better be there when Roscoe goes home from the hospital. In the meantime, you get back to calling those banks. I want to know exactly how much Leon Walsh borrowed."

"You going to confront Walsh?"

"Damn right. But even with the Osiris–Pluto connection, we're still guessing at what happened. I need to know about the money before I force a showdown."

Toward the end of the day Eberhart had tracked down a total of seventy-five thousand dollars' worth of loans Leon Walsh had taken out over a three-week period. "The last place that gave him a loan was Dollar Savings Bank, and they let him have only three thousand. After that, everybody said no—Empire Savings, Bankers Trust, Central Federal, bunch of others. He'd already borrowed on his own *Summit* shares to buy Sussman's, he didn't have any more collateral, and he was in debt. Not exactly what you'd call a good risk. Did your Wall Street contact find out how much Sussman's shares cost Walsh?"

"Exactly the amount he borrowed the week after Sussman's death," Murtaugh said. "So we can forget about that—this three-week flurry of borrowing was for something different. Seventy-five thousand. The amount in 'The Man from Porlock' is one hundred thousand. Well, maybe Walsh just inflated the figure for the sake of the story."

"Or maybe he did get the other twenty-five. There are still a couple hundred banks I didn't check, Lieutenant. The credit bureaus don't cover them all."

"Would he go to a shark? Does he know any?"

"I wouldn't think so. Do you want me to start calling those other banks?"

"I've got a better idea. Do we know which bank Leila Hudson keeps her money in?"

"His ex-wife? No, why should we? You think he got the rest of the money from her?"

"It's possible, isn't it? Walsh doesn't have all that many people to turn to. Look, go talk to her. She may still be at work—get the address from the Sussman file. She works for some television production company."

"I'm on my way," Eberhart said.

Leon Walsh had been a mistake. Leon Walsh had been a very bad mistake. Conceivably Leon Walsh was the worst mistake he'd ever made in his life. And what a way to find out about it! In print! Right there, for the whole world to see.

Pluto closed the copy of *Summit* and sat brooding over his mistake. Leon Walsh was a lulu, all right. Was it egotism or infantilism that made a man reveal his personal story in just that self-dramatizing way? Pluto glowered at the cover of the magazine.

A lightly sarcastic laugh drifted over from the table next to his. "That bad, huh?"

Pluto looked up to see a young woman watching him. Sparkle in her eyes, body tense. No make-up, but her jacket had been chosen to match the green of her eyes. "Just one story," he answered her. "But it was bad."

"Let me guess. 'The Man from Porlock'?"

He didn't even try to hide his surprise. "Now how did you know that?"

"It's a stupid story," she muttered. "He never should have published it."

"By 'he' I assume you mean, er, the editor?"

She nodded. "Asshole."

Pluto made a show of opening the magazine and checking to see who the editor was. "Leon Walsh?"

"That story made me change jobs," the young woman said unexpectedly.

What was this? Pluto considered a moment and then picked up his drink. "May I join you?" When she nodded, he moved over to her table. The tavern was crowded; two people quickly sat down at the small round table Pluto had just vacated.

"I'm Fran," she said.

"Nick," he answered. "How did 'The Man from Porlock' cost you your job?"

"It didn't *cost* me my job. I quit. Because of that asinine story. I used to be the fiction editor at *Summit*," she explained.

"Ah." It was beginning to make sense.

"The blasted story came in over the transom—no agent. I started reading in the middle the way I always do and the damned thing put me to sleep. How could anyone take a story like that seriously? Anyway, I rejected it, but Leon told me to take another look at it."

"The editor."

"Right. So I read it all the way through ver-y carefully, but the thing was even worse the second time around."

"But Leon overrode your decision. Why? What does he think is so great about it?"

Fran lifted her shoulders, let them drop. "No idea. I asked him, but he couldn't give me any real reason for wanting to print it. He just said he thought Kellerman's was a talent worth nurturing. I said 'What talent?'—and that ended the conversation for that day."

"Maybe this Kellerman is a personal friend he's trying to help."

"I wondered about that." She took a swallow of her drink. "But I don't think so. You see, Nick, Leon doesn't have a lot of friends. Not outside the magazine. The people he's close to, well, he talks about them. But he's never so much as mentioned this Kellerman."

"Well, then, some kind of power play going on at *Summit?*" Pluto suggested innocently. "Maybe Leon felt the need to assert his authority over you?"

She shot him a hard look. "Odd you should say that. I'd just about decided that's what was behind it. Leon and I went round and round about the Kellerman story— until we got to the point where I just felt I had to resign." She smiled wryly. "Hell of a way to get rid of your fiction editor, isn't it?"

He made a noncommittal sound. "Where are you working now, Fran?"

"I'm at the *New Yorker*. I don't have the status there I had at *Summit*, but there's room for advancement." She finished her drink. "Here I've been nattering on about myself all this time—what about you?"

"I'm a management consultant," Pluto said. "Not nearly as interesting as what you do."

She laughed, the tension draining out of her face.

"That's what people always say when they don't want you to ask questions." She looked at her watch. "I've got to go. Well, Nick, it was nice talking to you."

"Same here, Fran." He watched her go, feeling slightly relieved. Better that she go on thinking Leon Walsh published "The Man from Porlock" as a move against her in what was obviously a long-running clash of wills. Not that she was likely to start asking embarrassing questions now, not after she'd left *Summit*. There must have been a lot of tension between Walsh and his fiction editor for Fran to tell tales out of school like that. It was a common enough reaction to conflict, though; a combatant felt the need to talk, and it was easier (and safer) to pour it all out on a stranger. Pluto got a lot of his information that way. He ordered another drink.

Fran had called Leon Walsh an asshole, and in Pluto's opinion she was being generous. What on earth had possessed the man? He was acting like a heart-on-his-sleeve, gut-spilling adolescent. He probably wore a T-shirt that said *Love Me*. Perhaps Walsh should be punished for his impropriety—the same way Roscoe Malucci had been punished.

No: this was not the time to make such a decision. "The Man from Porlock" had disturbed Pluto; he was still upset about it. He came to understand *how* upset only when he realized that in his talk with Fran, he'd completely forgotten to put on his English accent.

CHAPTER

9

Leila Hudson's office was almost as messy as her ex-husband's. Sergeant Eberhart wasn't exactly sure what a television production manager did, but from the evidence of Leila Hudson's office it took a lot of paper to do it. The office was small and cramped, but it did have a window. One wall was covered with title graphics, another held a series of sketches of living room settings.

Leila saw him looking at the sketches and said, "You have a measly fifteen-by-twenty-foot space to work with, a budget that keeps shrinking with each new memo from the accounting office, and instructions to create the interior of a Rockefeller-type mansion. What would *you* do?"

He laughed. "Hire a wizard."

"I wish I could," she sighed. "My designer hates me. There's a chair under that pile of transparencies if you want to sit down."

Eberhart made himself a seat. "How long have you been doing this kind of work?"

"About eight years," she said. "I've been with this production company only two, though."

"I've got to ask you a question."

She nodded. "Didn't think you were here to make small talk."

"Has Leon Walsh asked you for money lately?"

She leaned back in her chair and gave him a long look. "Why do you want to know?"

That means yes. "We have reason to think he needed a large sum of money recently. He was borrowing heavily from the banks, but he wasn't able to get all he needed."

"How much did he need altogether?"

"We think a hundred thousand."

Her eyebrows rose, settled back down. "What did he need the money for?"

Eberhart answered the question with another. "Did you let him have some money, Ms Hudson?"

"So you don't want to tell me." She picked up a ruler and played with it. "Sergeant, is Leon in trouble with the law?"

"He hasn't been charged with anything."

She slammed down the ruler. "Damn it, stop giving me evasive answers." She stood up angrily and walked around her desk to face him. "You don't tell me anything but I'm supposed to tell you whatever you want to know! Sergeant, I don't like your rules. I don't want to help you build some sort of case against Leon."

"Look, I know you want to protect him—"

She shook her head vigorously. "No, I don't—not any more. Leon's on his own. But I don't like not knowing what's going on. What has he done?"

Eberhart gave a big audible sigh. "Since we're still in the process of gathering evidence, you know I can't answer that. Ms Hudson—sit down, please."

"I don't want to sit down."

"Will you just sit down? Please?"

Her mouth twitched in amusement. "And if I obey, then you'll reward me by telling me what I want to know? You like that game, do you, Sergeant?"

Eberhart tried to look stern but ended up grinning at her. He liked Leila Hudson. She was a good ten years older than he was, but he found himself attracted in a way that just might interfere with the business at hand. "I guess I can tell you this much. We've traced Walsh's borrowing pretty far—we've got him down for seventy-five thousand. All we want to know is whether he got the last twenty-five from you. It would just complete the picture, you see. You wouldn't be telling us anything new."

She looked depressed. "He's done something he shouldn't have, hasn't he?"

What the hell. "I'm afraid so. I *think* so. Did you let him have the money?"

She nodded reluctantly.

"How much?"

"You named it—twenty-five thousand. On the button." Leila walked to the window and stared out without seeing anything. "I can't say I'm surprised. I knew something was dreadfully wrong."

"How—from his manner, from something he said? What did he say?"

She made a visible effort to pull herself together. "Leon played an unbelievably shabby trick to get me to lend him the money. Don't ask me about it—I'm not going to tell you. But it was the sort of thing a man does only when he's reached the end of his rope. If he's a man like Leon, that is. It really was underhanded, Sergeant. But I decided to give him the money he needed

121

to get out of this scrape he was in, whatever it was—and then I'd have nothing more to do with him. Ever."

"Can you do that?" Eberhart was surprised. "Just walk away after all this time?"

Her face brightened a little. "Oh, yes! I can do that. I feel no more obligation to Leon Walsh—I've done all that can reasonably be expected. More."

Sergeant Eberhart felt a surge of high spirits. "No regrets?"

"Thousands," she laughed. "But none about saying good-bye to Leon. Why am I telling you this?"

Because you've sensed my interest. "I have one of those faces. Just let me ask one more thing. *Is* it a loan? Or is it going to end up being a gift?"

"No, it's a loan," Leila said. "He's already paid back twenty-five hundred of it. Leon's not a deadbeat, thank goodness. He really does try to do the right thing. It's just that it's usually more than he can manage."

"How's that?"

She left the window and absently perched on the edge of the desk, trying to find the best way to put it. "You see, Leon does only one thing in life well, but he does it far better than most other people do *their* things. He's a damned good editor—one of the best, when he's given a free rein. His own editorial writing is a bit pedestrian, but he has a way of putting his finger on what's good or bad in other people's writing that's downright uncanny. He never misses. Do you read much fiction, Sergeant?"

"Afraid I don't."

She nodded, expecting that answer. "Well, if you did, you'd be impressed by the number of established writers who got their start in *Summit.* Did you know Leon has had four novels dedicated to him? *In gratitude,* they all said. As long as he's shut up in that office editing his manuscripts and putting the next issue together, he functions beautifully."

Eberhart understood. "But once he comes out of that office—"

"Yes. He gets rattled easily, and he ends up making guesses when he should be making decisions. Leon is . . . well, he's just filled with heroic aspirations—but he always manages to slip on a banana peel on the way into battle. He's simply not equipped to handle the normal conflicts we all have. So if he should come up against some really desperate situation—Sergeant, don't make me beg. *What has Leon done?*"

Eberhart stood up, replaced the transparencies on the chair—stalling for time. "*If* he's done anything, you'll know in a day or two. I'll call you myself. But I can't tell you now. Besides—we might be wrong, you know."

"But you're not wrong, are you?"

"I don't think so."

Unexpectedly she smiled at him. "I'm putting you on the spot, aren't I? And you know something? Doesn't bother me a bit! You ought to tell me *something.*"

He returned her smile. "I wish I could."

Leila saw him to the door, a matter of about four steps. Just as he was leaving, Eberhart turned to her and said, "Have you read this month's issue of *Summit?*"

She looked vaguely around the paper-laden office. "I have a copy here somewhere. I haven't gotten to it yet."

"Story in there you might find interesting. It's called 'The Man from Porlock.' "

It took her a second, but then she caught on he'd told her something important. She touched his sleeve lightly. "Thank you, Sergeant."

Eberhart nodded and left.

• • •

Captain Ansbacher watched the machine to make sure the cup dropped down before the ersatz coffee started squirting itself down the drain. Double "whitener", no sugar. *Plop*—ah.

" 'Lo, Captain."

He should have known the voice, but Ansbacher had to turn around and look: Sergeant Hanowitz. Ansbacher frowned. Hanowitz was one of those men who always looked as if they had a hangover even when they didn't. Bleary eyes, gray skin. Ansbacher grunted a greeting, wondering what the little toady wanted this time.

Hanowitz put his money in the machine and punched the button for chicken broth. "That stuff gives me dyspepsia," he said, pointing a thumb toward the cup in Ansbacher's hand. "How are things going with the Parminter investigation?"

Ansbacher kept his face expressionless. "You have a special interest in the Parminter case?"

"No, just wondering, that's all. Making any progress?"

"Talk to Grogan. He's in charge."

"Haven't seen him around for a while. Real funny how Parminter stole those plans. Wonder if he'd been doing that all along."

Ansbacher didn't say anything, knowing Hanowitz would get to the point without any help from him. The man was about as subtle as a heart attack.

"Some of the guys are thinking Parminter and the Sutton Construction Company must have had something going for a long time—they did a helluva lot of business with the city. But me, I think it's just talk. I don't believe any of those stories going round."

Ansbacher understood he was supposed to say *What stories?*—but he was damned if he'd take his cues from this little weasel. "Good for you," he said tonelessly.

Hanowitz looked uncomfortable; he wasn't getting the response he was fishing for. He took a big swallow of chicken broth and burned his tongue.

"First time I've ever known that stuff to be hot," Ansbacher smiled as Hanowitz dashed for the water fountain. The Captain finished his coffee and headed back toward his office.

Footsteps, hurrying to catch up. "Hoo, my tongue hurts." Hanowitz sucked in air. "Those stories we were talking about—I think they're just so much sour grapes myself. Murtaugh got sore because you pulled him off the Parminter investigation, that's all."

"Murtaugh?" Ansbacher said before he thought, and was annoyed to see the corners of Hanowitz's mouth twitch.

"Yeah, he doesn't really have anything. He's just mad. He's even asking around about cases you pulled him off years ago—Christ, what a sorehead." Sergeant Hanowitz was almost smiling now; he had Captain Ansbacher's complete attention. "I think it's kinda sneaky myself. Goin' behind your back like that, I mean. But it'll all fizzle out once Murtaugh cools down. Irish temper, I guess."

"Some people carry grudges," was all Ansbacher would volunteer.

Hanowitz laughed. "Well, he's carryin' one big enough to make Arnold Schwarzenegger sweat. Man, he is asking questions about *everything*. He's even asking how many cars you own." He laughed again. "Ever hear anything so stupid?"

Ansbacher stopped in front of his office door and stared at Hanowitz until the other man started to fidget. "Well, I gotta be going," Hanowitz said and hurried off, feeling Ansbacher's eyes burning holes in his back.

· · ·

"Twenty-five thousand from Sterling National Bank and Trust," Murtaugh read from his notebook. "Thirty thousand from Chase Manhattan Bank. Six thousand from Franklin Savings. Five thousand from Citibank."

Leon Walsh's lips moved soundlessly; his face was ashen. Sergeant Eberhart stood by the closed door of the editor's office, his arms folded across his chest.

"Two thousand each from First Federal Savings and Loan, Lincoln Savings, and Dry Dock Savings. Three thousand from Dollar Savings. And last, twenty-five thousand from Leila Hudson." Murtaugh snapped his notebook shut. "Grand total, one hundred thousand dollars. That was a busy three weeks you spent, Walsh."

Walsh had to swallow twice before he could speak. "Why are you still checking up on me?"

"One hundred thousand dollars," Murtaugh repeated. "Exactly the amount needed to pay off the killer in 'The Man from Porlock.' "

"What?! That's just a *story*, for crying out loud! You don't think—"

"Who is J. J. Kellerman?"

"Uh, a writer. A short-story writer."

"You know him?"

"Not personally, no. I've published his work before, though." Walsh cleared his throat. "Good writer."

"Where does he live?"

"What?"

"You heard me. Where does he live? You had to send him a check, didn't you? That means you have an address."

Walsh gave a totally unconvincing laugh. "Lieutenant, you don't think I carry my writers' addresses around in my head, do you?" He buzzed his secretary and asked her to bring in the Kellerman file. "Why are you asking about Kellerman?" Walsh said, obviously preferring this line of inquiry to the earlier one.

Won't work, Murtaugh thought wryly. "Why did you take out a hundred thousand dollars' worth of loans over a three-week period?"

"Excuse me, Lieutenant, but that's none of your business."

"Excuse *me,* but it's very much my business. Now do you want to tell me here or do you want to come down to the station and tell me there?"

Walsh got a moment's reprieve when his secretary walked in with a manila folder. When she'd left, Walsh looked through the folder, taking his time. "Well, well . . . I'm sorry, Lieutenant, but we don't seem to have Kellerman's address. Somebody goofed."

I'll say. "Then how did you send him his check?"

"We obviously did have his address at one time, but somebody forgot to write it down in the file."

Eberhart strode over to the desk and took the file from Walsh. "No address," he confirmed.

"You can't just take things out of my hands that way," Walsh protested.

"Tell us about it." Murtaugh sniffed; what a poor liar Leon Walsh was. "Look, Walsh, enough of this pussyfooting. We know you and J. J. Kellerman are the same person and—"

"That's crazy! Where'd you get an idea like that!"

"And we know 'The Man from Porlock' isn't just a story you made up. It really happened that way. You needed the hundred thousand to pay off Sussman's killer."

"This is insane! *You* are insane! Just because I published a story about a killer . . . somebody else's story, I didn't even write it. You put *me* in the story and claim

I . . . do you really think I'd meekly hand over one hundred thousand dollars to some homicidal maniac who . . . who goes around calling himself *Osiris,* of all things?"

"Not Osiris. Pluto."

Until then Murtaugh would have said it was impossible for Walsh's face to turn any whiter. For a long moment none of the three men either spoke or moved. Then Walsh slowly lowered his face into his hands. Eberhart resumed his post by the door, a conscientious sergeant-at-arms.

"You understand, we do know what happened," Murtaugh said quietly. "Pluto watches the growing conflict between you and Sussman—and when your partner is on the verge of selling you out to UltraMedia, Pluto steps in and kills Sussman. Then he sends you a bill. He waits a while, giving you time to raise the money. You hit the banks for loans, borrow from your ex-wife. Then he calls with instructions where to leave the payoff. You comply."

Walsh lifted his face from his hands and stared blankly at Murtaugh. He said nothing.

"But then your conscience gets to bothering you," Murtaugh continued. "You start feeling that since you paid Sussman's killer the fee he demanded, you have in fact sanctioned the killing. You try living with the guilt, but it's too much for you. You need to tell somebody about it, about how it really was. But you can't. Then you hit on the idea of telling *everybody* about it—in the form of fiction. So you write 'The Man from Porlock' and publish it in *Summit.* Did it work, Walsh? Did it make you feel better?"

Walsh looked on the edge of collapse. "You don't understand."

Murtaugh snorted. "That's what my seventeen-year-old nephew says every time somebody disagrees with him. What don't I understand, Walsh? Make me see it."

"Why are you talking to me like this? I didn't order Sussman's killing!"

Eberhart spoke up. "But you paid for it. We want the bill Pluto sent you, Walsh. The killer in the story sent a bill. So you got one. From Pluto."

"I, I don't have any bill."

"Jesus Christ, Walsh!" Murtaugh exploded. "Are you going to go on pretending you don't know anything? You're not our only source. How do you think we knew the killer's name is Pluto? You're not the first person who's paid him off and you won't be the last. We've got to find this killer and stop him. *Now where's the goddam fucking bill?*"

He shook his head. "I got rid of it. I tore it into small pieces and flushed it down the toilet."

"Terrific," Eberhart grunted.

"All right," Murtaugh sighed, "tell us what you know about him. Ever meet this Pluto face to face?"

"No. We just talked on the phone."

"How many times?"

"Three altogether. I'm afraid the first time I was rather incoherent. You see, I couldn't really believe it was happening. Everything was going so well until this note came in the mail asking for a hundred thousand dollars. Well, I didn't know what to think—would *you* have believed it, Lieutenant? Did you ever get a bill from a murderer? I just couldn't believe it. So I hadn't done anything about raising the money the first time Pluto called."

"So what happened?"

"He threatened me. He *threatened* me, Lieutenant! He said if I wanted to live to see the next issue of *Summit* on the stands I'd jolly well better get the money up PDQ. He said there was no place I could go where he couldn't find me."

" 'Jolly well'?" Eberhart echoed. "He actually said that —'jolly well'?"

"That's what he said."

"Is he English?"

Walsh shrugged. "He's either English or he wanted me to think he is. I couldn't really tell—the accent sounded pretty authentic."

"Then what?" Murtaugh asked.

"Well, he convinced me. What can I say? I thought my life was in danger—and I still think he would have killed me if I hadn't paid him."

Or shot your hand off, Murtaugh thought. "All this is still the first phone call?"

"That's right. The second time he called, I'd raised seventy-five thousand and I asked him if he'd settle for that."

"And he said no."

"He said no. By the third phone call, I had the entire hundred thousand and he told me where to leave it."

"Which was?"

"The men's room at the Mark Hellinger Theater. Inside the paper towel dispenser."

"Anybody in there?"

"No, the place was empty."

"So you never saw Pluto at all?"

"Never."

"And you never got a receipt, either," Eberhart said, an edge of sarcasm in his voice.

Walsh flared up. "Why do you keep on at me about it? I tell you my life was threatened and you treat *me* like the criminal! *I* didn't threaten anyone and I certainly didn't kill anyone!"

"But you did pay a fee to the man who killed your partner."

"Because I had no choice! What else could I do?"

"You could have called us," Eberhart pointed out.

Walsh wouldn't look at either policeman, obviously rattled.

"He's right, you know," Murtaugh said reasonably. "Why didn't you call the police?"

Walsh muttered under his breath.

"What was that?"

"He told me not to."

"Pluto? When did he tell you that?"

"During that first phone call. The same time he was threatening me."

"But you could have called for help before that, couldn't you? When you first got the bill? But you didn't say a word."

Walsh glared at Murtaugh. "I told you I didn't believe it. Why should I call the police about a . . . a crank letter?"

"Oh, you believed it, Walsh. You believed it right from the start. It's only lately you've convinced yourself you didn't believe it—it makes a better story that way. Or at least it makes you look better. Not such a pushover."

Walsh had the wounded look of a child unjustly accused of eating all the Christmas cookies. "Why do you hate me? What have I done to you?"

Murtaugh closed his eyes and rubbed the bridge of his nose; he wasn't enjoying this. "Nothing. You never did a thing to me." He had only just then realized how much he disliked Leon Walsh. Even Walsh's *Why do you hate me?* annoyed him. The man was in a peck of trouble and couldn't be expected to behave rationally; it was just that Murtaugh had a low tolerance for self-pity. He opened his eyes and looked at Eberhart. After a moment's silent communication, Murtaugh muttered, "We have to."

Eberhart nodded and started to speak. "You have the right to remain silent. If you—"

"Wait a minute, wait a minute—*hold on!*" Walsh yelled at them. "What is this? Am I being arrested?"

"Yes, you are," Eberhart said.

"Why? What's the charge?"

"Accessory after the fact."

"Accessory . . . ? But I told you, I paid that money because my life was threatened!"

Murtaugh pulled at his ear. "It's a peculiar situation. You were the victim of extortion, that's true. But when you paid off the extortionist, you made yourself an accessory to murder. I don't know how the courts are going to handle this one. You could plead extenuating circumstances—a good lawyer can probably get you off. But that's not my concern. My business is bringing in lawbreakers. And, Mr. Walsh, you broke the law."

"How?" he screamed. "By protecting myself? By saving my own life?"

"By cooperating with a murderer," Murtaugh snapped. "By concealing knowledge of a crime. Every time someone like you pays off without a fuss, you're just paving the way for the next murder. And the next. And the next. This Pluto is a leech—don't you see that? He needs people like you to feed off of."

"So you're saying I shouldn't have paid him? You're saying I should have just stood around and waited to get shot?"

"No, I'm not saying that. We don't expect you to take

on a murderer by yourself. But we do expect you to inform us if you're being pressured by a self-admitted killer. How can we help you if you don't let us know what's going on? If you'd called us in the minute you got the bill, we could have had a line on Pluto by now."

"You don't know that," Walsh said weakly.

"But you don't know otherwise. And not only do you fail to call the police, you also destroy the one piece of evidence that might have given us a lead." Murtaugh looked at the crestfallen man in front of him. "Look, Walsh, we're not unsympathetic to your position. I know killing Sussman was Pluto's idea, and I know you were scared out of your skull. But you did pay a *killer* for *killing*—we can't just pat you on the head and say 'Oh, that's all right.' You are accountable for what you've done. We have to arrest you. What happens next isn't up to us."

"It might not even go to court," Eberhart said helpfully. "It depends on what the prosecutors decide to do. But we still have to take you in and book you."

Walsh had no arguments left; all the fight had gone out of him.

"Let's go," Murtaugh said.

Sergeant Eberhart was talking to Leila Hudson's answering machine when she cut in.

"This is Leila Hudson live," she announced. "Sorry about the machine—I thought it might be someone I didn't want to talk to. Are you calling about Leon?"

"Unfortunately, yes."

"Oh. That doesn't sound good."

"We've just placed him under arrest. Accessory to murder. The money he borrowed from you and all the rest of it—it was to pay off Jerry Sussman's killer." There was a long silence. "Leila?"

"I'm here. Did it happen like—was it like the story you told me to read? 'The Man from Porlock'?"

"Almost exactly. Walsh wrote it, you know—did you recognize his writing?"

"I suspected it was Leon's. Do you really have him in jail? It seems to me he's the victim, not the, ah, perpetrator. He was trying to save his own life. You don't put people in jail for that."

"It's a tricky problem, all right," Eberhart admitted. "But it's one the courts are going to have to solve, not the police. As for Walsh's being in jail, he'll be out in a matter of hours. He's talking to his lawyer right now."

"You aren't going to keep him locked up, then?"

"Naw. If he was a dealer or a rapist, he'd be out already. But since he's part victim, that complicates things."

"God, you sound cynical."

"Sorry. It's been a long day." And it wasn't over yet. "Leila? What if he turns to you for help again?"

"I don't know what I can do to help. You said his lawyer was there, didn't you?"

"You know what I mean. What if he comes to you for, well, support, encouragement?"

"You mean what if he wants me to make him feel good." She took a deep breath. "Sergeant Eberhart, I don't even know your first name."

"Dave."

"Well, Dave, what I told you before—I meant it. Leon's on his own now. I'm through being a Provider of Comfort. It's a tiresome, second-rate kind of role to have to play all your life. Does that bother you?"

"Not in the least," he said happily. "Can I do anything to help?"

"Not right now, I need a few days. Call me later in the week?"

"I'll do that."

He ended the conversation feeling less tired than when he'd started it. He wondered why two such dissimilar people as Leila Hudson and Leon Walsh had ever married in the first place.

CHAPTER

10

The plainclothesman watching Roscoe Malucci's front door on East Ninety-first Street was sitting in a black sedan that looked as if it had been washed and waxed only two minutes ago.

Murtaugh bent over by the driver's window. "Anything?"

The plainclothesman shook his head. "The nurse has been in and out. A Dr. Riley came once, and the kid's lawyer, guy named Wagner. Other than that, nobody."

"What about Roscoe—has he been out yet?"

"Nope, he just sends the nurse out when he wants something."

"Is she in there now?"

"*He*—and yes, he's in there now."

The man who answered the door looked more like a bodyguard than a nurse. Fortyish, mashed-in face, sleeves of a white T-shirt rolled up short to display oversized biceps. Fortunately his manner of speaking matched his profession rather than his appearance. "Lieutenant Murtaugh?" he said when Murtaugh showed his identification. "I thought someone named Billings was in charge of the investigation."

"He is," Murtaugh said. "I'm investigating a murder, and it looks as if our murderer is the same man who shot Roscoe."

The other man grimaced. "In that case, you'd better come in. My name's Bowers, by the way."

Bowers led him to a rather fussily decorated sitting room in which the sole inhabitant stuck out like a living anachronism; the blue jeans and sports shoes didn't go with the heavy Victorian décor. Roscoe Malucci was stretched out on a stiff-looking sofa, the old-fashioned quilt he'd kicked off lying in a heap on the floor. He glared at Murtaugh sullenly.

"Hello, Roscoe, I'm Lieutenant Murtaugh. Do you remember me?"

"No," Roscoe said shortly. "Am I supposed to?"

Murtaugh smiled. "We met briefly when you were still in the hospital. The doctor had you doped up on painkillers at the time."

Roscoe shrugged. "I don't remember."

"It doesn't matter," Murtaugh said, seating himself without an invitation. Bowers moved over to stand protectively by his patient. "We did talk in the hospital, though. You told me about Pluto."

"That crud!" Roscoe screamed, making Murtaugh jump. "That pile of shit! You see what he did to me?" He waved the bandaged stub of his left wrist in the air. "I thought he was puttin' me on, man! How was I supposed to know he meant it? And look what he did!"

"Whoa, whoa—back up. When did you first hear from him?"

"When? Oh, musta been a couple of months ago. He sent me this bill, see—"

"Do you still have it?"

"Shit, I don't know."

"It's here," Bowers said, starting out of the room. "I'll get it."

"Then he kept calling me and calling me," Roscoe went on. He sat up and swung his feet around to the floor. "He kept saying he'd killed my grandmother—hell, anybody coulda read about that in the papers! I thought he was just some creep trying to rip me off. He wanted me to pay him, he really wanted me to pay him for killing her! Shit."

"What did you tell him?"

"I told him to stop bugging me. I told him I didn't believe him."

Bowers came back with a blue envelope in his hand. "Here it is, Lieutenant."

It was a regular window envelope, the kind everybody used for mailing bills. How very businesslike of Pluto. Murtaugh took the envelope by the edges and carefully removed the note.

Pluto was not a man to waste words. A one-hundred-thousand-dollar fee for services rendered. *One murder, arranged to coincide with establishment of Cape Cod alibi.* "Roscoe, did you notice any accent when you talked to Pluto?"

"Oh yeah, yeah, just like my man Bertie."

"Who?"

"Bertie Steffans," Bowers volunteered. "An English rock singer."

"Did he threaten to shoot off your hand if you didn't pay up?" Murtaugh asked Roscoe.

"Man, he made all kinds of threats! I didn't pay no attention. I thought he was bullshittin' me."

"Did you tell all this to Detective Billings?"

"I told him a guy named Pluto had been threatening me, but I didn't tell him what happened after I got home from the hospital. Because I ain't *seen* him since I got back. Nobody's been here from the police. Nobody cares."

"I care, Roscoe," Murtaugh said patiently, "and I'm here. Tell me. What happened?"

"What happened was that ghoul called and asked me how I'd like to lose the other hand. *Shit*. I didn't argue—not this time. He's crazy, man."

"Wait a minute—are you saying you paid him the hundred thousand?"

"You're damn right I paid him. Paid him just this morning."

"This morning?" Murtaugh was astonished. "How'd you manage that?" he asked—and then knew the answer. He turned to the nurse. "You?"

"I dropped the money off about an hour and a half ago," Bowers said. "A hundred thousand dollars in a grocery bag."

"Where'd you leave it?"

"Madison Square Garden. They're having some kind of Modern Living Show there—model displays of interiors, you know the kind of thing. Pluto said go to the kitchen model called 'Rosetta' and leave the money in the breadbox. It was one of those built into a drawer."

"Did you talk to Pluto?" Murtaugh asked.

"I talked to him," Roscoe said as Bowers shook his head. "Those were his instructions. Put the money in a breadbox. *Crap*."

Murtaugh looked at the two of them a moment before

BARBARA PAUL

he said anything. "Roscoe, you just handed a hundred thousand dollars over to the man who killed your grandmother. Didn't it occur to you that paying him off might make you an accessory to murder?"

Roscoe hooted. "Don't you preach at me, man! You still got both your hands."

He had a point, Murtaugh conceded. "What about you, Bowers? You must have thought of the legal complications?"

"Yes, I did," Bowers admitted. "But it wasn't my decision to make, Lieutenant. I'm just here to help."

"Why didn't you call the police?"

Roscoe abruptly lay back down on the sofa. Then he reached down and picked up the quilt from the floor, covered himself up so that only the top of his head was showing.

"We were afraid," Bowers said, tactfully pluralizing the pronoun.

Murtaugh nodded. "Well, lucky for Roscoe, he's not the first one we found out about. We've arrested a man who paid Pluto's fee—he's been charged with being an accessory. Preliminary hearing comes up in a couple of weeks—it's a test case. That hearing will determine whether *Roscoe* has committed a crime or not. Plus a lot of other people we don't know about yet, no doubt. But until then, Roscoe, I don't want you to leave town. Roscoe—do you hear?"

A mumble came out from under the quilt.

"He says he's not going anywhere," Bowers translated.

Murtaugh handed Bowers his card. "If you hear from Pluto again, give me a call at that number. Good-bye, Roscoe. Don't worry—we'll get him."

Roscoe didn't even bother to mumble that time.

Bowers led the way back to the front door. "Why'd he have to shoot him in the hand, Lieutenant?" the nurse wanted to know. "Why not the leg or even an arm? Evidently the only thing Roscoe really cared about was playing his guitar—and now he'll never be able to do that again."

"And that's exactly why he was shot in the hand. Pluto doesn't like being told no. See how quickly he collected this time?"

Bowers muttered something unintelligible.

Murtaugh paused on the doorstep. "Bowers—you did leave the money where Pluto said leave it, didn't you? You know if you tucked it away somewhere for yourself, you just signed that boy's death warrant."

Bowers's body tensed. "That's a hell of a thing to say to me, Lieutenant."

"So it is," Murtaugh agreed. "Or maybe you left *most* of it in the breadbox? You deserved a little something for your trouble, right?"

Bowers was making a visible effort to control himself. "It's a good thing you're a cop, buddy, or you'd be nursing one busted nose."

"I still haven't heard any denials."

"You're hearing one right now. I put that money in the breadbox and I put it *all* there—I didn't help myself to a cent. Even if I wanted to cross the kid, you think I'm fool enough to play games with that Pluto? I did exactly what I was told to do. I'm not messing with any guy that goes around shooting hands off."

"Wise of you," Murtaugh sighed, believing him. "Sorry, Bowers—I had to ask."

"I have to go now," the nurse said stiffly. "Time for Roscoe's medicine—there's still danger of infection."

141

"Right. Well, good-bye. And Bowers—I'm glad to see Roscoe is in such good hands."

Bowers nodded acknowledgment before he closed the door, partly mollified. Murtaugh didn't linger; he was in a hurry to get Pluto's bill to the crime lab. And to send Sergeant Eberhart to the Modern Living Show at Madison Square Garden. Perhaps someone there had noticed that extraordinary interest in breadboxes earlier in the day.

Leon Walsh sat staring hopelessly at the old black Remington in his home. He'd filled four pages with meaningless words, phrases, sentences. But his old trick of typing anything at all just to get himself started hadn't worked this time. Nothing came; no plot idea, no line of dialogue, nothing.

He needed money again. He'd given himself a raise as editor of *Summit*, and that helped. But his bank loans and his obligation to Leila were weighing heavily on him. He had a dividend coming from his *Summit* shares, but that wouldn't be for another four months. The only sure way he could put his hands on money quickly would be to sell himself another story.

But not one written by J. J. Kellerman; that pseudonym was useless to him now. Damn that Lieutenant Murtaugh! Because of him, it would come out in the hearing that Leon Walsh had been publishing his own work under an assumed name. God. How humiliating. But . . . maybe he should put a brave face on it, capitalize on the revelation that Kellerman and Walsh were the same person—maybe he should go on writing under the name of Kellerman and dare the literary world to make of it what it would! But he knew he'd never do it. Bra-

vado like that required a certain kind of pushiness that
Walsh had always found distasteful. No, he'd have to find
a new name to write his new story under.

What new story? He rolled a fifth sheet of paper into
the typewriter, but that sheet wasn't any more magical
than the first four: it remained perversely blank. Good
god, of all the things that had happened to him lately,
you'd think *something* would lend itself to story form,
something should be transmutable into fiction. The three
hours he'd spent in jail, for instance.

Whatever he wrote, Walsh wouldn't have any trouble
publishing this one. *Summit*'s new fiction editor was far
more amenable to suggestion than the departed Fran
Caffrey had ever been. But before Walsh got to that point,
he had to have something down on paper. He stared at
the blank sheet in the typewriter and ordered himself to
write.

An hour later he was still staring at the same blank
page. It just wasn't going to come this time. Walsh's back
and underarms felt clammy. He couldn't afford not to
write, and he couldn't afford to put it off. His attorney
was optimistic that the hearing coming up in ten days
would end with the charges against him being dropped—
but what if the attorney was wrong? What if Walsh had
only ten days of freedom left? He dealt with that possibility by not thinking about it.

He pushed back from the typewriter; no help there.
He wandered around his study for a few moments,
stopped in front of the shelves that held a complete run
of *Summit* magazine. He pulled down half a dozen of the
first issues, published back in Summit, New Jersey, back
in the days before Jerry Sussman had appeared on the
scene. And Walsh had thought he had problems then! He

laughed humorlessly. That early struggle to get the magazine established was beginning to take on the coloration of The Good Old Days.

He carried the old copies of *Summit* back to his desk and sat leafing through them, remembering. He came across one story that made him grunt out loud: "Talking of Michelangelo"—by J. J. Kellerman. That had been the first one, the one that had started his subterranean writing career, if it could be called a career. It had also been the story that had evoked no comment whatsoever, pro or con.

Walsh read it through. Not a bad little story for a first effort—could do with some beefing up here and there. And some stylistic slickening wouldn't hurt either. But the basic idea was sound; all it needed was a little cosmetic help.

The idea came to him then.

He thought about it; he thought about it long and carefully and decided he could probably get away with it. Change the title and the names of the characters, think up a new pseudonym for the author. Fiddle with the setting, add a little here, cut a little there. Same kind of editorial work he did all the time—shouldn't be too hard. *Plagiarizing myself, cannibalizing my own work,* Walsh thought dryly. The thought had only just occurred to him, but already his ethics were hurting. Like an aching tooth. But he decided to go ahead with it anyway; it was the only solution he could see.

Of course, there was the danger that some sharp-eyed reader with a long memory would see that the new story was just "Talking of Michelangelo" in different clothing—but that was a chance he'd have to take. He didn't think it likely to happen, since the story had made no impression when it first appeared. The more Walsh thought about it, the more certain he became he could pull it off.

It wasn't as if he were doing something illegal. After all, he was stealing from nobody but himself.

Murtaugh came in in a bad mood. He and Ellie had quarreled that morning, about nothing at all. They'd both just felt like quarreling. It happened.

His mood wasn't helped any by the debris left on the desk by the night officer who used the office before him—scraps of paper, overflowing ashtray, a half-eaten candy bar. Two Styrofoam cups, each with half an inch of cold coffee in the bottom.

Sergeant Eberhart came bouncing into the office with an energy Murtaugh found almost indecent. "Morning, Lieutenant—I got something here that'll cheer you up!"

"How do you know I need cheering up?" Murtaugh snarled.

The younger man stopped short. "Uh, it's Monday morning and everybody needs cheering up on Monday morning."

That drew a wry smile. "Oh, good recovery! All right, Eberhart, sit down and tell me what you've got."

"Right." Eberhart pulled a chair up to Murtaugh's desk and hesitated. He grabbed a wastebasket and swept last night's leavings off the top of the desk. Murtaugh thought about the leftover coffee mixing with the cigarette ashes but said nothing. Eberhart muttered something about people who don't clean up their own messes and sat down, spreading out a few papers in front of him.

The Sergeant had been unsuccessful in his attempt to find a witness to Pluto's pickup of Roscoe Malucci's hundred thousand dollars at the Modern Living Show in Madison Square Garden. The people who ran the show said this year's crowd were touchers—opening drawers and doors, turning on (unconnected) faucets, etc. Dead end.

So now Eberhart was glad to have something positive to pass on. "Crime Lab report on the bill Pluto sent to Roscoe Malucci. Only fingerprints are those of Roscoe himself and Raymond J. Bowers, the nurse. The envelope has a whole mess of smeary prints—postal workers. But the paper itself is a help. Distinctive watermark, a stylized tiger's head. Heavy—twenty-pound weight. Kokle finish, odd color called 'bluebell'. Documents Section was able to identify the manufacturer as Yarborough Paper Products, operating out of Stamford, Connecticut."

"Have you called them yet?"

"Yep. The lady I talked to, a Mrs. Fertig, knew the line from the tiger's-head watermark. It comes in six different colors—and here's where we had a bit of luck. Mrs. Fertig said they were thinking about discontinuing the blue, or else substituting a different shade for the one they have. Seems that 'bluebell' isn't a good seller— it's too dark. The black ink of a typewriter ribbon doesn't show up as well as on white, and blue ink from a pen even less. Hard to read."

"So they don't have much call for it?"

"Not a whole lot. And get this—anybody wanting that shade of blue *with window envelopes* has to special-order them!"

"Great! Direct from Stamford?"

"No, the orders are placed through retail stores, stationers and the like. I asked Mrs. Fertig how many special orders had come through from New York City within the past year. She pushed some buttons on their computer and came up with four orders. Over eight million people in this burg, and only four of them like that shade of blue!"

"No wonder they're thinking of discontinuing it," Murtaugh smiled, his bad mood forgotten.

"Those four orders are just for business stationery and envelopes, remember," Eberhart said, "and just in this immediate area. That blue might be a big hit in Dubuque —who knows. However. Mrs. Fertig read me the names and addresses of the special order places, and here they are!" He separated one sheet of paper from the rest and handed it to Murtaugh with a flourish.

Murtaugh tried to make sense of Eberhart's illegible scrawl. "You can read this, can you?"

His sergeant was insulted. "Of course I can read it. Two of the orders came from the same place, an office supplies outfit on Broadway. The third order came from one of those high-toned places that call themselves fine paper merchants. The fourth was from a stationery shop in Brooklyn."

"So why aren't you calling them? What are you waiting for?"

"I'm waiting for the stores to open, Lieutenant. It's only eight-thirty."

Unbelieving, Murtaugh looked at his watch: eight-twenty-seven. "So when did you have your conversation with Mrs. Fertig?"

Eberhart grinned. "They start early in Stamford."

Murtaugh nodded, musing. "Special orders—the customers would have to leave their names. Our hundred-thousand-dollar killer wouldn't use his real name, of course, but maybe somebody'll remember him."

Eberhart was doing a little musing of his own. "One hundred thousand dollars. Jeez. Remember the Echeverrias?"

Murtaugh remembered; he'd helped bring them in. Raul and Juanito Echeverria, first cousins who'd murder anybody for six hundred bucks. That was six hundred dollars for the *team*, for both of them. Three hundred each.

Now Eberhart was thinking of something else. "Lieutenant, that English accent Pluto has—you think it's real?"

"Probably not. An accent is an easy way to disguise your voice."

"But why would he want to? Does he know any of these people he calls?"

"I think he's just being cautious. We don't know how long he's been doing his, ah, speculative killing. But if he's been getting away with it for any length of time, it's because he doesn't take any chances he doesn't have to."

"You don't think this is something he's just started."

"Hell, no, it's too slick. I'm going to see if the computer can help us. What we need is a list of unsolved murders that follow a specific pattern. The murder rather spectacularly benefits one certain person, and that person not only has an iron-clad alibi but is also in a position to come up with one hundred thousand dollars on short notice. And I can tell you a good place to start. Carolyn Randolph. You know—the landscape architect who was almost done out of a city contract by William Parminter? I want you to run a financial check on her, see if she needed a hundred thousand shortly after Parminter's death. I'm willing to bet next month's salary that the lady paid Pluto for killing Parminter."

Eberhart looked uneasy. "Lieutenant, if Captain Ansbacher hears you're back on the Parminter case—"

"I'm not back on the case, I just want to know if Carolyn Randolph needed a lot of money in a hurry. But leave that until after you've checked the stationers. If you can't get a line on Pluto through the four orders you know about, then call back your friend in Stamford, I've already forgotten her name—"

"Mrs. Fertig."

"Call Mrs. Fertig and get a list of last year's orders—you know the drill. What time do stationery stores open?"

Eberhart started calling at nine-thirty, and Murtaugh found the computer could indeed tell him what he wanted to know. Nine other unsolved murders fitting the pattern Murtaugh specified in the past year alone, but only two to four a year for the preceding ten years. Even if some of the cases were discounted as coincidence, the record still indicated a pronounced increase of murderous activity within the pattern during the past year. Why? What was behind it? Why did Pluto get greedy all of a sudden?

By nine-forty-five Eberhart had hit pay dirt. "Tobin and Sons," he told Murtaugh. "Stationers, on Lexington—it's gotta be them. The two orders at the office supplies store on Broadway were placed by businesses—Di Gennaro's Ceramic and Marble Cleaning Service, and Lasky and Appelbaum, a jewelry firm. Both of them ordered the company name imprinted on the bill paper and the window envelopes. The Brooklyn order was also for imprinted work—a specialty foods store called Popo's. The only order with no imprinting was at Tobin and Sons. I talked to the clerk who took the order—and Lieutenant, she said, 'Oh, yes, I remember him. That's the English fellow, isn't it?' "

Murtaugh's grin stretched from ear to ear. "What's he look like?"

"The clerk says he's a bit on the chunky side, average height. Dark blond hair, worn long. Age, thirty or forty. Or maybe fifty. I'm quoting."

"Hm. What name did he give?"

"Nicholas Ramsay. No address, but he left a phone number—I called it and it's an answering service. They wouldn't give out any information over the phone, so I'm going to have to go over there and flash a badge at them."

"I'll do that—you stay here and start the check on Carolyn Randolph's finances. That was good work, Eberhart. What's the name of the answering service?"

"Backtalk Telephone Service. It's on—hell, I forgot to write it down. I'll get the address for you."

"Okay. Nicholas Ramsay, huh?"

"Right. Lieutenant—why'd he buy this exclusive paper and envelopes? If he's so damned cautious, why didn't he just use a cheap paper anybody could pick up anywhere?"

"Vanity, I'd guess. Remember 'The Man from Porlock'? Leon Walsh kept talking about the killer's enormous ego. Cheap paper wouldn't suit Pluto's sense of style."

Eberhart thought of something. "Are you going to tell Captain Ansbacher?"

Murtaugh looked pained. "Yes." Eberhart nodded and went back to his desk to start phoning.

The Lieutenant didn't want to tell the Captain; Murtaugh wouldn't feel safe from his superior's interference until he actually had Pluto (alias Nicholas Ramsay undoubtedly alias something else) safely under lock and key. But he'd have to share information with Billings, the detective in charge of the Roscoe Malucci shooting, and Billings had to report to Ansbacher. There was no way around it—Ansbacher had to be told.

Might as well get it over with. Murtaugh walked down the hall and knocked on Ansbacher's open door.

"Not now, Murtaugh. Come back later."

"Fine with me. Thought you might like to know we have a line on Sussman's killer." He walked away.

"Come back here!" Ansbacher roared after him. Murtaugh went back. "Billings says that's the same gun that shot off the Malucci kid's hand."

"Same gun, Captain." Murtaugh filled him in on what they'd found out. " 'Ramsay' has got to be an alias, but the answering service might give us a further line. Also, we can get an Identikit picture of his face—the clerk at the stationer's remembers him."

Ansbacher was nodding, making notes. "What about an all-points?"

"As soon as we get the picture."

"Okay, I'll say we have a suspect, picture to follow."

"You'll . . . what?"

Ansbacher checked his watch. "I have a press conference downstairs in ten minutes. I'll include an announcement about your Pluto and how he operates. A splash of publicity might be just the thing to keep him quiet for a while."

Murtaugh's mouth fell open. "You can't be serious!"

"Of course I'm serious!" Ansbacher eyed him with annoyance. "Don't tell me how to do my job. You're still taking orders from me."

"I wasn't—"

"You don't decide policy around here, *I* do. Got that?"

God—how jealous of his authority he was! "Captain—"

"Why shouldn't I make an announcement? It'll all come out at the Walsh hearing next week anyway."

"That still gives us a week. Captain, there are other people out there who've been finagled into paying Pluto for killing their enemies—Leon Walsh and Roscoe Malucci aren't the only ones. You go down there and spill the beans to the news media and we're going to get zilch from those people who paid Pluto. Especially if you tell them about Walsh's hearing. Nobody's going to talk to us if they think they can be charged as accessory to murder!"

"It's your job to get them to talk. Who are these people anyway?"

"I got a list of possibles from the computer. I could use some more men, Captain."

"Can't spare any. Send me the list—I'll pass it on to Billings or somebody."

Murtaugh felt his face turning red. "At least wait until after Walsh's hearing before you go public. Chances are Walsh'll get off—then the people who paid Pluto won't be so reluctant to talk. But if they clam up now, they might never open up to us."

"What if Walsh doesn't get off?"

Murtaugh gestured helplessly. "A week, Ansbacher. Just *one week*."

Ansbacher stood up behind his desk. "I'm going to be late," he said, and brushed by Murtaugh on his way out.

11

What a laugh. Nobody could identify him from that silly drawing, he was sure. He was almost sure. A police drawing based on a description given by a stationery store clerk who'd seen him only twice, and that was months ago. It looked like a cartoon, not a person. It certainly didn't look like *him*.

Maybe he should grow a beard?

Pluto took a large pair of scissors and cut the sketch out of the newspaper. He pinned the drawing to the corkboard wall of his study. He walked around, looking at it from different angles. He tried squinting his eyes. No, he just could not see himself in the drawing. If that was all the police had to go on, he didn't need to worry. So, no beard. Good; he hated the idea of all that hair sprouting out of his face. But an ounce of precaution never hurt—he'd compromise: a mustache.

Pluto had had enough time to get over the initial shock of hearing his name on the six o'clock news several nights earlier. A police captain who looked like a bulldog and talked like an elocution teacher had announced to the world that the NYPD had only recently learned of a murderer-for-hire named Pluto—who killed first and collected afterward. The captain's name was Ansbacher and he told the reporters shouting questions all about Leon Walsh and Roscoe Malucci (Pluto's two big mistakes). Ansbacher said they were investigating other cases that Pluto may or may not have been involved in—the thought of which made Pluto a bit nervous. But he cheered up considerably when he heard Leon Walsh had been charged with being an accessory to murder.

Of course, he would have preferred total anonymity, but Walsh didn't really know anything to tell the police. Every step Pluto had ever taken to protect himself had been chosen with this eventuality in mind: that someday, somehow, the police would learn of his existence. But if anybody was going to jail, Pluto sincerely hoped it would be Leon Walsh. Evidently Roscoe had shot off his mouth just as much as Walsh and had even given the police the bill Pluto had sent. But Roscoe Malucci was a fool, an empty-headed nitwit who'd never be anything more than what he was at that very moment. Walsh, on the other hand, was an educated adult, a professional man, someone who ought to know how to conduct himself in tight situations. Leon Walsh offended Pluto's sense of decorum.

That time when Captain Ansbacher first announced that the police were on to Pluto—that had been a *bad* moment. Pluto had had to fight an unseemly urge to throw a few things into a suitcase and catch the first plane for Switzerland. But then he reflected that, all things considered, it was rather thoughtful of the good captain to keep him informed of police goings-on. Pluto might have blithely gone his usual way and walked right into a trap, a setup. Now . . .

Now what? Pluto read every newspaper account he could find over the past two days, including today's publication of the police Identikit sketch that was supposed to represent his face. He tried to remember the stationery store clerk who the papers said had helped the police with the sketch, but he came up blank. Since the police had traced the blue paper to the store where he'd ordered it, that meant he wouldn't be able to go on using the Nicholas Ramsay alias any longer. And *that* meant he'd have to change answering services, find a new mail drop. What a bother. Oh well, he'd have had to do all that eventually anyway; might as well be now as later.

At first Pluto thought Captain Ansbacher had done all the investigating himself, but such turned out not to be the case. The man in charge of the Jerry Sussman murder investigation and the one who'd arrested Leon Walsh was a Lieutenant James T. Murtaugh. Ansbacher had failed to mention Murtaugh in his television announcement and in fact had identified him only in response to a direct question from a newspaper reporter the next day. A little interdepartmental rivalry there? Something worth looking into, perhaps.

But he wasn't even going to be able to cross the street from now on without looking both ways twice. All these years he'd been practicing his profession without the police tumbling to what was going on—they hadn't had a *clue*. Now his unique approach to staving off personal economic crisis was smeared all over television and the newspapers for everyone to see. Pluto knew as well as he knew the sun would rise out of the smog the next morning exactly what was going to happen next: imitators. Before long the police would be blaming *him* for copycat killings he wouldn't even know about! What a revolting development.

Perhaps it was time to retire. The chalet between Lausanne and Geneva beckoned. But the chalet wasn't furnished in the early-rich-man style Pluto wanted, and he didn't have enough for that *plus* the lavish style of living the money-worshipping Swiss so heartily encouraged in their alien residents. Besides—wouldn't it be better to stay in New York where he could keep an eye on things? Pluto didn't think it would be too difficult to stay ahead of the grandstanding Captain Ansbacher.

He turned back to the newspaper clippings, skimming through until he found what he was looking for. Leon Walsh's hearing was scheduled for the following Monday.

Monday, Pluto mused. Perhaps he should drop in, just to see how things went.

"Lieutenant, she's just not talking. Not even yes or no when we ask her if she wants coffee. We're not going to get anything out of that one."

Murtaugh thought Sergeant Eberhart had a harried look to him. "Does she have a lawyer?"

"She didn't ask for one. She's just sitting there with her mouth shut, waiting us out." Eberhart plopped down on a chair in Murtaugh's office and stuck his feet out in front of him. "We can't hold her much longer."

"I know," Murtaugh said quietly. "But she paid Pluto —I'm sure of it. You confronted her with the evidence that she'd had to raise a hundred thousand dollars in a hurry, didn't you? What did she say then?"

"Same as she said to everything else—nothing. She didn't say 'None of your business' or 'Bug off' or anything. She just keeps her mouth closed and her gaze fixed on the wall behind us. She *ignores* us, Lieutenant. Carolyn Randolph isn't going to tell us a thing."

"Hell. She's the one I wanted the most."

"How about trying for a search warrant? For her home *and* her office—we might have probable cause. If we could find the bill Pluto sent her—"

Murtaugh cut him off. "Nothing doing there—I already asked. Besides, anybody cool enough to outwait a police interrogation isn't going to leave incriminating evidence lying around where we could find it. Damn. I especially wanted Carolyn Randolph to talk."

Eberhart thought he knew why; there was some hidden connection among Carolyn Randolph and the late William Parminter and Sutton Construction Company and Captain Ansbacher. Not for the first time Eberhart wished Murtaugh would take him into his confidence; he wanted to know exactly what the Lieutenant had on Ansbacher so far. But Murtaugh was keeping him out of it; to protect him, no doubt. Right now, though, the problem was the speak-no-evil Carolyn Randolph. "So what do we do with her?"

"Let her go." Murtaugh sighed. "If the charges against Leon Walsh are dropped, maybe she'll talk to us then."

"I don't think so." Eberhart stood up to go. "She's not like Walsh and Roscoe Malucci, Lieutenant. She knows we got *nothing* on her without her cooperation."

Murtaugh nodded, waved him out. So forget about the Randolph woman; she wasn't going to help. Better to concentrate on one of the other possibles, somebody like the opera singer, what was his name—Bàccolo, Luigi Bàccolo, that was it.

Although he wasn't any too clear on what he hoped any of them could tell him, Pluto's . . . what? Customers, clients? Murtaugh thought the Walsh arrangement was probably typical, and Pluto never came face to face with the people he billed for one hundred thousand each. Roscoe Malucci was the exception to the procedure, the dumb bunny who'd failed to understand what very real danger he was in. Even then Pluto hadn't shown his face.

The answering service Pluto had been using sent a monthly statement to Nicholas Ramsay at the Knickerbocker Mail Address Service on Fifth Avenue. Both services said that Ramsay had been a customer for only four months. That meant Pluto periodically changed his name, his mailing address, and his telephone number. A careful man.

Pluto. A red-hot devil? No. Not by any stretch of the imagination. This had to be the most cold-blooded son of a bitch ever to walk the streets of Manhattan. The man must be totally without conscience. What other kind of person could impartially survey a conflict between two human beings he didn't even know, dispassionately pick one of them to champion, and then coolly destroy the other one's life? Pluto had had no compunction about shooting down Roscoe Malucci's grandmother, an elderly woman with no defenses, with no idea even that she was in danger. Poor old woman. What chance do the Mrs. Maluccis have against a Pluto?

That was the thing about Pluto that Murtaugh hated the most: Pluto sucker-punched his victims. They had no warning, not even a hint of what was coming. People living together in society had to trust one another to an extent; they had no choice. You had to trust the short-order cook not to sprinkle arsenic on your hamburger because he was mad at the world and wanted to hit back; you had to trust your life to the *drivers* of the world, taxi drivers and bus drivers and pilots, all of them strangers; you had to trust that the man sitting so close to you in a theater that your elbows touched wouldn't suddenly slip a knife between your ribs. It was a trust that was a little harder come by every year, and someone like Nicholas

Pluto Ramsay could wipe out what little was left without half trying. One Pluto equaled several thousand cases of paranoia. He had to be stopped, and he had to be stopped soon.

"*Murtaugh!*" The word was a shout; Murtaugh looked up to see Captain Ansbacher looming over him. "What do you think you're doing? *What the hell do you think you're doing?*"

Murtaugh stood up uneasily. "What do you mean, Captain?"

"What do you mean, Captain?" Ansbacher mimicked viciously. "You're not going to try the wide-eyed innocent shtick, are you? Aren't you a little old for that?"

Murtaugh counted to five. "I don't know what you're talking about."

"Don't lie to me, Murtaugh. You know exactly what I'm talking about. Who told you to bring Carolyn Randolph in for questioning?"

"Who . . . ? Nobody told me, Captain. I think she paid Pluto for killing William Parminter—after the fact, of course."

"You *think*. No, Murtaugh, you don't think—that's your trouble. You don't think, and you don't listen. I told you to keep your hands off the Parminter case."

"It's the same killer, both Parminter and Jerry Sussman were killed by the same—"

"There, that's a perfect example of what I'm talking about," Ansbacher interrupted smoothly. "You just don't listen. When was the last time you had your hearing checked, Murtaugh? Maybe you have a physical disability."

Murtaugh fought down the urge to punch this vicious bulldog in the snout, said nothing.

"I pulled you off the Parminter case so you could concentrate on nailing the Sussman killer. Then the minute I'm not looking you're back sticking your nose in the Parminter investigation, meddling in somebody else's case."

"I'm not interfering with the investigation—"

"You hauled Carolyn Randolph in, didn't you? What do you call that? I call it interference."

"Captain—"

"And you didn't report to me what you were doing. There's only one way I can read that, Murtaugh—you were going behind my back. You disobeyed my orders."

"Now just a minute, Captain," Murtaugh said angrily. "This has gone far enough. I was ordered to investigate the murder of Jerry Sussman and that's what I'm doing. I turned up a killer-for-hire named Pluto—is that supposed to be the end of it? We don't have Pluto in custody, we don't even know his real identity. Do I just drop the whole thing because he may be the man other investigators are looking for in other cases? What do you expect me to do?"

"I *expect* you to obey my orders."

"Do you mean I'm just to stop my investigation or—"

"I mean what I say," Ansbacher said, deliberately vague. "If you can't follow directions—Murtaugh, listen up because this is the last time I'm telling you. You are not to interfere in the Parminter case. You are not to question anyone associated with that case. You're not to bother Carolyn Randolph again."

"How can I follow up on the Sussman case if—"

"You're supposed to be the bright boy around here, you figure it out. But take this as an official warning, Murtaugh. If I find you anywhere near any case other than the Sussman murder, I'm going to have you suspended. Now I can't make it any plainer than that. Do you understand?"

"Yes," Murtaugh said shortly.

Captain Ansbacher lumbered out without another word.

Murtaugh sank back down into his chair, his skin hot and a tight knot in his stomach. He had never, never before in his life been tempted to strike a fellow policeman. But he had come *so close*—god, if he'd let Ansbacher have it, that would have been the end of his career. Murtaugh wondered if the man had been deliberately baiting him, trying to provoke him into striking out.

He wasted nearly half an hour just cooling down to the point where he could think rationally again. Murtaugh wondered if Pluto had any idea of the extent of the trouble he was causing. He'd probably be pleased if he did know—that one had to have a gargantuan ego to do what he did. But maybe that could work to the police's advantage. Pluto had been supercareful so far, and there was no reason to assume he'd abandon his usual caution now. But he was not omniscient, and that ego might lead him to expose himself in a way he hadn't anticipated. Besides, Murtaugh still had a trick or two up his sleeve.

They now had a greatly improved version of the Identikit picture of Pluto. The people who had come face to face with Nicholas Ramsay were few and far between, but Murtaugh had found one of them. Nobody at the answering service Pluto used remembered talking to him in person, but a young Englishman working at the Knickerbocker Mail Address Service remembered him quite well. "I can always spot an American trying to pass as British," he'd said with a smirk. With the Englishman's suggestions, they'd been able to fill in the original outline so that now it looked more like a real face.

Murtaugh had "forgotten" to forward a copy of this new sketch to Captain Ansbacher; he didn't want it splashed all over the newspapers. The city's patrolmen had copies; ordinary citizens almost never fingered suspects for them solely on the basis of sketches in the newspaper. Murtaugh thought it was a bad mistake, letting Pluto in on what they knew.

Behind my back, Ansbacher had said. He wouldn't like it when he found out.

Pluto—so what answering service and mail drop was Pluto using now? Which ones had he used before he went to Backtalk Telephone Answering Service and Knickerbocker Mail Address Service as Nicholas Ramsay? With the new sketch, there was a good chance of getting a fresh line on their killer. Still a lot of leg work to be done. Murtaugh had been planning to ask Ansbacher once again for more men, but there was no point in that now. It was all up to him, to him and Sergeant Eberhart.

Murtaugh stood up resignedly. Better get on with it.

Leila Hudson was the first one out of the courtroom. She was uncomfortable in there, as if *she* were the one on trial, the target of all those staring eyes. She leaned against the wall of the hallway and wanted something— a cigarette, a drink, something. She'd come down to the Criminal Courts Building on Centre Street for Leon's hearing and was only now realizing the extent of her emotional investment in the outcome.

The charges against Leon Walsh had been dismissed. The prosecutors hadn't exactly strained themselves prosecuting, Leila noticed; they probably had too many real criminals to worry about without wanting to go after half-and-half types like Leon. When the defense attorney introduced the matter of Roscoe Malucci and how his hand had been shot off when he failed to pay the killer, the Assistant District Attorney hadn't made so much as a token objection. Defense and prosecution alike seemed convinced the same man was responsible in both cases. Dave Eberhart had told her the hearing was a test case; the D.A. and the police simply wanted a ruling to establish precedent. With precedent, they'd have a legal guideline for dealing with the other people who'd paid Pluto off. *What other people?* she'd asked. *Dozens of them,* Dave had said.

What a monstrous thing. So Leon had been only one of a series of people whom Pluto had "helped out"—to the killer's way of thinking. Poor Leon; how frightened he must have been. Getting caught in a situation like that would strain the resources of anyone. It must have been Roscoe Malucci's missing hand that convinced the judge; that gruesome bit of evidence ruled out the possibility that Leon was exaggerating the potential danger to himself. Yes, Leila thought, that must have been the clincher. The man sitting next to her thought so too, some Englishman with the beginnings of a mustache. The judge had decided Leon Walsh was more sinned against than sinning—he'd actually said that. But whatever had convinced him, Leon was now free.

And Leila was free of Leon. She'd felt the need to see this last bit of trouble through, more out of self-respect than anything else. What kind of person would turn her back on a man she was once married to, at a time his whole life was in danger of collapsing? But the danger had passed, and Leila felt her final responsibility to Leon Walsh was discharged. Leon was truly on his own now. He had no criminal charges hanging over his head and he had no Jerry Sussman interfering with his work. Leon should do all right now. He *was* deeply in debt—but then who wasn't these days? Leon would have to get out of that hole by himself.

When she'd first arrived at the courthouse, Leila had hoped to slip unobtrusively into the back row and then out again at the end of the session. But the courtroom was much smaller than she'd expected, and Leon had spotted her right off. He'd probably looked for her to rush down front and congratulate him at the conclusion of the hearing, but Leila shrank from that kind of public display. Besides, it was Leon's victory; let him enjoy it.

"Leila." He stood close to her; she hadn't seen him approach.

"Congratulations, Leon," she smiled at him. "I'm happy for you."

"Thank you. And thanks for coming."

Like a funeral, she thought.

Leon himself was strangely calm. "It hasn't really hit me yet," he explained, half-apologetically. "So many things have happened lately—it's all left me kind of numb."

Leila nodded. "But at least your story has a happy ending, Leon. It all worked out right. The police—or I guess I mean the prosecution—*somebody* could have made it rough for you. But nobody did." She was thinking of "The Man from Porlock"; Lieutenant Murtaugh had testified that the story was what had tipped him off to Pluto's free-lance murders. But no mention was made of the fact that the ostensible author was someone named Kellerman; Murtaugh had simply identified Leon Walsh as the author, to no objection from the defense. Leon's reputation as an editor of integrity had been sort of protected. "They could have shot you down, Leon," Leila said, "but they didn't."

He looked puzzled. "Shot me down?"

She lowered her voice. "I mean the Kellerman business."

"Kellerman?"

He really could be obtuse at times. "I'm talking about the *story*."

"The story?"

"Leon, do you suffer from echopraxia?"

"Echo—"

"*Stop repeating everything I say.*" She took a deep breath. "Forget it. Just forget I said anything."

"No, I want to know. What about Kellerman?"

All right, if that's the way you want it. "I just meant they could have made a big thing out of your publishing your own fiction under a pen name."

"Is that what you think?" His eyebrows climbed upward. "That I wrote 'The Man from Porlock'? You're wrong, you know. I told Kellerman what had happened to me and he wrote it up."

Oh, Leon! She looked at him sadly, saying nothing. Even his close brush with imprisonment had taught him nothing. Still the transparent liar, still thinking he could fool people.

"Leila, let's not quarrel," he said abruptly. "Let's go somewhere and have a drink. I want to celebrate! Come help me celebrate."

She shook her head. "I'm waiting for someone."

"Oh." A possibility that clearly hadn't occurred to him. "Well. Ah. When will I see you then?"

How easily he assumed they *would* be seeing each other. "Let's not make any plans," she said.

"I see." An uncomfortable silence grew between them. "If it's your money you're worried about, I'll be making another payment next week," he said sharply.

"Oh, Leon, I'm not worried about the money!"

Just then Dave Eberhart came up to them; he had been a witness in the hearing. "Congratulations," he said to Walsh. "I'm glad the charges were dropped."

"Thank you, uh, Sergeant," Walsh said, obviously not remembering Eberhart's name. "I have to say that sounds a mite peculiar coming from you." *Since you're the one who arrested me*, he meant.

"Yeah, I know," Eberhart grinned. "But it's such a freaky situation we had to get a court ruling on it. Especially since you didn't call in the police yourself."

"But why me? Why not the Malucci kid?"

"We didn't know about him yet. You were the first."

Walsh started to say something sarcastic but changed his mind. Why bother.

"I'll say this," Sergeant Eberhart went on. "You sure got the *cleanest* hearing I've seen in a long time. Not muddied up by a lot of extraneous stuff, I mean. You go into any normal trial courtroom and you find the prosecutors and the defense attorneys all doing exactly the same thing. They just snow the judge and the jury with as much picayune detail as they think they can get away with—a real trial is not the clear-cut, one-thing-at-a-time kind of argument you see on television. And if one side says a thing is true and the other side says no, it's not—then more often than not it's just dropped and the issue is never resolved. There are dozens of loose ends like that in every trial. Of course, this was only a preliminary hearing and there wasn't any jury—but it was still the cleanest inquiry I've ever sat through."

"How very interesting," Walsh said dryly.

166

Eberhart turned to Leila. "The car's five blocks from here. You wait down front while I go get it, okay?"

"Sure," she said. Eberhart waved casually to both of them and left.

Walsh was staring bug-eyed after Eberhart. "That's the one you were waiting for? That *cop*?"

"He's a very nice cop."

"But he's younger than you are!"

Leila's mouth twisted into a cynical smile. "Shocking, isn't it? We all know it's the woman who's supposed to be younger. Younger, smaller. Less."

"Oh Leila, for crying out loud, act your age. You know better than to—"

"Butt out, Leon." She spoke so harshly that a passerby turned to look. Leila shook her head in dismay; this wasn't how she'd meant it to be. "Leon, I don't want to fight with you. Can't we just say good-bye without making a big thing of it? All I want is for us to—"

But she didn't get to finish saying what she wanted them to do, because Leon Walsh had turned his back on her and walked away.

12

They were parked on Tenth Street. "A regular garden of delights," Murtaugh coughed, glaring at the small mountain of garbage five feet away. Yellow and blue Chiquita Banana Puree drums topped with plastic bags, a good half of which were split open and spilling their contents on to the sidewalk. "Jesus, what a place to meet."

"His home turf," Eberhart said apologetically.

"Which ought to be a good reason for meeting somewhere else."

"Yeah, well, he's not too bright."

Murtaugh grunted. "Where'd you get this guy?"

"Inherited him from Grivalski." Grivalski had been Eberhart's predecessor on the job, an exhausted and cynical cop who'd quit the force to become police chief of a small desert town in New Mexico. "I've used him four or five times."

"What's his name again? Barnaby what?"

"Barnes, Barnaby Barnes," Eberhart said. "That's his

168

real name, too, I checked it out. Just don't call him Barney—that makes him mad."

Barnaby Barnes was an on-again, off-again police informant. He picked up a living as best he could—mostly on the fringes of other people's operations, many of which were even legitimate. When he worked at a steady job, he liked to sell women's shoes. At least he used to like it, before so many women started wearing trousers all the time.

"Here he comes," Eberhart said.

A man in his late thirties, tall and clumsy, was trying to make himself smaller by hunching his shoulders. He slid into the back seat of the car. "Drive," he rasped.

Yessir, bossman. Eberhart started the car. "This is Lieutenant Murtaugh, Barnaby. You tell him what you got to say."

"Outa here," Barnaby commanded, slouching down in the seat. Eberhart dutifully turned uptown.

Murtaugh unfolded one of the drawings of Pluto's face. "You know this man, Barnaby?"

"You gotta understand something first," Barnaby said. "I ain't talking for myself. I'm just the intermediary."

Murtaugh nodded. "Understood."

"My friend that sent me, he wants to know what's in it for him."

"Now, Barnaby, you know that depends on what you got to sell," Eberhart put in.

"What I got's worth a hundred."

"Must be good," Murtaugh said. "Let's hear it."

"Okay. This friend, he sold your man Pluto a forty-five. And don't ask where it came from because he don't know."

"Then how'd he get it?"

"From another friend. Look, I said don't ask, okay?"

"When was this?"

"Coupla years ago . . . yeah, about two years, that was it."

"So why are you telling us now, Barnaby?" Murtaugh asked. "A two-year-old sale of a single firearm isn't what I'd call red-hot news."

"Willya let me finish? My friend, he seen this Pluto again, just a coupla days ago."

"And?"

"And that drawing you got ain't exactly right. He's got a mustache now."

Eberhart glanced over at Murtaugh. "We put out a third version?"

"Looks like it," Murtaugh said. To Barnaby: "Handle-bar, pencil-line, cookie-duster, Fu Manchu, what?"

"I dunno, just a regular mustache. Kinda full."

Murtaugh reached over the seat and handed him the flyer with the sketch of Pluto and a pencil. "Draw it in."

"Car's jigglin' too much."

Eberhart pulled into an alleyway and turned off the engine. Barnaby drew in the mustache and handed the picture back.

"You're sure that's the way he looks now?" Eberhart asked.

"I'm sure."

Murtaugh said, "Where did your friend see Pluto a couple of days ago?"

"Gettin' out of a taxi on Fifth Avenue."

"Fifth and what?"

"Uh, he didn't say."

"Sure he did, Barnaby," Eberhart said. "Think."

Barnaby thought. "Fifty-fourth or Fifty-fifth, around there. I can't be sure."

"Anything else?" Murtaugh asked. "Like where he went when he got out of the taxi?"

"Naw, that's it."

Murtaugh nodded. "Pay him, Eberhart." Eberhart held out a fifty-dollar bill to the man in the back seat.

"Hey, I said a hundred."

"Oh, come on, Barnaby, you know better than that," Eberhart laughed. "What did you tell us? That Pluto has a forty-five. We already knew that. You told us he got it illegally. We knew that too. So what you're asking a hundred for is the mustache. No mustache is worth a hundred bucks, Barnaby. Take the fifty."

"Shit," Barnaby said. He took the fifty, got out of the car, disappeared down the alley.

Murtaugh watched him go. "He told us more than he knows, but I would have thought twenty was enough for a mustache."

"Inflation, Lieutenant," Eberhart grinned. "They won't even bother calling you for a twenty any more."

"Is he reliable?"

"He has been before."

"Did you know he was selling illegal firearms?"

"Nope, that was news to me. He said two years ago, but he might still be picking up a buck or two that way. Jeez, if Captain Ansbacher would only loosen up and give us a few men! We could have Barnaby tailed, find out his source—if there still is one. Do you want me—"

"No, let Barnaby go—you and I have another job. We have to check shops on Fifth Avenue between Fifty-fourth and Fifty-fifth." Murtaugh paused, tasting bile: a full lieutenant, doing flunky work. "You have a copy of the drawing?"

"Yeah, right here."

"Be sure to sketch in the mustache. And keep an eye

open for any officers on the beat—maybe we can recruit some help. All right, let's get going."

While Murtaugh and Eberhart were checking the stores on Fifth Avenue, the man they were tracking walked into a different business establishment fifteen blocks away. The store on Seventh Avenue was so brightly lighted that not even the corners of the room had shadows. Decals were pasted up here and there announcing the presence of an alarm system connected directly to the Midtown South Precinct station on West Thirty-fifth Street.

The clerk was leaning his arms on top of the counter, flipping through a gun catalogue.

"Good awftuhnoon," Pluto said in his best Sir Reginald manner.

"Help you?" the clerk said without looking up.

"I do hate to interrupt your reading, but I'm in need of ammunition."

The clerk looked up, suspecting sarcasm; but his customer was smiling cheerily. "What size?"

"Thirty-eight. Four boxes." The clerk was staring at him, not moving. "That's thirty-eight-caliber?" Pluto nudged. "Point three eight?"

"Oh. Yeah, yeah. I'll get a box. Don't go away."

"Four boxes," Pluto called after him. "And of course I won't go away!" *What a peculiar clerk.*

The peculiar clerk returned with four dull green boxes covered with black lettering. He slid them across the counter and stared at Pluto some more.

Pluto raised one eyebrow. "I don't suppose I could prevail upon you to wrap them, could I?"

"Oh. Yeah, I'll wrap 'em." He did, shooting little glances at Pluto all the while. The clerk cleared his throat, and after one false start managed to say, "Doing a little target shooting?"

"That's right," Pluto answered evenly.

"Where do you go to shoot?"

Pluto narrowed his eyes. "Why?"

"Oh, uh, my customers sometimes ask me to recommend places and I, uh."

Very peculiar. "I do all my target shooting in New Jersey," Pluto said frostily, ending the conversation. He paid for his package with a hundred-dollar bill, waited for his change, and then left without another word. The clerk didn't take his eyes off him until he was out the door.

Outside, Pluto paused to glance through the gunsmith's window. He watched the clerk study a legal-sized sheet of off-white paper and then pick up the phone and dial a number he read from the same paper.

Pluto moved away, thinking.

Captain Ansbacher sat in his office with the door closed, thinking of his dead friend. Smith. A simple man with a simple name. With Smith there had been no complications, no hassle—just a quiet understanding. Smith had been Ansbacher's man in the Commissioner of Police's circle. For nearly eight years Smith had run interference for his old friend Ansbacher; that was part of their understanding.

But then Smith had up and died on him; Ansbacher ground his teeth every time he thought about it. Smith had had no ambition beyond laboring on as one of several Deputy Commissioners; he should have been good for another ten or fifteen years. But now this pansy who had taken Smith's place . . .

The pansy's name was Turnbull; he was thirty years old, had a master's degree in sociology, and dearly loved to tell Ansbacher how to do his job. He was careful to preface everything he said with *The Commissioner wants you to . . .* but oh, how he enjoyed it! All that smirking, every time he passed on an order. Ansbacher couldn't stand a man who smirked. Women, okay; men, no.

Turnbull had just left. The day before Ansbacher had had a lengthy phone conversation with the Commissioner himself. They were supposed to be talking about several cases pending, but the Commissioner had kept coming back to Pluto and demanding more and more details about what the various investigators had been doing. And today that pansy Turnbull had shown up to say the Commissioner thought Lieutenant Murtaugh was probably the closest to a solution and Captain Ansbacher might want to coordinate all investigatory efforts under Murtaugh's command.

Murtaugh.

It had been a suggestion, not an order. Ansbacher hadn't hesitated; he'd told the Deputy Commissioner straight out what he thought of that suggestion. Murtaugh wasn't qualified for that big an operation, he'd said. In that case, Turnbull had replied, could he at least reassure the Commissioner that Captain Ansbacher would see Lieutenant Murtaugh had all the assistance he needed? The Commissioner didn't like it that this Pluto was still free to go on killing whenever he wanted to. The Commissioner didn't like it at all.

Murtaugh.

Ansbacher hadn't made captain by being overly defiant of his superiors' suggestions. He'd promised Turnbull that Murtaugh was getting everything he needed,

KILL FEE

and he could see no way of getting out of that one. His sneaking Lieutenant who'd gone around asking questions behind his back—he'd been just about to lower the boom on Murtaugh when the Commissioner sends word to *be nice*. This one was going to take kid gloves.

There was a knock at the door. Lieutenant Murtaugh stepped in and closed the door behind him. "Captain, we have a new line on Pluto."

Ansbacher nodded. To indicate his interest.

Murtaugh told him about Barnaby's tip. "We traced Pluto to a tailor on Fifth Avenue, Farrell Custom Tailoring. He'd gone in for a fitting. Now he's using the name P. N. Wolfe, and the phone number he left is another answering service. We checked the service, and they gave us an address that's another mail drop—what you'd expect."

Ansbacher asked, "Why two places for mail and phone calls? Why doesn't he use the same service for both?"

"Less chance of drawing attention to himself by repeated visits to any one place. And he's got a mustache now." Murtaugh hesitated; then with ill-concealed reluctance he handed a single sheet of paper to Ansbacher. "Here's the updated sketch we're sending out."

Ansbacher studied the face on the paper; their mysterious Pluto had become a recognizable human being. "You say he's calling himself Wolfe now?"

"P. N. Wolfe. So far we've got only the three places he's used the name—tailor's, answering service, mail drop."

Ansbacher let the drawing fall to his desk and leaned back in his chair, folding his hands over his stomach. "Well. And to what do I owe this sudden sharing of information? I'm flattered you've decided to take me into your confidence."

Murtaugh's face darkened. "I've got to have more help. Pluto went into the tailor's for a fitting—the final fitting. The tailor told me the suit will be ready this coming Thursday."

"Stakeout?"

"Eberhart and I can't do it alone. Farrell Custom Tailoring is a big establishment. Two main entrances and a service entrance through an alley. If—"

"He wouldn't use the service entrance."

"He might duck out that way. The tailor who's making his suit is a nervous type—he could get spooked and give the game away."

"Put Eberhart in his place."

"That would tip Pluto off the minute he walked in. A different tailor taking over somebody else's work? I want Eberhart inside, though—as another customer. But I can't watch both main entrances and the service entrance all by myself. Captain, you have *got* to give me more men."

Ansbacher reached for a pencil and a pad of paper. "How many do you want?" he asked, and watched Murtaugh's mouth drop open.

Pluto liked to think of the Pardee Club as his ace in the hole. The Pardee was a combination social and health club; it boasted a good-sized gym where members could work off the extra poundage they'd picked up in the Pardee's excellent dining room and bar. Or if that was too strenuous, there was a steam room where they could sweat it off. There were no Rockefellers at the Pardee; the membership was mostly minor capitalists, well-established men who were happy to have an aristocratic Englishman like Pluto among them. Not a single black, brown, or yellow face was to be seen.

Pluto was known by the name Willoughby at the Pardee; it was the only place he used it. The Pardee had rooms that members could rent overnight or even on a long-term basis; perhaps a dozen members were full-time residents. Pluto considered the club as a sort of personal safe house; if ever it became risky to return to his own apartment, he could stay at the Pardee until he figured out what he wanted to do next.

Pluto socialized just enough to avoid appearing mysterious. Most of his fellow members thought of themselves as concerned Americans, worrying over the government's meddling with the economy, the ever-increasing greed of labor, the Communist-inspired racial troubles, and the constant threats to the sanctity of the home. A conservative retreat in a traditionally liberal city. Pluto listened politely, for it was those same complaints that had led to the construction of what Pluto considered the Pardee's main attraction: a fully equipped firing range in the sub-basement.

Until he discovered the Pardee Club, Pluto had kept his hand in at a West Side pistol range. He didn't like it there, though; the tough-looking clientele made him uneasy. Most of his fellow shooters made him think they were practicing for their next liquor store holdup, if anybody ever did practice for such a thing. Pluto just hadn't felt *safe* there.

He felt safe at the Pardee, though, safe and warm. He liked to do his shooting in the mornings; the range was always fairly empty during the hours before noon. He'd waited until the weather was bad, wanting the range completely to himself; marvelous the way a little wind and rain could make otherwise stalwart types think, *Well, it can wait 'til tomorrow.*

Pluto rode down to the sub-basement in an empty elevator, humming a little cheerful Bach to himself. He started toward the firing range's check-in counter—and stopped. Stopped walking, stopped humming, almost stopped breathing. He was shocked to see his own face staring back at him from the oversized bulletin board next to the counter.

He looked around to see if there was anyone watching. He tore down the sketch, folded it and put it in a pocket, and got back into the elevator without being seen. Out on the street, he hailed a cab.

"Just drive." Pluto settled back in the seat and took out the drawing. A completely new police sketch, not the cartoonish one that had been published in the papers. How long had this one been circulating? The resemblance was uncanny! They even knew about the mustache— *that* would come off the minute he got home. Pluto's throat was tight and he felt lightheaded. It was the first time the police had ever gotten close.

He read the physical description under the picture; they had that part right too. Dark blond hair, height five-ten; weight one-eighty to one-ninety. No distinguishing marks. Speaks with an assumed English accent. *Hmm.* How annoying. He'd have to talk plain Amurrican from now on. Known aliases: Pluto, Nicholas Ramsay, P. N. Wolfe—ye gods, they had the Wolfe name too? Why, he'd barely used that one! He read on. Anyone spotting the suspect was asked to contact Lieutenant James T. Murtaugh immediately.

Pluto rapped on the plastic divider behind the cab driver's head. "New York Public Library," he said through the grid.

After an hour and a half at the microfilm machine, he had a sketchy idea of his adversary's career. He also knew what Murtaugh looked like; it was a rare man who worked his way up through the ranks to police lieutenant without ever getting his picture in the papers. Pluto picked out the clearest photograph and asked the librarian for a print copy.

Murtaugh had Pluto's picture, and now Pluto had his. The police lieutenant's was one face he couldn't afford to forget.

"Just like the flyer said," the gun store clerk was telling Sergeant Eberhart. "Dark blond hair, English accent."

"What about the mustache?" Eberhart asked.

"Yeah, he had a mustache. It was him, all right. He bought eight dozen rounds, that's four boxes—thirty-eight-caliber. I asked him was he planning some target shooting and he said yes and I asked him where and—"

"And tipped him off you were on to him," Eberhart groaned. "Hey, don't do our job for us. Just call us, okay?"

The clerk scowled at him. "I was trying to help you."

"And I'm trying to help *you*. The next time you spot somebody in a police circular, don't ask questions. Play dumb. This guy here kills awful easy—he could have popped you without thinking twice about it."

"Just trying to help." The clerk was sulking.

Time for fence-mending. "Yeah, I know—and we appreciate it. Most people we ask for help don't give us the time of day. We depend a lot on civilians like you, the ones who do help." The clerk was looking a little happier. "Anything else?"

"Well, he said he did all his target shooting in Jersey, but I think he was lying."

Eberhart grinned. "He probably practices anywhere but

Jersey. Look, thanks for calling us. You've been a big help." Out on the street, Eberhart hurried along, secretly exulting. In spite of the mild scolding he'd given the clerk, he was grateful to the man; now they had a new place to look.

Pistol ranges.

Pluto stood before his bathroom mirror. He turned his head as far to the right as he could and still see his image; left profile looked all right. He turned his head the other way and checked his right profile. Well, all right indeed! Oh, yes.

The salon had done a good job. First the perm, then the dye job. Instead of longish dark blond hair, Pluto's head was now covered with tight brown curls. The mustache was gone, and he'd bought a pair of tinted glasses. Pluto was quickly getting used to his new look; truth was, he liked it better than the old one.

Satisfied that he was no longer in danger of being identified from the police circular, he turned his full attention to the matter at hand. Pluto went into his study and stood staring at the corkboard-lined wall. Dead center was a picture of Lieutenant James T. Murtaugh. Pinned around the picture were newspaper clippings and neatly typed lists of what other information Pluto had been able to garner. Snapshots. Of the people Murtaugh worked with—Ansbacher, Eberhart, Billings, Montoya, a couple of dozen others. Of Murtaugh's wife, Ellie. Of the few friends Murtaugh had outside police circles. Murtaugh's only living relatives were a brother and his family who'd moved to Pittsburgh nearly thirteen years ago; forget them. Pluto felt he was coming to know James Timothy Murtaugh quite well.

"Ah, Lieutenant, Lieutenant," Pluto shook his head.

"Make a mistake. Goof. Get off on the wrong track." He sighed. "Don't make me do it."

Murtaugh raised his eyebrows. "Pistol ranges?"

"Man doesn't buy eight dozen rounds just to scare off burglars," Eberhart said. "So he's gotta have a place where he goes to keep his eye sharp. So we check pistol ranges."

"Does he need to?" Murtaugh asked. "Keep that kind of sharp, I mean. Jerry Sussman was shot up close—he went right up to the car Pluto was driving. William Parminter was shot in an elevator—another close job. Roscoe Malucci's hand was shot off from the other side of the street. But it's a narrow street and Roscoe had gone out *into* the street to stop a cab—shooting distance was only twenty feet or so. Hardly sharpshooter range."

"What about that Canadian singer—the one who got shot at Lincoln Center?"

Murtaugh frowned, concentrating. "You're right. That was a distance shot. But we don't know that was one of Pluto's jobs."

"Oh, come on, Lieutenant—you know it was!"

"I think so, but we don't *know*. It's damned tempting to hang every unsolved killing we got on our elusive friend. But okay, let's say Pluto needs to practice on a more-or-less regular basis. Our circulars for gun-related killings automatically go to firing ranges as well as gunsmiths. But they get so many of the damned things they hardly look at them any more. Your clerk in the gun store paid attention, but nobody else did—so, we go jog their memories for them. We'll need a list of pistol ranges and addresses—"

"Got it." Eberhart waved a sheet of paper in the air.

Murtaugh grunted approval. "Give me half. Captain

Ansbacher's letting me have five more men, but we don't get them until Thursday."

Eberhart folded the sheet of paper, tore it in half. "Here."

Murtaugh glanced at the paper and scowled. "For chrissake, Eberhart, don't you ever use a typewriter? I can't read this."

"All right, all right, I'll *type* it," Eberhart muttered, snatching back the paper. Some days even the best of lieutenants liked to make life bothersome for sergeants.

Pluto stepped out of his rented car and looked around for a place to stand—there, in that shop doorway. A man sitting alone in an automobile at night always looked suspicious.

Just as Lieutenant Murtaugh was looking suspicious. The lieutenant was across the street, sitting in his car, alone, at night. And it looked suspicious. Just a man waiting for his wife, but it did look odd.

The front doors of Murray Hill Academy opened and a harried-looking woman with a briefcase came out— that was Ellie. Pluto strained to get a good look at her. She got into the car with Murtaugh and they drove away.

Pluto wrote down the time in his notebook, knowing it was a detail he probably wouldn't be needing. But his methodical approach had stood him in good stead for too long for him to abandon it now. And he had so few details about Ellie yet.

Ellie. What about her? Pluto was having trouble deciding whether Ellie would have a role to play in the new scenario or not.

Dan Grogan was already waiting in Michael's Bar by the time Murtaugh got there. Murtaugh had known

Grogan for a long time; they'd been rookies together, seventeen—no, eighteen years ago now. Grogan had wanted Murtaugh to meet him.

Murtaugh picked up a beer and went over to Grogan's booth. "Trouble?" he asked as he slid on to the wooden seat.

Grogan shook his head. "I got what you wanted to know."

"Why not just call?"

"We're both on open lines, Murtaugh. No telling who could be listening in."

Murtaugh felt a mild shock. Grogan was the investigator Ansbacher had appointed to take over the Parminter case when Murtaugh began breathing too hard on the Sutton brothers and their tainted construction business. Grogan was also in charge of another "Pluto possible"—the murder of Metropolitan Opera tenor John Herman, the Canadian. Murtaugh had asked Grogan to check on the finances of tenor Luigi Bàccolo, to see if he'd had to raise money in a hurry right after the Canadian's death. But now, if Grogan was so afraid anything said over the phone might get back to Ansbacher, afraid that Ansbacher would find out he was doing a favor for Murtaugh—good god, things were even worse than he'd thought! "You didn't step on any Sutton toes, did you?"

Grogan laughed mirthlessly. "I'm not even allowed *close* to those two. You know your files have disappeared? The ones you put together on the Suttons and Parminter. So I'm left with no reason to investigate the Sutton Construction Company."

Damn that Ansbacher—all that work, down the drain. "That rotten son of a bitch," Murtaugh said bitterly.

Grogan looked uneasy. "Don't talk like that. You don't know who's listening."

Murtaugh stared at him. "What's the matter with you? You never used to be afraid of your shadow!"

Grogan stared back. "You don't know, do you?" He took a deep breath. "Ansbacher knows you've been investigating him. He knows you're out to get him."

A second shock ran through Murtaugh, a much stronger one this time. "How'd he find out?"

"Know a guy named Hanowitz? Works the Burglary Unit. He told him."

Murtaugh remembered Hanowitz, a weasely man he'd trust about as far as he could throw. "Hanowitz told Ansbacher?"

"Right out in the hallway, where other people could hear. That was weeks ago, Murtaugh. I thought you knew."

"No." Murtaugh was stunned; he'd more or less expected it eventually . . . what was Ansbacher doing, what kind of waiting game was he playing? "Christ."

Grogan looked at his watch nervously. "I've got to be going—"

"What about Luigi Bàccolo?"

"Oh yeah—almost forgot. He raised the money all right—a hundred thousand dollars, the exact amount. He had to be one of Pluto's customers too."

"Mm. What'd he say when you asked him about the money?"

"Well, first he claimed his poor old mother back in Napoli needed a series of operations. When we pointed out his mother has been dead for twenty-one years, he said, Did he say *mother*? He meant *aunt*, and she was in Palermo, not Napoli. He's changed his story a dozen times, and each time it gets a little more farfetched. No question, in my mind—he paid off Pluto. Bàccolo's one of those high-strung types—we got him sweating, it's only a matter of time. He'll tell us."

"Good, glad to hear it. And Grogan—thanks for letting me know."

"Sure. We owe you for the tip." Grogan wanted to get away. "Uh, tough luck about Ansbacher. I thought you knew."

Murtaugh shrugged a good-bye. Grogan left, and Murtaugh sat on for a while, watching his beer go flat.

Thursday.

Pluto was torn. He wanted to avoid taking any risk he didn't absolutely have to, but he also wanted to pick up his new suit. The tailor had promised it for two o'clock— but the tailor knew him as P. N. Wolfe and that could get sticky. The new police circular had the name listed right under the sketch that now would no longer identify him. But the false name—would his tailor know about it? Police circulars went to gun shops and like places, including (obviously!) private clubs with pistol ranges in their sub-basements. But what possible cause would the police have for notifying a toney haberdasher on Fifth Avenue? There was no reason for Lieutenant Murtaugh to connect the killings with Farrell Custom Tailoring— Farrell's Apparel, Pluto called it.

Pluto wanted that suit; he wanted it in the worst way. Irish tweed, softer than any he'd ever seen. From a distance the material appeared gray, but up close it was an understated green. Pluto didn't have any green clothing; green tended to make him look chubby. But not this green, not this masterpiece of soft-pedaling. It did make him look just a tiny bit sallow—but now with his newly brown hair . . . he decided. He'd go get the suit.

He approached the tailor's cautiously, stopping to look in store windows as he tried to spot any signs of a stake-out. The trouble was, he didn't really know what to look for. He peered around, looking for Lieutenant Murtaugh and those of his cohorts Pluto knew, but all he saw was an ordinary street scene, Fifth Avenue at two in the afternoon on an ordinary Thursday.

Pluto studied a window display of men's formal foot-wear and thought about using a messenger service to pick up the suit. But his tailor was such a prima donna Pluto knew he wouldn't let the suit go without one last fitting. At the very least sending a messenger would stir up a fuss, and the last thing Pluto needed was a fuss. So, no messenger.

Nothing ventured. Pluto pushed through one of the two main entrances to Farrell Custom Tailoring and— well, well. Look who was over there pretending to be a customer. Eberhart, David J., Sergeant. Lieutenant Murtaugh's right-hand man, talking to Pluto's tailor. Pluto bought a sixty-two-dollar pair of socks and left, going out the other main entrance and displaying prominently his designer plastic bag with the word *Farrell* on it.

This time Pluto spotted him: Lieutenant Murtaugh, standing in a phone booth, doing a good imitation of a man looking up a number in the directory. *Ah well,* Pluto thought philosophically. Maybe he just wasn't destined to wear green.

He moved off down Fifth at a brisk pace, leaving Murtaugh and Eberhart and five other men watching over Farrell Custom Tailoring, watching and waiting.

Watching. Hoping.

13

Murtaugh sank down into his desk chair spiritlessly. He'd finished his half of the list of pistol ranges. Nothing.

Eberhart still had a few to go on his half, but Ansbacher had put the sergeant to work on something else the minute he'd come in. Eberhart had been on the telephone all morning; he'd been phoning when Murtaugh left, and he was still phoning when Murtaugh got back. After lunch Murtaugh would get the names of the pistol ranges Eberhart hadn't gotten to and take care of them himself.

The five men Murtaugh had been given for the futile stakeout of Farrell Custom Tailoring—they'd been reassigned the next day. Now Ansbacher was stripping him of his only remaining help; when Eberhart finished his current assignment, Ansbacher would come up with another one for him. And then another one. And another one after that. When Pluto failed to show, Murtaugh had lost his last defense against Ansbacher. The Captain would win. It was only a matter of time.

Pluto, Pluto—where are you? Why hadn't he shown up at the tailor's, how had he known they'd be waiting for him? *How had he known?* No matter how close they got, Pluto was always one step ahead of them. Was he psychic? There couldn't be a leak inside the Department because only Murtaugh and Eberhart knew where the investigation was heading—Eberhart? No, out of the question. But only he and Eberhart knew . . . until he'd gone to Ansbacher for help with the stakeout.

"Jesus, I'm going nuts," he said aloud. Ansbacher was a shit and Murtaugh could believe almost anything of him. But to think of a police captain feeding information to a wanted murderer just to spite one of his lieutenants— well, that was really stretching it. "I'm getting paranoid," he muttered.

Eberhart stuck his head in the door. "Shoo flies." He disappeared.

Now what? Murtaugh thought in irritation. He needed meddlers underfoot the way he needed a hole in the head. Two men loomed in his doorway, a tall one and a taller one; Murtaugh knew neither of them.

"James Murtaugh?" the merely tall one said. "I'm Sanders of Internal Affairs, this is Karp." The other man nodded and stepped into Murtaugh's office; Sanders followed and shut the door.

"Come in," Murtaugh said dryly.

Sanders and Karp positioned themselves in front of the desk. "I'll get right to the point," Sanders said. "A charge of malfeasance has been brought against you. Suspicion of taking a bribe."

"*What?*" Murtaugh jumped to his feet. "A bribe? That's absurd! Who's supposed to have paid me?"

"The killer you're allegedly hunting. The one known as Pluto."

188

Allegedly hunting. "That's ridiculous. That's the stupidest thing I ever heard. Who brought the charge? Ansbacher?"

One of Sanders's eyebrows rose. "What a lucky guess. Or was it? You knew Ansbacher was on to you, didn't you, Murtaugh? He's had your number for a long time. I want your shield and your weapon. Now."

Murtaugh started to reach angrily toward Sanders, but Karp stepped in and Murtaugh thought better of what he was doing. *Stay calm,* he told himself. "That's all it takes?" he asked. "Ansbacher points a finger and you come running to do his dirty work?"

"You were overheard making plans to set up a phony stakeout."

"A phony . . . that stakeout was legit! You're talking about the one at the Fifth Avenue tailor's, aren't you? Why would I set up a phony stakeout?"

"A diversion, a ploy. Ansbacher has a witness who heard you making plans on the phone to steer the investigation into safe waters. He heard you call the person on the phone 'Pluto'."

Murtaugh felt paralyzed, as if some vital function in his body had been summarily switched off. He knew what his captain was capable of—why was he so surprised that Ansbacher had set him up? *Why hadn't he anticipated it?* He worked his jaw a couple of times and said, "Who's this witness who claims he heard me incriminating myself?"

"Hanowitz, in Burglary. He reported the conversation to Captain Ansbacher."

Hanowitz again. "That lying little ass-kisser. He'd do anything, say anything he thought would help him get a leg up!"

"You'll get to tell your side of it at the hearing," Sanders said. "In the meantime, get yourself a lawyer. And

Murtaugh—get a good one. A ranking officer who'd let a paid killer go free . . . let's just say he's going to need damned good legal representation."

"You've made your mind up already, haven't you?" Murtaugh said bitterly.

"You may be clean. I don't know yet. But your own captain has been suspicious of you for months, and we do have a witness. It doesn't look good. You're suspended without pay until our investigation is complete and a hearing is scheduled." Sanders dropped an envelope on the desk. "There's the authorization. I want your weapon and your shield. You're to leave now and not return until the time of the hearing. Take nothing with you—all your files are impounded, even the contents of your desk."

"Want to search me before I go?" Sanders didn't answer the sarcasm. Murtaugh put his badge and his gun on the desk. "How long until the hearing?"

"However long it takes us to complete the investigation, and buddy, we are going to investigate you good. Get a lawyer."

Murtaugh walked around the desk and stopped to stare at Karp. The taller man hadn't uttered a word the whole time; Sanders had done all the talking. "Why'd they send two of you?" Murtaugh asked Karp sourly. "Are you the muscle in case I get violent?"

"I'm a trainee," Karp said.

It figured. Murtaugh nodded and went on out.

Captain Ansbacher felt perspiration beading up on his forehead but resisted the temptation to reach for his handkerchief. A man mopping his brow never looked good on television; he lost stature.

This wasn't going the way it was supposed to. In all his years on the force, Ansbacher had never met a news reporter yet who didn't start to salivate at the merest hint of scandal inside the Police Department. Most of them found misbehavior on the part of New York's finest downright titillating; something to do with suppressed envy, Ansbacher supposed, a sexual reaction. But here he'd just handed them a nice juicy tidbit and they were all acting surly about it.

The man from the *Times* asked, "Does this mean you busted Lieutenant Murtaugh on the basis of one over-heard telephone conversation?"

Ansbacher enunciated his words carefully; reporters were so prone to misunderstanding. "There were other matters taken into consideration."

"Such as?"

"I'm not at liberty to discuss that."

There were several audible snorts from the reporters. A woman in an unnecessarily tight red sweater asked, "So what happens to the hunt for Pluto now? Who's taking over Lieutenant Murtaugh's investigation?"

"I am," Ansbacher said. "I will be coordinating the efforts of all our investigators—"

"You mean they haven't been coordinated up to now?" the woman interrupted.

"Let me finish," Ansbacher snapped. "I will be coordinating various lines of investigation *and* taking over Murtaugh's case load myself," avoiding her question. "I'll have—"

"How many cases did Murtaugh have?" asked a slightly overweight man with curly brown hair and glasses.

"I don't have the exact number at the moment. As I—"

"Wasn't it just one?" the man persisted. "The Jerry Sussman murder?"

"I'll have to get back to you on that. As I was saying, I will be organizing the hunt to bring in the killer we know as Pluto. And I'll tell you this. We're getting close. We have several strong leads that I intend to pursue personally. We're anticipating an arrest before long."

The man with the curly brown hair spoke again; the little fag wouldn't shut up. "Those strong leads you're going to follow—weren't they all developed by Lieutenant Murtaugh?"

"The leads came from many sources. This is a cooperative effort, you know—"

"Come on, Captain, isn't it true Murtaugh was the only one who was getting anywhere tracking down Pluto? And all of a sudden he's under investigation by Internal Affairs—what's really going on?"

"I've told you all I can at this point. Thank you for coming—this press conference is ended."

"Is Pluto a cop?" somebody shouted.

"*NO!*" Ansbacher roared. "That is a totally irresponsible question! Pluto is not, repeat *not*, a member of this police force—or any other police force so far as I know. He's a civilian just like you, and he's out there, and we're going to get him!" On that strong finish Ansbacher strode from the room.

Once away from the sight of the reporters and their cameras, he pulled out a handkerchief and wiped his gleaming face. Damn them! The fourth estate would have a long wait before *he* ever handed them an inside story again. Maybe he was getting an overexposure problem; might be best to low-profile it for a while.

Damned faggots.

Murtaugh heard Ellie's key in the lock but couldn't summon the energy to get up and go open the door. "Aren't you early?" he greeted her.

"A little." She gave him a quick kiss and settled on the arm of his chair. "What did the lawyer say?"

"Not a whole lot—it's too early, he needs to do some work first. He did say if this were a regular trial, the charge would be thrown out of court. Not enough evidence, even the false kind."

"Well, that's a good sign, isn't it?"

"Not really. The rules are different in a police trial board hearing. Crooks have to be proved guilty by a court, but cops have to prove their innocence. Ansbacher's opinion counts a lot more in a trial board hearing, for one thing. And since the so-called witness is a police detective, his word will carry a lot of weight."

"What about this witness—Hanowitz, is that the name?"

"Ah yes, Sergeant Hanowitz. A grabby little weasel who doesn't mind climbing over dead bodies to get where he's going. I can't say I'm surprised."

"You think Ansbacher promised him something? Help in getting a promotion?"

"I'd make book on it. But there's no way to prove it. As long as Hanowitz sticks to his story that he overheard me setting up a bogus stakeout . . ." He trailed off, not wanting to complete the thought. *As long as Hanowitz sticks to his story, I'm going to end up losing my pension.* The phone rang. "Don't answer it."

"Why not?"

"Reporters. They've been calling ever since I got in. People love hearing a cop is dirty." After the thirteenth ring the caller gave up. "I'll get the number changed."

Ellie squeezed his arm in sympathy. "I've been thinking. Why don't you go stay with Des for a while?" Murtaugh's brother Desmond, living in Pittsburgh. "You haven't seen him for nearly a year, and it would do you good to get away from New York. For a little while."

"Run away?"

"Of course not—you know I don't mean that. Just give yourself some breathing space. Have you thought about it—getting away for a while?"

Murtaugh made a noncommittal noise.

"It might help you to get outside the situation here. Find a different perspective, get rid of the cobwebs. You'll think of things in Pittsburgh you can't think of here—you're too close. Call Des. Do it, Jim."

"Hm," he said. "What about you? Could you come?"

"I can't get away right now, but I can come at the end of the week. Go call Des."

"You'd come on . . . ?"

"Friday. Late afternoon or early evening."

Murtaugh didn't need any more urging. He called his brother and invited himself to Pittsburgh. Des said to come ahead.

"Why, that's Willoughby!" old Mr. Rasmussen exclaimed in obvious surprise. "Surely the police aren't looking for Willoughby?"

Eberhart felt a chill of pleasure run down his spine. "Are you sure, Mr. Rasmussen? Take a good look."

The old man held the police sketch of Pluto's face at arm's length and studied it carefully. "Yes, that's Willoughby—no mistake. I sponsored him myself. He hasn't done anything illegal, has he, Sergeant?"

"He called himself Willoughby here?" *Here* was the Pardee Club, with its pistol range in the sub-basement; Eberhart had at last hit pay dirt. "Would you spell that?"

Mr. Rasmussen spelled it for him. "Isn't that his real name?"

194

"We don't know his real name. This guy has a new alias every time you turn around." Eberhart printed *Willoughby* in his notebook, in careful block letters so that even Lieutenant Murtaugh could read it easily—and then remembered the Lieutenant wouldn't be reading it at all. "First name?"

"Henry. Henry Willoughby. Sergeant, you must be wrong. Willoughby is an English gentleman who wouldn't be associated with—what do you think he's associated with?"

"Murder. And we have proof. He's a professional killer, Mr. Rasmussen." The old man blanched, and Eberhart wished he hadn't spoken so bluntly. "You say you sponsored him here—you mean a membership in the Pardee Club? Then you must know him from somewhere else."

"Well, I first ran into him at Holland's. Then we met at Burney's a few times and had a couple of drinks together and—"

"Hold on—what are Holland's and Burney's?"

"They're antique gun dealers. As I said, Willoughby and I had a drink together a few times and then I invited him here—to the Pardee—for dinner. We were both interested in guns. . . ." Mr. Rasmussen trailed off as he realized why the other man had been so interested in guns. "No," he muttered to himself. "I don't believe it."

"So you brought him here to the Pardee," Eberhart prompted.

But old Mr. Rasmussen couldn't tell him much more. They'd talked guns and the old man had shown his guest the pistol range in the sub-basement. "Don't shoot any more myself," he said, holding up a trembling hand in demonstration. "First the eyes go, then . . . well." Mr. Rasmussen had introduced his new English friend to some of the other members and had eventually sponsored him for membership.

Eberhart took down the names of the other members who knew "Willoughby"—although Mr. Rasmussen had not wanted to name them. "You're wrong about Willoughby," he said stubbornly. "I didn't get where I am by being a bad judge of character, Sergeant. And I'm telling you Henry Willoughby is no murderer."

Eberhart thanked him for his help and didn't argue. Mr. Rasmussen was like those people who kept insisting Richard Nixon was just misunderstood; they couldn't bring themselves to admit they'd made *that* big a mistake in judgment. Eberhart took the elevator down to the sub-basement and talked to the counterman at the pistol range. The counterman was fairly new on the job and had never seen Pluto, but he had seen the police sketch before. He'd put a copy up on the bulletin board but somebody stole it.

Wonder who? Eberhart thought dryly. That meant their police sketch was no longer any good, he was willing to bet. Pluto had come in to do some shooting and had spotted his face on the bulletin board. Now he knew *they* knew what he looked like, so the first thing he'd do would be to change his appearance. *Where are you, Pluto, and what do you look like now?* The opposite of blond and mustachioed was clean-shaven and brunet. Or red—no, henna was too easy to spot. Black or brown hair. Possibly a full beard? But Pluto wouldn't have had time to grow one yet and putting on a false beard every morning was a pain; to look realistic, it had to be pasted on strand by strand. Clean-shaven, then, and brown or black hair.

Lots of goodies. Eberhart had the names of five mem-

bers of the Pardee Club who'd known Pluto; surely one
of them knew something that could be helpful. Also, he'd
have another go at Mr. Rasmussen, after the old man had
had a little time to recover from the shock. And there
were those two antique firearms dealers to be checked.

Eberhart decided he needed help. Unfortunately, that
meant a face-to-face with Ansbacher. Those little con-
ferences with the Captain always left him feeling like a
fool, no matter how well he'd done his work. In instant
contrast, Eberhart heard in his mind Lieutenant Murtaugh's chronic but good-natured grumbling about Eberhart's handwriting; it was true you didn't appreciate
what you had until you lost it.

Eberhart missed working with Murtaugh. But he'd go
on being all willing cooperation and smiling sincerity
as far as Ansbacher was concerned. Because the man could
destroy you. And would, if he didn't like the way you
combed your hair.

What the fuck kind of stinking system was it when a
good man like Lieutenant Murtaugh could be falsely
accused and kicked out and humiliated—and a high-
ranking son of a bitch like Ansbacher just went on surviving and surviving and surviving?

Leon Walsh pressed the palms of his hands against his
burning eyeballs. His neck ached, his shoulders ached, his
back ached. But he felt that special kind of *good* that
came only once a month. After all these years he still got
a kick out of putting another issue to bed. The proof-
reading was done, the corrected dummy was on its way
back to the printer's.

A knock at the door, shave and a haircut. *"Entrez,"*
Walsh sang out.

The door opened two feet and Andy Gill slipped in. Andy was the fiction editor, Fran Caffrey's replacement; a thin, pale young man, quiet and unobtrusive. "Do you have a minute, Mr. Walsh?"

That was one thing Walsh liked about young Andy Gill; he was respectful and well-mannered. Fran Caffrey would have just barged in and started talking. Walsh nodded, and Andy closed the door behind him.

"I called the printer," the young man said. "They have the dummy—it arrived all right."

"That wasn't necessary, Andy. They have to sign for it."

"I know, I just wanted to be sure. It's all locked up now, isn't it? Nothing can be changed?"

"You know it can't. A Martian invasion couldn't make *that* issue. What's this all about, Andy?"

"May I sit down?" he asked, sitting down. "It's about a story in that issue—the one written by your friend Vincent Yates. 'Whipping Boy'?"

In spite of his good feeling, Walsh tensed. "Whipping Boy" was the new title for the rewritten version of his old story "Talking of Michelangelo"—and Vincent Yates was his new pseudonym. "What about it?"

"It's a lovely story, Mr. Walsh. I'm glad we printed it."

Walsh relaxed. "So am I."

"Your friend Mr. Yates has a lot of talent. Will we be getting more of his stories, do you think?"

"Oh, I'm sure we will."

Andy Gill nodded. "Did I ever tell you I've read every single issue of *Summit* magazine? Right from the very first one, when you were still publishing in New Jersey. Did I ever tell you that?"

The tense feeling came creeping back, and Walsh knew

this time it wasn't going to go away. He swallowed and spoke slowly. "No, I don't think you did."

"There's a story in the sixth issue that's awfully interesting. It's called 'Talking of Michelangelo'—remember that one?"

Walsh stared at him without answering.

"It's an incredible coincidence," Andy went on, "but 'Whipping Boy' had so many things about it that reminded me of 'Talking of Michelangelo' that I went back and read it again. The older story, I mean."

No. Not now. No.

The young fiction editor pulled a small spiral notebook from a hip pocket and opened it. " 'Whipping Boy' is set in Berlin while the action of 'Talking of Michelangelo' takes place in Paris, but they have the same themes and basically the same plot. And the characters of both stories have a great deal in common."

Walsh put his head back and closed his still-burning eyes as Andy Gill's featureless young voice droned on, comparing the two stories point by point. Walsh succumbed to a flood of self-pity; good God, couldn't he get away with *anything*? Probably the best line to take with young Gill was to pretend to be shocked, horrified, outraged by the plagiarism—and to swear loudly and convincingly that that was the last word by Vincent Yates *Summit* magazine would ever publish, by golly.

But Andy Gill wasn't finished. "Here's the part that's causing me trouble. 'Talking of Michelangelo' was written by J. J. Kellerman. You've published six of Kellerman's stories altogether, Mr. Walsh—I went through and counted them. 'The Man from Porlock' was the last one. But in your, ah, court hearing, and I surely am sorry about that, that you had to go through all that, I mean—

but at your hearing they said *you* wrote 'The Man from Porlock.' Isn't that right? That's how that police lieutenant, ah, figured things out, wasn't it?"

Walsh kept his eyes closed, not wanting to look at that accusing young face.

"So if you wrote 'The Man from Porlock' then you're J. J. Kellerman. And since you're Kellerman, that means you also wrote 'Talking of Michelangelo'—isn't that true? Then if 'Whipping Boy' is just a new version of 'Talking of Michelangelo' you must also be Vincent Yates."

Walsh forced himself to open his eyes. "What are you talking about, Andy? You know Vincent Yates is a friend of mine." Something more was needed; he snorted as if disgusted. "Some friend!"

Andy shook his head. "I know you *told* me Vincent Yates was a friend . . . but it just doesn't make sense, Mr. Walsh. You're too good an editor not to recognize a plagiarized version of one of your own stories. There isn't any Vincent Yates, is there?"

Walsh looked at him wonderingly, not knowing what to say. "Well." He cleared his throat. "I don't know what to say."

"You don't have to worry, Mr. Walsh," Andy Gill hastened to assure him. "I haven't said a word to anybody. And I don't think you have to worry about the rest of the staff. None of them were with you in New Jersey, were they? And if they haven't gone back and read the old issues already, they're not likely to now, are they? You really don't have a thing to worry about. I promise you, I'm not going to say anything about it."

It was going to work out? "I don't know what to say," Walsh repeated.

200

Andy Gill smiled broadly, making himself look boyish. "You don't have to thank me, Mr. Walsh. I know you're an honorable man at heart. You'll take care of me."

The temperature dropped. "What?"

"I said I know you'll take care of me. Working with fiction is fun, and I appreciate your giving me the chance. But I really would rather work with the whole magazine, not just the fiction."

"Oh, is that all?" Walsh asked sarcastically, at last understanding he was being blackmailed. "Would publisher be good enough for you?"

"Nothing so grand as that," Andy said modestly. "An associate editorship would suit me fine."

Walsh gaped. "Associate . . . I don't have enough budget to take on another associate editor!"

The young man's face clouded. "I'm sorry to hear that. I hate to think of one of those older people being turned out to make room for me—but if you don't have the money, you don't have the money. That's the way it goes."

Walsh couldn't believe what he was hearing. Whatever happened to the quiet, unobtrusive, respectful young man he'd hired to take Fran Caffrey's place? Even Fran would never have pulled a stunt like this. "Uriah Heep," he said bitterly.

Andy Gill blinked his eyes, looked hurt. "I'm sorry you feel that way."

I'm sorry you feel that way—the same thing young Hartley Dunlop had said to him, that day at UltraMedia when Walsh had come within a gnat's eyelash of losing *Summit.* Pull the rug out from under a guy and then say, *I'm sorry you feel that way,* when he yells. The young, conscienceless punks. They took whatever they wanted, and anyone who got in the way had better look out. Walsh wondered if he was destined to spend the rest of his life being one-upped by men half his age.

"Go away," Walsh said softly. "I don't want to talk to you right now."

"Yes, sir, I understand," Associate Editor Andy Gill said courteously and left the office.

Walsh leaned his head back and closed his eyes again. *Pluto, Pluto—where are you now?*

Desmond Murtaugh padded down the hall in his pajamas and bare feet toward the ringing telephone. It was six o'clock in the morning and he wasn't fully awake. "What couldn't wait one more hour?" he answered the phone.

"Des? It's Ellie. Wake Jim up—it's important. Hurry, Des."

Des padded halfway back down the hall to the guest room. He woke his younger brother the same way he had awakened him when they were boys, by taking hold of his big toe and shaking his foot lightly. "Ellie's on the phone. She says it's important."

Lieutenant James Timothy Murtaugh woke up faster than his brother did; he was down at the end of the hall before Des made it back to his own bedroom. "Ellie? What's wrong?"

"Jim, something ghastly has happened. Captain Ansbacher has been shot. He's dead." The silence that followed was so long that Ellie said, "Jim?"

"I'm listening." *O Captain, my Captain.* "How did it happen?"

"I don't know, I just know he's been killed. A man from the Deputy Commissioner's office called, somebody named Turnbull. You know him?"

"I know him."

"He wants you to come in to see him. He means right away, Jim, today. As soon as you can get a plane back to New York." Another silence. "Jim?"

"I'm on my way," he said.

CHAPTER

14

Deputy Commissioner Turnbull was on edge. He tried to hide his nervousness under an abrupt speaking manner; not his usual style, and he didn't carry it off too well.

Murtaugh wasn't inclined to help him out; he had a small case of nerves of his own to worry about. He was being reinstated; that was all he really cared about. But the departmentally regulated process of absolving him had opened a new can of worms.

"You know the charges against you have been dropped," Turnbull said shortly, in a hurry to get this part over with. "There'll be no hearing. Insufficient evidence now."

"What about Hanowitz? There's still his claim he heard me talking to Pluto."

"Funny thing about Hanowitz," Turnbull said dryly. "The minute he learned Ansbacher was dead he started having memory lapses. Like maybe he's not really sure it was *Pluto* he heard you say on the phone. And like he's not sure if it was a stakeout or a steak dinner you were talking about. He's mentioned a couple of times that Ansbacher had been pressuring him about it. He says he was just trying to be helpful."

"Hm. What's going to happen to him?"

"Oh, he's not getting away with it, don't worry. False accusation—that's serious stuff. If he'd stuck to his story . . . well, he still might have made trouble. But Hanowitz sounds like one of those pricks who change sides so often it gets to be a habit. His 'patron' is no longer around to back him up, so he's not going to try to put the screws on you by himself. How did a turkey like that ever make detective—that's what I'd like to know." Turnbull paused. "Lieutenant, the Commissioner wanted me to tell you that he's glad you're back. He never believed you were guilty."

It was the sort of thing police commissioners probably made a practice of saying to lowly lieutenants in need of encouragement, but it still gave Murtaugh a lift. He smiled for the first time that day.

Turnbull barked an uncomfortable laugh. "Good thing your papers were impounded after all. Sanders in Internal Affairs—you sure gave him a hell of a turn. When he came across your notes on Ansbacher, I mean. Two files of 'em! After he'd had a chance to study them he came to us and said he thought they were investigating the wrong man."

Murtaugh's eyebrows rose. "My notes convinced him?"

"Not exactly. You didn't have any hard evidence. But they made him suspicious—which ain't all that hard to do with Internal Affairs, my friend. But it was enough. They were about to open an official investigation when Ansbacher got shot." Turnbull cleared his throat. "Did he know what you were doing? Is that why he brought that trumped-up charge against you?"

"Yes and yes. Hanowitz told him I was asking embarrassing questions."

"Hanowitz." Turnbull made a face. "The Commissioner had no idea—about Ansbacher, I mean. Not even a whisper. He really was on the take, then."

"For a long time. At least fifteen years, probably more." So his surreptitious investigation had done some good after all. It had saved his neck. "My notes on Ansbacher—what did you do with them?"

"Buried 'em. As far as everybody outside the Department is concerned, Ansbacher died a hero. Can you live with that?"

Murtaugh nodded. "I wasn't out for blood, I just wanted him out of here. Any leads on the killer?"

"Not yet. The bullet was a twenty-two-caliber." Turnbull paused significantly. "No lands or grooves."

Murtaugh frowned. "No lands or grooves? That means a zip gun." He snorted. "Nobody uses zip guns any more."

Turnbull shrugged. "Street gangs?"

"When they can get the real thing so easily? No."

"Somebody under age. *Way* under age. Had he been rousting kids, do you know?"

"I don't know. Ansbacher didn't keep me informed. Who's heading up the investigation?"

"Dan Grogan." Turnbull looked uneasy. "We can't put you in charge, you understand. Right after he got you suspended . . . well, it would look peculiar, to say the least. We need somebody not involved."

"Sure," Murtaugh nodded agreeably. "Grogan'll do a good job."

"You're going to have your hands full anyway. Ansbacher had just started coordinating all the cases Pluto is thought to be involved in. Help yourself to what you need from his files. The Commissioner doesn't want you working on anything else—just catch Pluto, that's all."

"That's all, huh?" Murtaugh managed to grin.

"Yeah." Turnbull didn't return the grin. "The Commissioner also told me to give you what you want in terms of manpower and resources."

"For starters, I want Sergeant Eberhart."

"You got him." Turnbull made a note. "What else?"

"I'll need foot soldiers—begin with six. I'll get back to you on the rest as soon as I go through Ansbacher's files."

"Okay." Turnbull ran a hand through his hair. "Just one more thing. The Commissioner has a press conference scheduled for six o'clock and he wants you to be there."

"Six this evening?"

"Yes. He's going to make things right for you, Murtaugh. He's going to tell the reporters you were falsely accused and you've been reinstated. He's also going to say that your accuser has been suspended pending an investigation."

So Hanowitz is to be the goat, Murtaugh mused. Offhand, he couldn't think of anyone who deserved it more.

Turnbull went on, "One thing working in our favor is the short period of time you were out—only a matter of days. I don't know of any shorter suspension in the Department. Anyway, the Commissioner is going to announce you are now in sole charge of the Pluto-hunt. It'll be a sign of our faith in you and a smart move as well—since you know more about Pluto than anyone else in the Department."

"I think Sergeant Eberhart may be ahead of me now," Murtaugh sighed.

"But you're the one who's going to be at the press conference," Turnbull pointed out. "Be prepared to answer questions."

"Then I'd better get at those files." Murtaugh stood up; it was noon—he had six hours to do his homework and get organized. He was excited, even exhilarated. "Pluto's an elusive bastard, but I think I can get him, Turnbull. Now that I've got the full resources of the Department behind me—for the first time, I might point out. I can get him."

Turnbull nodded complacently. "We're counting on it."

The first thing Murtaugh did when he left Turnbull's office was call Ellie and tell her all was well. The second thing he did was go out and get something to eat; solid food in his stomach ought to help steady him. The third thing he did was go to the precinct station; he loped through the squad room, bellowing, "Eberhart! I need you!" without breaking stride.

"Yes, *sir!*" A beaming Sergeant Eberhart jumped up from his desk.

They went to Ansbacher's office, where Murtaugh explained they'd be going through the files looking for everything Ansbacher had accumulated on Pluto.

"What if we find something that might be related to Ansbacher's death?" Eberhart asked.

"Then it goes to Dan Grogan. He's in charge of the investigation—but I imagine he's already been through everything here."

Eberhart was puzzled. "Why Grogan? Why not you?"

"They wanted somebody not personally involved with Ansbacher." *They knew I'd be glad the son of a bitch was dead.* Murtaugh didn't even feel guilty. He *was* glad Ansbacher was dead. He hadn't been completely truthful with Turnbull; he had indeed been out for blood. Not this way, of course—but he'd take it.

"Lieutenant," Eberhart grinned, "you don't know how glad I am to see you back."

Murtaugh smiled, genuinely pleased. "Thanks." He was feeling better every minute. All because Captain Edward Ansbacher had taken a straight shot to the heart, a disquieting example of the very approach to problem-solving Murtaugh was sworn to oppose. "By the way, did you know Ansbacher was killed with a zip gun?"

Eberhart looked incredulous. "C'mon."

"No lands or grooves in the bullet. Zip guns aren't accurate more than a few feet, so it had to be an up-close killing. But that's Grogan's worry. We'd better get started here."

Ansbacher had taken the computer-generated list of possible past murders committed by Pluto (the list Murtaugh had given him, the one he hadn't thought to ask for himself) and used it as a guide. He'd pulled the files on all the names on the list, and at the time of his death had isolated five names other than the ones Murtaugh and Eberhart already knew about. And there were more names on the computer list still to be checked out.

"Now we're cooking," Murtaugh exulted. "Okay, Eberhart, bring these five in for questioning. All at once. Help's on the way, incidentally—I asked Turnbull for legmen. Anyway, when you get these five possible 'clients' of Pluto's in here, the first thing you do is tell them they're in no danger of being tried as accessories. Tell them about Leon Walsh's hearing and the legal precedent it set. Make sure they understand about that. It's the only way we'll get them to talk—let them see we know all about it, that they're only one among many and they're in no danger from the law if they cooperate. Might not

209

hurt to hint that they could be in trouble with the law if they do *not* cooperate. We've got to make that distinction clear."

"Right," Eberhart said. "You say legmen are coming? How many?"

"I asked for six. We can have more if we need them."

"Could I use one to follow up on the Pardee Club leads?"

"What the hell's the Pardee Club?"

Eberhart had put it all in a written report; it was there among Ansbacher's papers—Murtaugh hadn't gotten to it yet. The Sergeant explained about the private club with the underground pistol range. Pluto had been a member of the Pardee, Eberhart said, and had talked to other members. He also frequented shops that sold antique firearms.

Murtaugh felt like kissing him. "Eberhart, that's the best lead we've had yet! Take two men—three if you need them. Go call Turnbull's office and find out when they'll be here. And forget about hauling in those five earlier clients of Pluto's, I'll take care of that. This is your lead—checking on pistol ranges was your idea in the first place, wasn't it? You follow through on it. Git."

"Yes, sir!" Eberhart grinned happily and left. Now that was the way ranking police officers were supposed to act.

We're going to get him, Murtaugh thought with barely suppressed excitement. He knew the signs; he'd been there before. Things were falling into place; there were too many lines leading back to Pluto for one of them not to pay off. They even knew his exact body measurements now, thanks to the Fifth Avenue tailor.

So at a little after six o'clock Murtaugh was able to face the microphones and the cameras with composure and say, "We have quite a few leads to Pluto—no, don't ask me, I'm not going to reveal anything that might tip him off. Yes, we think he's still in New York." He went on in that vein for a few minutes, giving the reporters nothing substantive but doing it in so authoritative a manner that they went away reassured. At least that was the effect he had aimed for; when the Commissioner congratulated him later, he knew he'd succeeded.

The press conference had been televised live as part of the six o'clock news and a tape replay was to be shown at eleven. That meant the next day would be too early for what he was expecting.

During that next day four of the five of Pluto's clients Murtaugh had brought in admitted they'd paid a hundred thousand each to the never-seen hit man. The fifth admitted nothing, even though he was repeatedly assured he would not be charged with complicity in any crime. They could have made a mistake with that one case, but Murtaugh thought the man was just too ashamed to admit he'd paid off his wife's killer.

Then the day after that it came.

At home, not through the police mail room. Same blue window envelope, same blue note paper.

FEE FOR SERVICES RENDERED

One murder, arranged to coincide
with establishment of Pittsburgh
alibi

Payment due . . . My continuing freedom

Well, there it was. He'd known from the minute Ellie had called and told him Ansbacher was dead, but now he had it in writing. If it hadn't been for Pluto, Murtaugh would still be sitting in his brother Desmond's house in

211

Pittsburgh, anguishing over how to beat the frame Ansbacher had set up. One little zap from a zip gun, and Murtaugh's problems were solved. That simple.

Jesus.

Smart move, using a zip gun. That isolated the Ansbacher killing from the rest, one hell of a red herring. Now no one was likely to look at Murtaugh and think, *Hm, I wonder if he might not be a Pluto-client . . .* not that anyone would suspect him of being able to come up with a hundred thousand dollars for the payoff. But he could misdirect the search for Pluto, throw everybody off the scent, bollix it up so royally that Pluto never would get caught.

Which was exactly the price Pluto was charging for his service this time.

Jesus Christ.

And Pluto always collected. Poor dumb handless Roscoe Malucci was proof of that. Pluto didn't like being told no.

Murtaugh was beginning to feel a grudging respect for the man—the chubby, fast-moving killer who sometimes liked to pretend to be an English gentleman. He was efficient—oh, he was *deadly* efficient. He'd thought up this ridiculous scam combining intimidation and gratitude, and he'd made it work! A scam that left a trail of dead bodies behind him, a minor matter that didn't seem to bother him unduly. Even mob hit men tended to burn out after a while, to grow sick of the killing or lose their nerve, to notice the gun hand was beginning to shake a little. But not Pluto. Not kill-'em-and-bill-'em Pluto. Pluto rolled with the punches, bounced back, kept on going no matter what.

One familiar hazard of a long police career was the

policeman's susceptibility to a perverse change of standards: he could come to admire the criminal and feel contempt for the victim. Shifting guilt on to the victim was a self-exonerating response well known in psychiatric circles; but it was something not talked about much in the Police Department—too close to the bone. The victim-blaming attitude was mostly an unconscious one, based upon years of working with (and against) both doers and those-done-to. So much crime, so much viciousness—rare was the policeman who had never wanted to give a victim a good shaking and say *Why didn't you take better care of yourself?* Most of the time such a frustration-filled reprimand was out of place; most crime victims truly could not protect themselves. But was there a policeman anywhere in the world who had *never* thought that?

Maybe that was what was behind Murtaugh's own dislike of people like Leon Walsh and his reluctant admiration of Pluto. The slick, callous criminal versus the bumbling, helpless victim—cartoon figures, clichés. *We simplify not to understand but to persuade ourselves we do understand.* Leon Walsh was not an easy man to like. You had to share *his* background and enthusiasms before you could talk to him; he never made any real effort to venture beyond his self-proscribed world. Murtaugh thought Pluto must be more cosmopolitan than that, moving as he did through so many different environments. Or was he glamorizing Pluto, endowing him with admirable traits simply because of his distance, his unreachableness? Murtaugh grunted in annoyance at himself.

There was only one way to deal with the problem: get Pluto before Pluto got him. Murtaugh wondered if Pluto seriously thought that he, James T. Murtaugh, would pay the price demanded. Damnedest thing, though, he *was* grateful to the son of a bitch. He hadn't done such a good job of untangling the Ansbacher mess on his own; Pluto had just come in and cut the knot with one blow. Now Murtaugh knew how Leon Walsh must have felt when he first learned Jerry Sussman wouldn't be around to sell him down the river. But to expect Murtaugh to derail the investigation deliberately . . . ? It was preposterous.

If he stuck to his usual pattern, Pluto would follow up with a phone call before long. In his other arrangements he'd given his clients time to get the payment together— almost a month in Leon Walsh's case. But since Murtaugh was not expected to pluck a hundred thousand dollars out of the air, he wouldn't be allowed so lengthy a grace period. How long did he have before he heard from Pluto?—two days, three? Twenty-four hours?

Early the next morning he was in his office making plans. He requested more investigators from Turnbull; they had a lot of ground to cover. Other tailors. Every place in Manhattan that dealt in antique firearms. One of the members of the Pardee Club had told Eberhart that "Willoughby" had always worn Bally shoes, so that gave them another line to follow. Also, Sergeant Eberhart was sure Pluto had changed his appearance again, so they needed to check the more posh of the men's hair salons. Murtaugh didn't think Pluto was the type to attempt a home dye job.

Then one of the new legmen found a cab driver who'd picked up Pluto three times since the beginning of the year, always in front of the Pardee Club. Did the driver still have his destination sheet, Murtaugh wanted to know, could he look up where he dropped Pluto off? Didn't have to look it up, the driver said, he remembered. He always let him out in the vicinity of Fifty-second Street and Third Avenue. This guy never gave an exact address, y'unnerstand, he just said as close to Fifty-second and Third as you can get.

Home? Fifty-second and Third was near wherever Pluto called home?

Midtown, east of Fifth—high rise? townhouse? Doormen, building superintendents, realtors. Murtaugh made a series of phone calls, mobilizing a small army to invade the district in question, armed with sketches of Pluto's appearance up to the time he found his picture on the Pardee Club bulletin board. Murtaugh felt like rubbing his hands together; every day, a little closer.

The cab driver had said Pluto was clean-shaven the first two times he'd picked him up but had a mustache the last time; all three times he was blond. So no clue to Pluto's new appearance there. Murtaugh had instructed the foot soldiers he sent into Pluto's "home" area to ask especially about any tenants who'd recently changed their appearances. Or tenants who looked like the police sketch and who'd abruptly changed residences. Or anything else they could think of. A chubby blond man with a mustache and an English accent doesn't change into something else overnight without *somebody* noticing.

Twenty-four hours was all the grace period Pluto allowed him. The phone call came late at night. Ellie was asleep; Murtaugh, wide awake. Even as he answered, he knew who was calling.

"Hallo, Lieutenant? Pluto here." The English accent was back.

In spite of being prepared for the call, Murtaugh felt his stomach do a flip-flop. Here he was at last, the ever-elusive Pluto, only a telephone call's distance away. In contact at last—proof, as if he needed it, that he was getting close. "I've been expecting your call," he said cautiously.

"Ha! I'll wager you have. I'm calling from a phone booth, in case you were thinking of having the call traced. No point, old man. I have no intention of talking long enough for that. Do you understand my fee?"

"I understand it. Do you understand I have no intention of paying it?"

"Dear, dear. Most ungracious of you, I must say. You prefer being a defrocked policeman, or whatever it is they do to policemen? I rescued you, you know. I do think you could express a *little* gratitude."

"I'm not going to argue morality with you, Pluto—it'd be a waste of breath. But you've fallen into the trap of assuming everyone thinks the way you do. That's a bad mistake."

Something like a little-boy snicker came over the line. "Not so bad a mistake, Lieutenant. All those poor souls you're currently investigating—they all paid their bills with nary a whimper."

" 'Pour souls' is right," Murtaugh said. "They were so frightened they didn't dare *not* pay you. I'm not so easily intimidated."

"Oh, aren't you the brave one!" Again the snicker. "Ah well, a little chest-beating never hurts, I suppose. But come, Lieutenant, we've both been around. Do you really think my clients paid me only because they were intimidated? They *loved* having someone step in and do their dirty work for them. And you want me to think you've never figured that out?"

Too late Murtaugh saw he shouldn't have let the conversation take the turn it did. Change the subject. "Is

Carolyn Randolph one of your clients?" he asked abruptly.

"Carolyn who?" Pluto answered blandly, not missing a beat. "Enough of this chit-chat," his voice taking on a brisker tone. "You must understand I mean to collect."

"How? By shooting my hand off?"

A chuckle. "You're thinking of Roscoe Malucci, aren't you? Poor Roscoe. Probably talked his silly head off, didn't he? Roscoe and Leon Walsh, not an ounce of discretion between them. But you're different, Lieutenant. I know I can count on you not to talk out of turn."

"What makes you so sure? How are you going to force me to cooperate? Come on, Pluto, this is where you slip the threat in, isn't it? What do you think you're going to do to me?"

"Dear me. That has an almost masochistic ring to it, Lieutenant. Actually, I'm not planning to do anything to you at all. Not to *you*. Actually . . . it was Ellie I was thinking of."

Murtaugh's mouth went dry.

"She'll be a lot easier to get to than you, don't you see," Pluto went on conversationally, "even if you give her police protection. Besides, policemen themselves are more or less used to the idea of danger, but school administrators are not. What I mean to say is, if I threatened *you* I probably wouldn't get anywhere. But if you think Ellie is in danger—and you know she is if I say she is—well, then you're more likely to cooperate. Am I right, Lieutenant?"

Murtaugh made a strangled sound.

"I'll take that as an affirmative. You do understand, don't you, that I have no compunction at all about crippling her for life, or blinding her, or doing something equally nasty? I'm a very good shot, Lieutenant. I won't kill her—I don't want to lose my hold on *you*. But no matter what happens to her, just remember she'll always have something more to lose. Do you understand?"

"Yes," Murtaugh said tightly.

"Good. Then I can count on your cooperation?"

"I . . . I need some time to think."

"Of course you do," Pluto purred. "You need time to think of ways to 'get' me and protect Ellie . . . and time to see that nothing like that is going to work. How can you protect Ellie the rest of her life? Even if you both start life over elsewhere under new identities, you won't ever be sure I'll *never* find you, will you? And what a dreadful thing to do to Ellie! She'd have to give up her work, her friends, the life she's built for herself—and spend the rest of her days looking over her shoulder. *All because of you.* Do you think she'll love you for that? Seems to me that would put a strain on any marriage. But you need time to think all these things through for yourself. I'll call tomorrow night," he concluded. "Remember one thing, Lieutenant. I *always* collect."

The phone went dead in Murtaugh's hand.

He sat in a daze, holding the receiver until the cut-in signal reminded him to hang up. So that was it. Pluto would go after Ellie instead of Murtaugh himself. He'd go after her with intent to maim, to blind, to shoot out her kneecaps—and he'd succeed. Promising police protection to a witness was one thing; but when it was someone close who needed protecting, Murtaugh thought, the weaknesses of their protective system became glaringly obvious.

Murtaugh wasn't the first cop whose family had been threatened and he wouldn't be the last. But knowing that didn't make it any easier. He was shaken to realize he wasn't sure what Ellie would do when she learned

he'd put her in danger. She'd be outraged, he knew—
but she'd eventually forgive him. She would, wouldn't
she? He honestly didn't know, nor could he imagine how
he would feel if their positions were reversed. Ellie was
no yes-dear wife who accepted whatever came her way.
Perhaps he should try to keep her in the dark as long as
he could.

Murtaugh had enough objectivity left to realize he was
going through the very same thing every other one of
Pluto's clients must have gone through. The fear, the
questioning . . . the slowly growing conviction that there
was, after all, only one real way out. Murtaugh allowed
himself the sinful indulgence of supposing how things
would go if he agreed to Pluto's terms: Eberhart might
be a problem, but there was bound to be some way of
diverting him. The new men Turnbull sent wouldn't
question Murtaugh's orders; they'd not be familiar
enough with the investigation. The only real obstacle
Murtaugh could foresee was the difficulty of justifying
his ultimate failure to catch Pluto. The Commissioner
had made it clear, both through Turnbull and in person,
that Murtaugh's was an *or-else* assignment. Catch Pluto
or else.

If he gave in to Pluto's demands in order to protect
Ellie, how could he protect himself from the departmental wrath that was sure to follow? He was in a no-win
situation—god damn that Pluto! No matter what Murtaugh did, he was bound to come out on the short end of
the stick! *Now wait a minute, wait a minute,* he told himself—*Don't give up so fast.* One thing was certain: the
Commissioner would have his head on a platter if he
didn't find a solution to the Pluto problem. Unless . . .
unless Pluto would agree to move his operation out of
New York? That would make a difference, if the killings

219

stopped. Yes—perhaps an agreement was possible, a compromise of some sort. Dump our garbage in some other city. Then Murtaugh could make a case (semi-truthfully) that Pluto had been frightened off by the police investigation.

How tempting it was! Look at him, sitting there thinking about going through with it. Now Murtaugh understood Pluto's other clients a little better. How easy it was—just to give in and let things slide, take care of themselves. No more hassle, no more danger. Murtaugh thought of himself as a fundamentally honest man, at least an honest cop. But what if that honesty had never really been tested? Pluto's offer was like no other that had come Murtaugh's way. He'd never felt anything but contempt for crooked policemen, parasites dependent on the corrupt strength of others for their survival. It was the only thing that ever made him ashamed of his profession. He'd made no secret of his attitude; after his first few years on the force there'd been no serious attempt to bribe him. He fingered Pluto's bill that he kept in his coat pocket, the blue piece of paper that some voice of caution had kept him from adding to the ever-growing file on Pluto.

Murtaugh suddenly thought of something Sergeant Eberhart had told him, something he'd learned from Leila Hudson. Leila had told Eberhart that *Summit* magazine was having personnel problems; a lot of the long-time staff were leaving and Leon Walsh was having trouble finding people of equivalent caliber to replace them. It seemed folks were uneasy working for a man who was known to have paid off a killer—even when the payment had been made under extreme duress.

Murtaugh wondered about all the others the police had gotten to admit to paying off Pluto. How did their friends and families and co-workers treat them? Did they all shy away, ostracize the offender? Did they ever stop to consider what Pluto's clients must have gone through before agreeing to the killer's terms? The nausea, the fear . . . the shameful secret elation? Would any of the men Murtaugh worked with try to see his point of view if the truth came out? The answer to that was a resounding no.

But what was any of that compared to Ellie's safety? Nothing, nothing at all. Some choice he had. Ellie in danger—*you know she is if I say she is.* Some choice.

Murtaugh opened the bedroom door a crack. The only light source in the room was the red digital numbers on the clock-radio—4:01. Murtaugh opened the door a little wider, until the light from the hallway fell on the bed where Ellie was sleeping. She did not look like a child in her sleep. She looked exactly like what she was: a woman in early middle age, tired out from the rigors of keeping on top of a demanding job. Yet she could still surprise Murtaugh by waking him early in the morning, eager for lovemaking once she'd had her rest. How could he tell her of the danger he'd put her in? It wasn't his fault— and yet it was his fault. But if she ever found out he'd *not* told her . . .

He sat down on the only chair in the bedroom. He sat without moving, watching his wife sleep. Watching, and waiting for daylight.

15

Pluto was fighting an inappropriate tendency toward nostalgia. He hadn't even left New York yet and he was already beginning to miss the place. A sentimental reaction, one he had no time for. His luggage had gone out to Kennedy yesterday and the one-way ticket to Geneva was in his pocket. All he had to do was concentrate on getting through this little charade Lieutenant Murtaugh had dreamed up and he'd be on his way to Switzerland, free and clear.

But for only four or five years. He'd be back. That wasn't part of the deal, but Lieutenant Murtaugh didn't have to know everything.

The Lieutenant had come up with the one argument Pluto had no answer for. Murtaugh had said that he (Pluto) had used up New York—that he'd worked the town for all he could safely get out of it and now all the machinery of the law was converging on him in a drive that Murtaugh wouldn't be able to divert after much longer. It was a point Murtaugh had borne down on hard:

he could cover for Pluto only as long as he was in charge of the investigation. But if Pluto kept up his killing ways, Murtaugh wouldn't stay in charge very long.

Pluto had reluctantly admitted the Lieutenant was right; it was a conclusion he'd pretty much come to on his own. When Murtaugh suggested he take his operation to Philadelphia or Detroit, Pluto had murmured something about seeking a warmer climate and let the Lieutenant think he'd be heading toward Miami, perhaps Los Angeles. Dropping red herrings was second nature to Pluto.

Of course, he could just skip the cops-and-robbers playlet Murtaugh had come up with and get on his airplane and *go*. But there was a distinct advantage to being listed as dead on the NYPD records. No one ever went looking for a dead man. It certainly would make things easier when he came back, in four or five years. Who'd be expecting him? He could call himself Pluto Junior then— ha. Son of Pluto. Plutoson. But first things first. Today he had to see if Murtaugh was on the up and up. Because if he wasn't . . . well, Pluto had warned him he always collected.

What Murtaugh had proposed was such a perfect setup for a double-cross! Or a triple-cross, if it came to that. It was also a scenario that would work the way it was supposed to if it was played absolutely straight. And that, of course, depended solely upon Lieutenant James Timothy Murtaugh. Jim Tim. Pluto unaccountably felt a new stab of homesickness. *It's only a few years.*

Pluto shifted his weight, trying to find a more comfortable position in his rental car; so little leg room! He was parked across the street from the entrance to Murtaugh's apartment building, in the exact same spot where he'd parked two days earlier. That was the morning after the first time he'd spoken to the Lieutenant, the time he'd made all his threatening noises. The following morning he'd seen Ellie come scurrying out the door, escorted by good old Jim Tim and a man Pluto didn't know carrying a suitcase. The three of them had climbed into a sedan driven by a woman Pluto didn't know—and Ellie Murtaugh, her husband, and her two police guards had driven swiftly away. Pluto wondered idly where the Lieutenant was sending her. It didn't matter; just so long as she was out of the way.

That was two days ago. Then yesterday the Lieutenant had come up with his plan.

Ah, at last. Lieutenant Murtaugh's car came nosing up the ramp from the indoor parking area beneath the apartment building. Pluto glanced at his watch: still three minutes shy of seven A.M. The Lieutenant was putting in long hours these days.

Twenty minutes later Pluto let himself into the Murtaugh apartment; it had taken him a while to find the right combination of picks for the downstairs locks plus the four locks on the apartment door. Once inside, he put the canvas case he was carrying on the sofa and his tool kit on the end table. He measured the width of the front door: thirty-six inches exactly. Next, a kitchen chair to stand on. He drilled a small hole in the ceiling two feet in from the three-foot-wide front door, making a face as he did; Pluto hated messing with plaster, such dirty stuff. When he'd finished that he drilled another hole, this one right through the carpet directly under the hole in the ceiling. A tiny eyebolt buried in the carpeting, a small pulley in the ceiling. Then he rigged a vertical trip wire that would be triggered the next time the door was opened. Crude, but it had the virtue of being undetectable from the other side of the door.

Pluto dragged a heavy armchair into position and piled books (mostly Ellie's) into the seat. Then he opened the canvas bag he'd placed on the sofa and took out the shotgun. He fussed with chair and books until he'd fashioned a stable cradle for the firearm. Pluto didn't care much for shotguns. He'd stolen this one a few years ago just to try it out in his work. No good. Too big and clumsy to carry around easily; and the one time he'd used it, the scatter shot had only wounded, not killed. Lots of blood and mess, ugh; he'd had to finish the job with the Beretta he'd taken along as backup.

But for his present purposes the shotgun was exactly right. He made sure the two barrels were aimed low, knee-level. He didn't want to kill Murtaugh; no satisfaction in that. He did want to cripple the Lieutenant for life—*if* Murtaugh's plan was indeed a trap. But if Murtaugh played straight with him, Pluto would simply let the other man know what was waiting for him at home. Pluto fussed with the positioning some more and was finally satisfied. Some of the shot might go high enough to damage the Lieutenant's manhood. *Too bad,* Pluto sniffed. It all depended on the Lieutenant himself.

Pluto had never had any intention of hurting Ellie Murtaugh. If he did harm her, Pluto thought, Lieutenant Murtaugh would suffer horrible waves of guilt—at first. But that feeling would pass, perhaps even turn into resentment. Murtaugh was basically a decent sort and would resist longer than most men, but eventually he would start to rationalize away his part in his wife's tragedy and go on with his life as usual. But if he himself were forced to spend the rest of his days in a wheelchair—ah, that was quite different! So Pluto had to make sure it wouldn't be Murtaugh's wife who opened that door. The Lieutenant had responded to Pluto's threats against Ellie with heartening predictability; Pavlov would have loved him.

Pluto ran the wire through the trigger guard of the shotgun, testing the tension carefully before anchoring the wire to another eyebolt. His original plan had been to get Ellie out of the way and then rig the shotgun to fire into the floor—as a warning, to show Murtaugh that Pluto could get to him anywhere. Pluto had allowed all along for the fact that the Lieutenant would take more convincing than his usual clients. But then Murtaugh had offered him a deal, a scheme to convince the city of New York that Pluto had gone to his Eternal Rest, how sad. The shotgun then quickly transformed itself into an instrument of retaliation, a little surprise awaiting the Lieutenant if he was so foolish as to think he could double-cross Pluto and get away with it.

Connecting balconies ringed every floor of the building, each balcony exactly like every other one. Pluto stepped outside; the balcony was shallow, cramped, covered with New York grit. The only thing the balconies did was enable the landlords to charge a higher rent. With an expression of distaste on his face, Pluto climbed over the divider into the next-door balcony and let himself out through that apartment.

In the hallway he noticed a large ugly smudge of soot on his right knee. Now he'd have to fly all the way to Geneva in dirty trousers.

The building superintendent covered both ears against the whine of the drill. "You sure that warrant covers destruction of property?"

"Yeah, it's okay, don't worry about it," Sergeant Eberhart said with poorly concealed excitement. A police locksmith was working his way methodically down a row of seven locks. Eberhart handed the super the police sketch of Pluto. "Are you absolutely certain this is the guy who lives here?"

"That's him, all right. But he's got himself a fancy-schmancy hairdo now."

"Fancy how?"

"Brown and curly. Don't look natural."

Eberhart turned and grinned at the big man hovering over them. "Good work, Costello. You got 'im."

The big man grinned back. Costello was one of the legmen the Deputy Commissioner had provided, part of the army of canvassers Lieutenant Murtaugh had sent into the area of midtown Manhattan he suspected of being Pluto's home base.

Pluto had leased the apartment under the name of Bell, but undoubtedly that was no more his real name than any of the others he'd used. If nothing else, they should at least get a complete set of prints from the apartment, Eberhart thought. "Where are the Crime Lab people?"

"On their way," Costello said. "They told me they were leaving immediately."

"There you are, Sergeant," the locksmith said, opening the door. "Is that all?"

"No, hang around. We might need you inside."

Inside turned out to be one of those geometric apartments that always made Eberhart uncomfortable. Every piece of furniture looked like a drawing made with protractor and compass. "You look down the hall," he told Costello. The building superintendent had trouble deciding whether to follow Costello or stay with Eberhart; he stayed with Eberhart. The locksmith lounged against the door he'd just opened.

There wasn't much to search in the living room. No

desk, not even a table with drawers. "Modular seating pieces" instead of chairs and sofas. Pluto, hooked on the minimalist style of the seventies?

Costello was back. "Got a locked cabinet in here. Sergeant Eberhart, come take a look at this."

Eberhart, the locksmith, and the super followed Costello into Pluto's study. Eberhart whistled; one entire wall was lined with corkboard. "Hell of a bulletin board." He turned to the super. "What did he use it for?"

"Beats me. This the first time I've been here since he moved in."

"There's the locked cabinet," Costello told the locksmith.

Nothing was pinned to the corkboard wall except the pins themselves, a couple hundred of them lined up in two neat rows, one at each end of the wall. Eberhart spotted a typewriter on a small desk. Using his handkerchief, he started opening desk drawers and in the bottom one found what he was looking for: blue note stationery with matching window envelopes. "Costello, tell the Crime Lab to check this typewriter against the bill Pluto sent Roscoe Malucci."

"You think that's the one?"

"I know it is. Look at this blue paper. And Costello, go call Lieutenant Murtaugh and let him know what we got here."

"Sergeant." The locksmith had the cabinet drawer open. The four men stood staring at Pluto's collection of guns. A Colt Government Model .45. A Coonan .357 Magnum. Two nine-millimeter semiautomatics, a Beretta and a Browning HiPower. A Smith and Wesson .22. And what looked like a Czech CZ .75 automatic.

The super swallowed audibly. "Gawd."

"Where's the thirty-eight?" Eberhart muttered.

"Where's what?" Costello called back over his shoulder, on his way to phone the Lieutenant.

"He bought ammo for a thirty-eight. It's not here."

The men from the Crime Lab showed up and the roomy apartment was suddenly very crowded. Eberhart thanked the super for his help and told him he could go. On his way out, the super said, "Will you look at that—he's had a lock put on the hall closet!"

Without a word the locksmith got to work.

Pluto had turned the walk-in closet into a file room. Three four-door file cabinets and a small table with a reading lamp took up most of the space. All three file cabinets had combination locks. "Oh good," the locksmith smiled, and had all three open in no time flat.

Again using his handkerchief, Eberhart opened the drawer labeled "S–T." The drawer held only six file folders, but all six were fat ones. One of them was marked *Sussman, Gerald.*

Eberhart couldn't examine the files until they were dusted for prints, but he figured he could make a list of all the names on the folders. He pulled out a notebook and opened the "A–B" drawer.

The first name he saw was *Ansbacher, Edward.*

Ansbacher? Pluto had killed Captain Ansbacher? *With a zip gun?*

Eberhart didn't understand that. Why Ansbacher? Who profited? Who paid the killer's fee? And why did Pluto use such a clumsy weapon when he had so many sophisticated and well-cared-for handguns right there in the apartment? Eberhart shook his head; he'd have to think about it later.

He went through Pluto's file drawers in alphabetical

order, finding some unfamiliar names, some familiar ones. *Herman, John*—the Canadian opera singer. *Malucci, Rose*—Roscoe's grandmother.

Murtaugh, James Timothy.

Forgetting all about fingerprints Eberhart pulled out Murtaugh's file. Inside were photographs, newspaper clippings, typed and dated lists of the times the Murtaughs did certain things, Ellie's school schedule, names, addresses. Eberhart felt the hair on the back of his neck rise when he came across a snapshot of himself talking to Lieutenant Murtaugh in the street. Pluto had gotten close enough to them to take their picture and they hadn't even seen him? Good god. Telephoto lens, maybe. Either that, or the man didn't have a nerve in his body.

And now he was going after Lieutenant Murtaugh? Eberhart didn't understand that, either. Say Pluto eliminated Murtaugh. Someone else would just be appointed to take the Lieutenant's place; the investigation wouldn't stop. That couldn't be it.

Something Eberhart had thought peculiar at the time. Just a couple of days ago Lieutenant Murtaugh had assigned two police officers to guard Ellie and had sent all three of them out of town. Nobody else saw anything odd about that, considering how dangerous a man it was they were hunting. But nobody else had worked as closely with Lieutenant Murtaugh as Eberhart. The Lieutenant's forcing his wife to run and hide without some *specific* reason just didn't ring true.

Eberhart looked at the file again.

Lieutenant Murtaugh had heard from Pluto—that had to be it. But why, how? The only time Pluto got in touch with someone was when he wanted to collect his fee . . . *Ansbacher?* Pluto was collecting from Lieutenant Murtaugh for Ansbacher's murder? Was that it? And the fee

—this time was it something other than money? And Ellie, hiding somewhere under guard—Pluto must have threatened *her* to get the Lieutenant to pay. Aw god, no. Not Lieutenant Murtaugh! But the Lieutenant had to have heard from Pluto or he wouldn't all of a sudden have thought Ellie was in danger. He'd heard from Pluto, and he wasn't telling anybody.

He wasn't telling anybody.

Sergeant Eberhart stood there a long time, trying to decide what to do.

He felt a rawness in his throat, a tickle in the nasal passages. Hell of a time to come down with something.

When he was a boy, his father had refused to take any medication for anything: a burly weekend ballplayer who loved to boast: *Naw, I'll just throw it off.* Thanks, dad o' mine; as a consequence he and brother Desmond had gone through one cold after another, catching every bug his father had ever "thrown off." Murtaugh took a couple of aspirin at the drinking fountain; anything stronger might make him sleepy.

Maybe it was psychosomatic.

Murtaugh looked into the squad room; everything seemed okay. He'd sent Eberhart out to check on a possible identification one of the legmen had turned up. He'd arranged for the other special assignees from the Deputy Commissioner to be out too, following up one lead or another. All except Jacoby, the juniormost member of the team. The baby.

Time to make his move. "Jacoby! Come in here."

The young investigator hurried into Murtaugh's office, his eyebrows asking questions.

"Sit down, Jacoby. Got something to write with? All right, now listen carefully. I just got an anonymous call—

man said he was paying off Pluto today. One hundred thousand dollars, just like the rest of them."

Jacoby's eyes were saucers. "Who . . . anonymous, you said?"

Murtaugh nodded. "He said if we could catch Pluto and recover his money for him, then he'd come forward and identify himself. He gave me a code word so I'd know him. He's playing it safe—doesn't want to antagonize Pluto in case we blow it."

"Where's the drop?"

"On the Circle Line sightseeing boat, the one that makes a three-hour cruise around Manhattan? Our anonymous caller said he was instructed to take the boat that leaves at ten-thirty this morning—probably their busiest trip of the day."

Jacoby looked at his watch. "It's a quarter to ten now."

"I know. The boat departs from Pier Eighty-three, foot of West Forty-third Street. I'm going there now. What I want you to do is get on the phone and see how many of the men you can round up. Plainclothesmen only—no uniformed officers." Murtaugh was counting on the shortness of time here. "But don't spend more than twenty minutes on it. Then get out to Pier Eighty-three yourself —I've got to have at least one man. Get going."

"Right." Jacoby was up and gone.

The Lieutenant smiled in nervous satisfaction; Jacoby still had a lot to learn. Sergeant Eberhart would have asked a few pertinent questions first, such as: where on the boat was the money to be stashed?

Murtaugh put on his jacket and left, missing by fifteen minutes Costello's call with the news that Pluto's apartment had been found.

. . .

Librarian or schoolteacher, Pluto thought. "What is it you do back in Grand Rapids?" he said aloud.

"I operate a chain of garages," she answered surprisingly. "My brother and I were co-owners, but he died last year. So now I run things by myself."

"Must be a big job for one person."

"It is, but I enjoy it. It's something I'm used to."

They were still docked at Pier Eighty-three. The woman didn't look like a small-scale business tycoon, standing there by the rail of the excursion boat. She did look like an out-of-towner, a middle-aged tourist here to see the sights in the big city. Some gray in her hair, brand new clothes purchased just for her vacation trip.

And she was alone. As long as she was willing to talk to Pluto, then he was part of a couple instead of the single man Lieutenant Murtaugh was undoubtedly trying to spot at that very moment. A woman with a child would have been better, but all the children on the boat seemed to have come equipped with two parents instead of just one.

The garage lady from Grand Rapids was fidgeting; she kept looking at the few people still milling about on the pier. "Shouldn't we have left by now?"

"Five more minutes."

One of the people still on the pier was Lieutenant James Timothy Murtaugh. Who was obviously waiting for somebody. Murtaugh had come aboard for a quick check around. Now he was back on the pier waiting for his straight man to show up. Murtaugh had promised Pluto it would not be Sergeant Eberhart but a less experienced man.

"Where are you from?" the garage lady asked tentatively.

"Deer Falls, North Dakota," Pluto said.

She nodded. "I didn't think you were a New Yorker." She smiled at him, feeling safer.

Pluto speculated over the thinking process Murtaugh must have gone through to come up with his plan. He would have to convince his superiors that the dreaded free-lance killer known as Pluto was dead, dead, indubitably dead; *and* that he had died in such a way that his body could never be recovered. How to make a corpse disappear—even a police lieutenant would have to give that one some thought. Fire and explosions always left traces. There were no volcanoes or quicksand in Manhattan. Meat-grinders and acid vats were easily accessible only in Vincent Price movies, and a one-way rocket to the planet Mercury wasn't even on the drawing board yet. Earth, air, fire, and water—Lieutenant Murtaugh had opted for water.

The middle-aged lady at Pluto's side was chattering away, making small talk. Pluto was grateful. He answered an occasional question, asked one or two himself, kept the conversation going.

There he was: the patsy. Murtaugh's straight man had shown up, his semi-witness. Pluto thought he looked very young; it shouldn't be too hard to get the drop on him. Murtaugh had wanted Pluto to come up and hit the patsy from behind at a time he was being distracted by Murtaugh himself. But Pluto had very quickly rewritten that part of the script; he had no intention of revealing himself to Murtaugh. The Lieutenant's plan was to claim he'd struggled with Pluto and Pluto had gone overboard—such melodramatics! But Pluto had agreed, once Murtaugh had given in on the point of the semi-witness. Pluto's attack on the young officer was necessary to give credence to Murtaugh's story.

Then Pluto was to slide one of his guns under the unconscious officer for Murtaugh to find, a gun that could be connected to a recent killing. Murtaugh had said that would serve as evidence that the man who'd gone overboard was indeed Pluto. Pluto had thought about it a while and then had agreed to that too. He had confidence in his own ability to spot a trap if there was one. He'd selected the Ruger .38, the gun that had killed the thieving landscape architect William Parminter, among others; it was untraceable because it had been stolen instead of bought.

In spite of himself, Pluto felt a flutter of excitement. He'd never allowed an adversary to get this close before. As far as he could tell, there were no other police on board; Sergeant Eberhart certainly was nowhere in sight. Pluto had looked for Sergeant Eberhart *very* carefully. So far, it looked as if Murtaugh were keeping his side of the bargain. If all went well, Pluto would see to it that the Lieutenant didn't go home to face a shotgun blast after all.

"At last!" the garage lady said. "We were supposed to leave five—oh, look. Somebody running for the boat."

Pluto looked, and then looked again. The "somebody" was Sergeant Eberhart—running like crazy, gripping the handles of a bright red Gimbels shopping bag flapping at his side.

He made the boat.

When Murtaugh first learned that Pluto had probably changed his appearance, he was astonished to see how many slightly overweight men with dark hair there were in New York; every fourth or fifth man he passed on the street seemed to fit that general description. So he wasn't particularly surprised when a dozen or so turned up on the excursion boat. Some wore glasses, some had mustaches, all had companions. There was no way he and Jacoby could watch them all; he'd have to rely on the script as written.

Jacoby, when he finally arrived, was excited. "They've found his apartment!" he blurted out. "Costello called in just before I left. Filing cabinets *full* of evidence, Costello says."

"Slow down—start at the beginning."

Jacoby repeated in detail everything Costello had told him about Pluto's home base. "And oh yeah—Sergeant Eberhart sent word he has two files he needs to talk to you about immediately."

"Which ones?"

"He didn't say. I told Costello you got a tip Pluto'd be on this boat—but Lieutenant, Costello's the only one I talked to. He'll tell Eberhart, but I couldn't get hold of anybody else. Not enough time. Can we hold the boat? Until Costello or Eberhart gets here?"

"No, that would tip him off—we don't want to spook him now that we've finally got this close. You and I'll have to take him by ourselves." Murtaugh checked his watch; Pluto had had enough time to spot them and familiarize himself with Jacoby's appearance. "Come on, let's get on."

Once on board Murtaugh took Jacoby on a quick tour of the boat. They were climbing down a companionway from the top deck when the boat pulled away from the wharf. Murtaugh's heart was in his throat. The news about Pluto's apartment should have left him jumping for joy—but why couldn't Costello's call have come just a few minutes later? *After* Jacoby had left. Jacoby had told Costello about the excursion boat and Costello would report to Eberhart. And Murtaugh didn't want Eberhart

knowing anything about the upcoming little drama until
it was over and done with.

"How long did you say this trip takes?" Jacoby asked.

"Three hours."

Timing was so important. Murtaugh had told Pluto
the fake struggle would have to take place at the exact
moment the boat was passing Battery Park, rounding the
southern tip of Manhattan to start its way upriver. The
rivers themselves could be dragged and sounded—but not
New York Bay. There was too much water, too much area
for the Harbor Patrol to cover. It was a good place to
lose a corpse; no one would really expect Pluto's body
to be recovered, Murtaugh had told him.

Pluto bought it. He had agreed to Murtaugh's plan.

Murtaugh had tried to think of everything; he'd even
included something in his plan for Pluto to reject so the
killer would feel he was controlling the situation. The
crucial point had been whether Pluto would agree to
leave a gun by Jacoby or not; once he said yes, Murtaugh
knew his plan had a real chance of succeeding. Pluto was
so sure he could outsmart any opponent; Murtaugh had
counted on that ego to bring him to agree. Murtaugh was
sorry about the lump Jacoby was going to have to take;
he didn't like putting anyone in danger, even when that
danger was slight. But he had to have somebody to act as
unintentional bait, to help maneuver Pluto into position.
Sergeant Eberhart was too sharp; he'd never let Pluto
sneak up behind him. Jacoby was the other extreme—of
all the men under Murtaugh's command, Jacoby was the
least qualified to help bring in a killer.

The "struggle" was scheduled to take place on the
New Jersey side of the boat; the tourists would be on
the New York side, gawking. He picked out his spot and
stationed Jacoby there, telling him it was near the deck

locker where Murtaugh's fictional anonymous caller had said Pluto's payoff money would be stashed. Murtaugh had told Pluto he himself would be on the other side with the tourists until Pluto had taken care of Jacoby and planted his gun, but in truth he didn't plan to be far away. There weren't many places to hide on an excursion boat, but he'd found a small concession storage area nearby that would do nicely. Then once Pluto had disarmed himself . . . .

Murtaugh checked his watch again; enough time for one more quick scout around. He left Jacoby standing by the starboard rail, trying to look like a tourist fascinated by the New Jersey river bank.

"I have a confession to make," the garage lady from Grand Rapids said uncomfortably. "I don't own a chain of garages. I don't even own one garage. I *work* in a garage. I'm a bookkeeper."

Pluto looked at her in surprise. "Then why the fairy tale?"

She sighed. "Women my age who travel alone—well, you've got to understand we're simply treated better when people think we have money. The little courtesies, friendly treatment on the part of clerks and waiters— you'd be surprised how fast it all disappears once people learn you work for a living just like everybody else. So I lie a little."

How extraordinary. Pluto asked, "By 'people' do you mean men-people?"

"It's women, too, but the problem is mostly men. There's a certain kind of man who seems to live on boats like this one or in hotel lobbies and the like. The kind of man that's always on the lookout for well-to-do widows. They're very attentive until they find out you've had to save for two years to make the trip. But until then they can be quite helpful, you know, in a strange place."

Pluto was delighted. "And you think that *I* . . . ?"

"Oh no, no, I don't," she said, distressed. "It's because I *don't* think you're one of those men that I'm telling you. My saying I owned a chain of garages—well, that was just habit, I'm afraid. Little excursions like this boat trip are always so much more pleasant if you have someone to talk to, don't you think? That's all I had in mind."

"But at first you *did* think—"

"Well, I couldn't be sure—"

Pluto laughed out loud. "Dear lady, I am immensely flattered. I've been mistaken for many things in my time, but never before for a gigolo. Hush now—don't say a word! I *like* the feeling." He laughed again. The lady smiled uncertainly.

They heard the tour director's voice over the loudspeaker direct their attention to the World Trade Center. That was Pluto's cue; Battery Park, coming up.

He stood up. "I could use a cup of coffee. How about you? Shall I bring you one?" When his companion didn't answer, he said, "Perhaps a soft drink? Lemonade?"

"Black coffee," she sighed, suddenly listless.

"I'll be right back."

"Sure you will," she said expressionlessly.

She thinks I'm walking out because she doesn't have money. Pluto stood looking down at her, thinking fast: something he could use here?

Lieutenant Murtaugh might be playing straight, might be trying to pull a fast one. Sergeant Eberhart certainly hadn't tried to slip aboard unseen—what a flamboyant entrance, with that great red shopping bag flapping with every step! But *something* was not going as planned; Eberhart wasn't supposed to be there at all. It occurred to Pluto that it might not be a bad idea to take a human shield along with him.

"Why don't you come with me?" he said to the lady from Grand Rapids. "We'll have to go to the other side of the boat, that's where the concession counter is—but I don't think we'll miss much. We can always watch from the back—oh dear, they don't like you to say 'front' and 'back' on boats, do they? We can watch from the *stern*, that's better. Let us go fetch our coffee and then remove ourselves to the stern of this noble vessel and watch from there. What do you say?"

Utterly charmed, the lady rose and took Pluto's arm. He maneuvered her around to the other arm, where there was no danger she might feel the .38 nesting in his shoulder holster.

Sergeant Eberhart made his way among the crowds on the main deck, his red shopping bag banging against his legs. Where the hell was Lieutenant Murtaugh?

He shouldn't have brought the files. If Pluto really was on board—well, one thing at a time. But he'd been obsessed with the thought that he had to get both Murtaugh's and Ansbacher's files out of Pluto's apartment before anyone else saw them. The shopping bag was one he'd left on the back seat of his car; now Eberhart was afraid to let bag and files out of his sight.

Eberhart was trying to sort out supposition from fact. What he *knew* had happened was a bit on the skimpy side. First, Pluto had investigated the Lieutenant and Ansbacher the same way he investigated his clients and his victims. Two, Ellie Murtaugh had been hustled out of town under police guard. Three, Lieutenant Murtaugh had received an anonymous tip that Pluto would be making the ten-thirty cruise around Manhattan.

Correction. Lieutenant Murtaugh had *said* he'd received an anonymous tip that Pluto would be making the cruise.

What if Pluto had threatened to kill Ellie Murtaugh unless the Lieutenant agreed to . . . to what? Had Pluto and Lieutenant Murtaugh collaborated on some sort of scheme? Was the Lieutenant supposed to muddy up the investigation? He couldn't get away with that for very long; no, it had to be something else. Pluto didn't know his home base had been penetrated; he still thought he was safe, he was still making plans. What did he want from the Lieutenant? What were they planning?

The answer came to him like a door opening. They could be planning to fake Pluto's death.

Eberhart leaned against a railing and stared down at the river water. Would Lieutenant Murtaugh let a serial murderer go free in exchange for Ellie's life? Or put it the other way: would the Lieutenant sacrifice Ellie for the satisfaction of bringing in Pluto? No, of course he wouldn't. A lot of ambitious men would make the exchange, but Lieutenant Murtaugh wasn't one of them. The Lieutenant would cooperate with Pluto. And Eberhart was standing there with a shopping bag full of incriminating material, documents, and photos that would link Murtaugh and Pluto in a way neither one of them wanted.

The Lieutenant would cooperate. Unless.

Unless he refused to accept the proposition that he had only two alternatives: to let Pluto go free or to watch something terrible happen to Ellie. Lieutenant Murtaugh was too good a cop just to give in to that. Maybe he'd come up with a third possibility, a way of stopping Pluto once and for all before he had a chance to hurt Ellie. Had the Lieutenant figured out a trap?

And was it to be sprung here, on this boat, right now?

Eberhart pushed away from the railing and resumed his search for the Lieutenant, fighting against a sense of urgency. He didn't know how much time he had; it couldn't be much. The Lieutenant could use some backup. It suddenly occurred to Eberhart that he might be proceeding on wishful thinking. There had to be a reason the Lieutenant hadn't taken him into his confidence. Eberhart admitted he couldn't guess whether the Lieutenant was trying to capture Pluto or whether he was trying to help him escape.

He moved away from the crowds toward the other side of the boat, which was virtually deserted. He saw a few stray sightseers—and one familiar figure. "Jacoby! Where's the Lieutenant?"

Before Jacoby could answer, Eberhart heard his name hissed from behind him. He turned to see Lieutenant Murtaugh beckoning from behind a barely open door. "Get in here!"

The Lieutenant was in a small storage room; Eberhart crowded against plastic bags full of Styrofoam cups as Murtaugh closed the door to a crack. "What's going on, Lieutenant?"

"Keep your voice down. What the hell are you doing here?"

"Costello said—"

"Never mind, tell me later. We're expecting Pluto to show any minute. To pick up his money." He glanced at the red paper bag Eberhart was carrying. "Fine time to go shopping."

Eberhart frowned. "He's coming here to pick up his money? And Jacoby's standing right there in plain sight?"

"He doesn't know Jacoby."

"How can you be sure of that? Lieutenant, tell me what's really happening. I can help."

Murtaugh didn't say anything, gestured impatiently.

Eberhart took a deep breath. "I know Pluto got in touch with you. I think he threatened your wife." He hesitated. "I don't care what you're planning, Lieutenant. Either way, I want to help. Let me help."

Murtaugh gave a big sigh, and then smiled ruefully. "You're right. There was no anonymous tip—I made that up. It's just as well you know. You'll need your weapon. I'm not sure I can take him alone."

Eberhart felt a lifting of the spirits; a trap, then. "But you're not alone. What about Jacoby?"

"Jacoby is scheduled to take a fall—but he doesn't know it. That's why I couldn't tell anybody. I set the kid up."

"I don't get it."

"Look, there's no time to explain everything now. I had to work out a plan that would get Pluto here and convince him I was staging a phony death scene for him. He's going to knock Jacoby out and leave one of his guns—proof he was here, he thinks."

"And then as soon as he gets rid of his gun we jump him?"

"Then we jump him."

"It must be the thirty-eight."

"What?"

"The gun he's going to leave. There was no thirty-eight in his apartment. Six others, but no thirty-eight."

"Six? What—no, save it. We can't talk any more. It's almost time."

Eberhart slipped his pistol out of its holder and removed the safety catch. Outside on the deck, Jacoby started a series of isometric breathing exercises to calm himself down.

"You said black, didn't you?" Pluto handed the lady from Grand Rapids her coffee.

The concession counter was crowded, but as soon as the tourists got what they wanted they headed back to some better spot for sightseeing. The loudspeaker told them they were passing Battery Park.

It was time.

"Let's walk back along this way, shall we? Miss the crowd."

The lady agreed easily, now that she was convinced Pluto was just another tourist like herself, open to a little temporary companionship. They strolled casually along the starboard side, passing the young man Pluto had earlier seen talking to Lieutenant Murtaugh. He was stationed exactly where Murtaugh had said he'd be. Except for the unexpected appearance of Sergeant Eberhart—which could have been as big a surprise to Murtaugh as it was to Pluto—everything was going exactly as planned. He took a quick look around: no Murtaugh, no Eberhart. He didn't need his human shield after all. Pluto made a show of taking out a handkerchief and blotting some imaginary coffee from his lips.

Don't go through with it.

The thought astonished Pluto with its intensity; he hadn't realized his own reluctance. How easy it would be just to complete this little boat trip like any other tourist. Leave the young man alone, don't leave the .38 for Murtaugh. Finish the cruise, take the lady from Grand Rapids for a leisurely all-afternoon lunch at the Rainbow Room, and still be at Kennedy International in plenty of time for his night flight to Geneva. Get rid of the .38 before boarding the plane—perhaps drop it over the side of the boat? Just walk away from it all. And let a disappointed James Timothy Murtaugh go home, open his front door to the little surprise Pluto had left for him, and spend the rest of his life as an emasculated cripple. That part didn't bother Pluto.

What did bother him was the thought that if he did walk away from Murtaugh's plan, he'd never be able to come back to New York. Aside from his unwillingness to give up the city, Pluto thought it wouldn't be too smart to close any door behind him. And the police were getting close—Pluto knew that as well as he knew his own name. No, he had to get the New York police files closed on Pluto-the-hundred-thousand-dollar-killer. And Murtaugh's plan was the way to do it.

Pluto and his companion had turned a corner; the patsy Murtaugh had stationed by the starboard rail was out of sight. "Oh—I've lost my handkerchief," Pluto said. "I must have dropped it back there. I'll just nip along and take a look. Wait here for me?"

"I'll be here," the lady said.

Murtaugh had said the man would be young and inexperienced; this one certainly was. He kept looking in the same general direction instead of keeping his eyes in constant motion. It was easy.

Pluto used the butt of the .38 to catch the young man a good clip in the occipital region of his skull. He used his free arm to lower the slumping figure to the deck and then knelt down, the .38 still in hand.

"What are you doing?" said a woman's voice—high, alarmed. "What have you done to that man?"

Pluto whipped the .38 around so the nozzle pointed in her direction; he heard her gasp. "You shouldn't have followed me," he told the lady from Grand Rapids. "You should have stayed where I told you."

"I, I just wanted to help you look, I . . ." she stammered.

"You shouldn't have followed me," he repeated, and took aim.

A door four or five feet behind the lady burst open—and Murtaugh and Eberhart were both pointing guns at him. "Drop it, Pluto!" the Lieutenant shouted. "Drop it now! Get down, lady!"

A trap! It was a trap after all!

Pluto and Murtaugh stared at each other, face to face for the first time. An electric shock ran between the two men—it was anybody's guess which one would recover first.

Pluto fired. *The lady from Grand Rapids dropped like a stone ka-pow and Murtaugh grabbed his own arm his face twisted in sudden pain two for one not bad but before he could get off another shot*—a bomb exploded in his chest.

Sergeant Eberhart lowered his pistol.

Pluto was on his back on the deck, perfectly numb, feeling nothing. He looked up to see Lieutenant Murtaugh bending over him, grimacing with pain. Pluto closed his eyes.

"She's dead," Eberhart's voice said.

Pluto opened his eyes, looked straight at Murtaugh, said, "Surprise for you," and died.

Murtaugh stood up straight. That was it? That was all there was to it? This pudgy, lifeless creature was the great Pluto who'd had them all running in circles for so long? He heard Eberhart speak again. "You say she's dead?" Murtaugh asked.

Eberhart nodded. "You all right, Lieutenant?"

"He killed that woman just because she got in the way?"

"Because she was there. That's all the reason he ever needed." Eberhart was looking in her purse. "Name's Georgia Maxwell. From Grand Rapids, Michigan."

Murtaugh was vaguely aware of agitated voices; the gunfire had drawn attention. Jacoby was groaning, beginning to come to. "Georgia Maxwell," Murtaugh repeated, tasting the name. "Georgia Maxwell is dead because I wanted to protect my wife. I traded one woman for another."

"Georgia Maxwell is dead because Pluto shot her," Eberhart said harshly. "Don't start that, Lieutenant."

Murtaugh stood looking down at Pluto's body, waiting for a feeling of satisfaction that would not come. *God, his arm hurt!* He looked at the dead woman, back to the dead man. "You rotten son of a bitch," he said quietly. Ellie Murtaugh was alive and well but Georgia Maxwell was dead, and she'd died without even knowing why. Abruptly Murtaugh found himself thinking of two other women, Rose Malucci and Carolyn Randolph. An old woman who'd been shot down without a second thought, and a young one who'd come through the Pluto wars without a scratch. Some women were allowed to live, some were not.

Jacoby was sitting up. "What happened?"

Out of the corner of his eye Murtaugh caught a glimpse of movement; he turned just in time to see Eberhart heave the red shopping bag overboard. "What was that?"

"Just some trash I should have gotten rid of earlier. Are you okay, Lieutenant? You don't look so good."

"I don't know, I've never been shot before." He half-laughed in apology. "I never knew a gunshot wound was so, so *hot*. My arm's on fire."

247

"Why don't you sit down on the deck—here, let me help. I've got to go get them to stop this tub."

"I think I'm going to faint," Murtaugh said, and did.

Four hours later Lieutenant Murtaugh leaned against the wall of the elevator car, let Sergeant Eberhart push the button. His arm was in a sling, the pain damped down to a generalized discomfort.

"You okay?" Eberhart asked.

"Yeah, now that everybody's stopped telling me how lucky I am."

I'm okay, you're okay. The doctor had told him his wound would not have hurt so much if he'd gone into shock as a protective reaction. Perhaps Murtaugh was in an overly defensive mood, but he would have sworn there was a note of reprimand in the doctor's voice. *I apologize, Doctor, for not going into shock.* The light in the elevator seemed dimmer than usual; the car was barely crawling.

"I wonder what his real name was," Eberhart said.

"We'll find out—more things to work with now, fingerprints and such. It'll come out."

Eberhart shrugged. "Maybe."

Murtaugh concentrated all his efforts on not sliding to the floor—the shot the doctor had given him had just about knocked him out. Not much farther; all he had to do was make it to the apartment and then he could collapse. He looked forward to oblivion. He needed oblivion. He had a lot he wanted to blot out. "Stupid," he said aloud, bitterly.

Sergeant Eberhart pretended not to hear.

He had handled it all wrong. He'd let his fear for Ellie's safety blind him to correct procedure. His plan had been stupid—so stupid that a woman had died of it. An innocent woman from Grand Rapids, Michigan, had wandered into the crossfire and died, gratuitously and senselessly. Pluto's bullet had gone straight through her neck and lodged in Murtaugh's upper arm; she had shielded him. That made her Murtaugh's victim as much as Pluto's. And to a lesser extent, so was Jacoby. The way Murtaugh had set him up—that alone could cost him his shield, if Eberhart ever decided to talk.

Murtaugh had never before in his life been so cavalier about other people's safety. That's what contact with Pluto had done to him: he'd lost his perspective, he'd lost his plain common sense. True, the hundred-thousand-dollar killer had been stopped. But *he* hadn't been the one to stop him—Sergeant Eberhart had been quicker. And Sergeant Eberhart wasn't even supposed to be there.

What a royal mess.

Murtaugh glanced at the younger man in the elevator with him; Eberhart was watching him with a worried look on his face. Murtaugh forced himself to smile. "Did I thank you for my life?"

Eberhart made a dismissive gesture, embarrassed.

It was gradually dawning on Lieutenant Murtaugh just how much he owed to his sergeant. It was something he'd have to think about later; he couldn't handle anything more today. So tired. Right now all he could think about was making it to the apartment—where he could just collapse.

The elevator finally shuddered to a stop. Eberhart took his superior's good arm to steady him when he began to weave down the hallway; Murtaugh did not object. At the door he stared at the four locks—which doubled and then tripled even as he watched. He shook his head to clear his vision; didn't work. He handed the keys to Eberhart: "You do it." Murtaugh leaned tiredly against the wall by the door, out of the way.

Eberhart took the keys, fitted the right ones into the right locks, and opened the door.